Billy's Ink

NINA GRASIA RENND

A Griffin

Copyright © Sandra Ashton 2020

The moral right of the author has been asserted.

All characters and events in this publication other than those clearly in the public domain are fictitious and any resemblance to real persons, living or dead, is purely coincidental.

All rights reserved worldwide.

No part of this novel may be reproduced, stored in a retrieval system, or transmitted, in any form or by any means, without the prior permission in writing of the author, nor be otherwise circulated in any form of binding or cover other than that in which it is available here and without a similar condition including this condition being imposed on the subsequent purchaser.

Design: Diseñolibros.com

Dedications and acknowledgments

This book is for my family, Tracey, Linda, Mike and especially my Mum, for their encouragement and love. To all my friends, that put up with me talking about writing, until I bore them silly, but still remain true friends.

Thanks to Rosie Reay, for proof reading the book with me. Also, thanks to the members of the writer's groups and, especially the Ladies of Spain group, who gave so much input into the book cover. I really appreciated all your help.

Thank you to Melissa Levine of Redpen Editing for all her had work editing. Fantastic job!

Also, to my cover designer and his team at Diseño Libros for helping me achieve a dream and a fantastic cover.

Prologue

Billy had made several mistakes in his life. One was falling in love. He hoisted himself up and made his way to the highest rung of the scaffold. At least here maybe, he could think straight.

He sat, dangling his legs over the edge. Dorrie had prepared him lunch and coffee. He placed them beside him on the wooden planks that made up the platform. Looking out over the city, he could see the cityscape of London. In the distance the dome of Saint Paul's Cathedral and the ferries wheel of the London Eye.

London was home. This is where he had met Elizabeth, who would set him on the road to his destiny. He had done the right thing. He was convinced he had, even though the cost would be high. Maybe too high.

He looked at the people below scurrying about their business. Protecting themselves against the cold wind, blowing around the city. The grey clouds, threatening to unleash the usual torrent of rain, catching some unaware. Just as Elizabeth had caught him. She was so unexpected.

Would his loved ones understand why he had done, what he had? The result of his action was both his joy and sadness. He started to feel cold, shivering. He was too exposed to the elements.

After today everything would be different. He imagined himself standing erect. His suit and a pressed shirt. Witnesses stood both sides of the room, waiting to play their roles.

He was unfocused on his surroundings, unhearing of the crowd. Sounds muffled, except a repressed cough. Sunlight shone hazily through windows making everything seem dream-like.

Was this just a dream? Was he really here?

How did the direction of his life change so dramatically and so quickly? His mind drifted back.

Chapter One

London November

"I'm getting a new ink this weekend Mum, this one's only costing me a hundred and sixty quid, it normally costs six hundred, but I've sold Matt the de sign, so he's given me a really good deal", Billy gushed enthusiastically. Whenever he spoke about tattoos, he would become animated, sometimes to such an extreme, the words spewed out of his mouth so fast, he had to stop to take a deep breath.

"That's nice sweetly, the picture you've been working on?"

"Yeah, the one with the Griffin. This is the last one", he said adamantly. "I've decided everything has been told and, in the future, I'll just design and sell them either to Matt or online."

Dorrie had heard 'it's the last one' so many times she didn't place much note on it.

"Well that's lovely. Have you told your dad about it?"

"Sure, at least three times a day." He smiled and winked at Dorrie; she smiled and winked back.

"You'd best get yourself off to work or you'll be late."

He grabbed his jacket off the rocking chair in the kitchen. Dorrie handed him his lunch as he strode out the door. Billy was a builder and scaffolder, it paid very well, especially for a guy that was good at it and didn't mind heights; Billy actually loved heights and never lacked work.

Once a scaffold was at a decent height, you'd find him sitting somewhere quietly looking out over the scenery. Sometimes a small village or town, or else a big city like London and on rare occasions somewhere special, like Windsor Castle or Portsmouth, overlooking the sea. Even when it was raining you could usually find him looking at the view during his break, quietly contemplating life and the minions of people below.

He didn't like strange, crowded pubs or cafés and his mates knew it. They said idiots who reacted to how he looked were not worth giving a shit about, but it always hurt, just a little, even though he was used to it.

People's first reaction to Billy would be to shy away. He'd been a big boy even when young, his biological Mum told him he took after his Dad. His dad was a big bloke, well-built and so was Billy.

His work, lifting metal poles and building all day long, had made him muscular. He was tall to boot, standing six foot two in his socks. His size fourteen boots intimidated people as they imagined him kicking some poor sucker on the ground. But, why would anyone shy away from a tall well-built bloke? Billy was a skinhead and has a fully tattooed body which made him stand out like a sore thumb. The ones that covered his neck and half his head, were the ones that caused unease. He didn't mind too much; he knew why people thought the way they did.

You never see a shaved, tattooed man portrayed in a good light, not in the papers, the news or films. They're always shown at Nazi rallies, or in fights and people are good at assuming the worse of someone.

The few people that actually took the time to look at Billy's ink and get to know him found a gentle artist. Billy and his siblings, Derrick, two years his senior and Lesley two years younger were brought up, first by their birth parents and then by their adopted parents after their own died in a car accident when Billy was twelve.

Dorrie and John Johnson had been fostering for years, then social services arrived with three young kids that needed a temporary home until they could place them permanently.

Unfortunately, not many adopting parents would take on all three, so they were likely to be split up and Dorrie couldn't accept that, neither could John for that matter. After six weeks, Dorrie spoke with John.

"John, how do you feel about adopting these three? We can give up fostering and give them a home, otherwise they could be scattered and never see each other again."

"You know, Dorrie, I was thinking along these exact same lines." With his approval and that of social services it all went through and they became a family.

It wasn't easy. Derrick would often tell them.

"I'm fourteen and I can take care of Billy and Lee on my own." But, of course he couldn't.

Billy was twelve and just wanted to back up his brother and stop his sister from crying all the time. Lesley, who was ten, just wanted her Mum and Dad back and the two substitutes just didn't fill her loss. It took a couple of years, but with lots of love from both Dorrie and John and John's way of reasoning things out with the boys, things eventually settled down.

When Derrick was sixteen, he wanted to leave school and get a job, but John insisted he study for a degree. They compromised, Derrick got a part-time job and took his teaching degree online with the Open University. He went to work as a PE teacher in Manchester, where he eventually met his wife Jenny, an English teacher. After getting married the pair managed to get a job in the same town, Surbiton, which wasn't too far away, so they were able to visit regularly.

Then it was Billy's turn and again his Dad insisted on him getting a degree. Billy wanted to study and got a place at Newcastle University studying History and Math. He found he had a love for history and in his second year decided first to go for his teaching degree and then carry on for his masters. At twenty-five, he had a bright future and couldn't wait to get started. He decided to take a year off to travel and then settle down into his career and hopefully meet a girl like Derrick did before starting a family. Of course, with the decision he made to start getting tattoos, then, with the way it became an obsession, meant that things were not going to work out as he had planned.

The same rules had applied to Lesley who was plain sailing as she was desperate to get away from the overprotectiveness of her parents and brothers and couldn't wait to get into university.

Billy remembered the day she chose her subject.

"I want to be a doctor. It's a long course. Medicine would entail me having to do five years at University, plus at least two years residence, but it's what I want to do. Bristol is a great university for medicine, and I think I can get accepted there." She hoped also to find some freedom from her over protective parents and brothers.

She found she loved the academic side, and went on the get her masters in medical science so that she could teach, instead of becoming a medical doctor.

Billy missed them, but they kept in touch via Skype at least twice a week.

Billy was beginning to worry about Dad, now in his early eighties who was suffering with Alzheimer's and forgetting who Billy and Dorrie were at times.

"Hi Dad, did you have a good day?"

"Who... Who are you? This was last night's greeting. "It's me, Dad Billy."

"I don't know no Billy. Where's Brenda?" Brenda not being my adopted Mums' name.

"It's me, Dad, your son, Billy. There's no Brenda here Pops only

Dorrie, and me."

"I don't have any son, what you talking about, I'm not even married you idiot."

Billy knew, Dad was off somewhere else, and so left to find Dorrie and see if he could help with dinner.

The doctor had explained Dads Alzheimer's' would get worse, and he would need to be cared for in a home eventually, but Billy would have none of it. Pops would stay here and Billy would take care of him, which he did, from getting him up and dressed in the mornings to putting him to bed at night. Billy paid for a home help to come in during the day; she was company for Dorrie and also helped around the house when Pops was resting.

When Billy got home, he would sit for hours speaking with him until it was time to put him to bed.

If Dad didn't know who he was, he'd talk about anything that was playing on his mind. He knew he wasn't really being listened to, but hoped the sound of his voice soothed his father. After he would sit with Mum for an hour reading a good book and discussing its merits, watching something she liked on the telly, or just quietly drawing.

***

I wonder what her name is.

One evening he spoke with his dad.

"I've seen a lady going in and out of the house we are working on in Belgrave. I'm not sure whether she works or lives there. Mind you, she's well out of my league. I've been watching her. Not in a creepy way. I just watch her in a, wish-I-could-meet-her, kind or way."

He hadn't told anyone else about her. She was his secret. His mates would give him nothing but flack if they knew he fancied her like crazy, so he kept her to himself. He kept an eye out for her as she turned into the street, which he could see from the third tier of scaffold.

He first saw her three weeks ago, when they came to price the job. They didn't deal with her directly; the quote was given to some toff in a pin-stripe that looked down with disdain having to deal with common workers. *Maybe she's his wife, secretary, mistress.*

As soon as he set eyes on her, something happened, no big explosion or fireworks or any soppy stuff like that, but a smile came to his face, a tightening in his chest and a sigh from his mouth. For some reason he felt calm. He noticed she came there at the same time nearly every day, so he took to taking his break closer and closer to the entrance.

Every day he would dare himself to say a few words to her, find out who she was, but every day he chickened out. She'd probably take one look and run a mile thinking she was about to be mugged. *How can I approach her? When am to speak with her? Well I'd better do it soon, or the job will finish and I'll be moving off then I'll lose the chance forever.*

Billy didn't find it easy speaking to new people, especially people of the female variety, and if he thought about it long enough, he didn't like talking to anyone, not even his family. Instead he spoke his thoughts and feelings through his ink art, now there was a story!

As luck would have it, Bret the foreman forced the meeting.

"Excuse me."

Oh no, it's her.

"Sorry to bother you, but there's a bucket just above your head that looks as though it could do real damage and it looks as though it's about to totter off."

Billy looked up and two layers above, Bret had placed a bucket of screws and bolts onto a plank without securing the handle. It did indeed look as though the whole lot was about to come crashing down. Billy jumped to the ground and moved the woman to a safe distance, then called up to Bret.

"Hey, Bret, Bret, you fucking moron secure your bucket."

A head and face appeared, "Oh shit, sorry, I got distracted."

"Well your distraction could cost a life. Get your bloody act together mate."

He turned around to the woman he had moved out of danger. She stood, looking –to him– like an angel. Her white raincoat tied tightly, long blonde hair dancing in the wind in unison with a shock pink scarf; the two performing a mid-air flamenco, *Olé*. She smiled and at that moment he realized the language he had used. His eyelid dropped in embarrassment and his face felt heated, he pulled a bit of a grimace.

"Damn, I'm so sorry about the foul language, Miss, Mam, Madam."

"Don't worry", she laughed, "I'm a big girl and I'm sure I've used just as bad a language when I've been scared. And you can call me Elizabeth."

She was so relaxed with him. He quickly glanced behind to see if there was someone else standing behind him, but of course there wasn't. She was looking straight at him with beautiful, green, smiling eyes.

"Oh, I wasn't scared", he started, "well, I was, but not for me, for you. These guys are a good team, this stuff doesn't happen, but Bret should know better. You just can't...." He was speaking without pause, like he did when he spoke about his ink. *You sound crazy.*

"It's Okay, really it is, nothing happened, it's fine, I'm fine, you moved me out of the way of certain death and I appreciate you looking out for me."

Did he just see her wink at him? She was definitely smiling in a very cheeky way. He decided there and then that he was going to ask her out one day, if she wasn't married to the jerk, whose house they were working in, or any other jerk come to that. Maybe she was one of those rich women that tease the pool man as seen in American movies. He didn't mind, it was just a bit of fun. *I would enjoy having fun with this woman.*

Then the mind of experience took over, the mind that had spent the last fifteen years being discriminated against because of the way he looked. The self-doubt started chattering its negativity, *Come on Billy, this is a classy lady. Do you seriously think she is being anything but polite, which is what classy ladies do? Be serious man! Look at yourself and look at her. Can you imagine taking her for dinner or a boat ride along the Thames? She'd laugh at you.* He felt himself shrinking, knowing his mind was right. He'd been here many, many times before, not with someone classy like her, but with people in general. They would say his looks didn't bother them, but as soon as they were seen in public, their tunes change. Other people's stares would make them tense and uncomfortable. *You never know Billy, this one might be different and if she is, how great would that be? Shut up mind.*

She was looking at him.

"I have a question. Do you think I could sit with you for a few minutes one day and look at you, ask you some questions about your tattoos? No, no this is terrible of me, I know. It's just that I've noticed you, but I've been too shy to approach. It would be such a shame if someone like you were here and I didn't take the opportunity to... Oh, my goodness, I'm so rude, I'll leave, sorry for disturbing you."

She's leaving, move you idiot, say something, stop her, she's moving away, Billy wake up Billy NOW!

"No, Miss I'm sorry. Please don't go and by all means, what kind of questions do you have about my ink?

Billy didn't care if she were only interested in him as a specimen to examine, a circus curiosity, it would mean spending time with her.

Chapter Two

Thirty-two Eaton Place, SW1 was on the corner with Belgrave Place and you didn't get posher than this in London. This was the place with embassies and embassy personnel, the city apartments of the rich. Billy would never see this sort of *rich* in all his life but this was Elizabeth's norm. She had grown up with it, had always known it, so she accepted it, just as he accepted the three-bedroom semi, he had grown up in.

As it turned out, she didn't work at the house. She did in fact own it, although in truth, it was a family property, one of several it emerged.

It came to light soon after their first meeting. Elizabeth appeared outside.

"Hello, Billy. Do you have some sort of cover you could put over my window? My flats on the second floor and I'm getting a lot of powdery dust coming in the lounge."

So, she has a flat here. "Yes, sure Elizabeth, I'll find you something and rig it up. Must be expensive living in this neighbourhood. Do you work close by?" He knew he was trying to gather intel on her.

"I'm lucky, my parents own the building. My father, Omar Hudson rents it to me. I doubt I could afford it on my wages if he didn't give me a generous discount."

Lady Bethany Dowels and Lord Omar Hudson were landed gentry. The Belgrave house was being redesigned on the fourth floor. The house stood five stories high if you counted the basement. Each floor having been turned into flats with the fourth being the last. Elizabeth as stated, lived on the second floor.

Their job at Eaton Place was to reconfigure the internal structure, from two huge bedrooms and one bathroom, to two bedrooms, two bathrooms, a kitchen, lounge and guest washroom. The apartment, when finished, would be just as classy as the woman herself. The lounge overlooked the street of Eaton Place, full of fine stucco houses, whilst the main bed room overlooked the Belgrave Place. Another bedroom was an interior adjacent to the next house, both large with their own en-suite, a washroom serviced visiting guests. The kitchen was modern with an open-plan layout. He wondered whether Elizabeth's apartment was the same.

On their first outing they had walked along to Lennox Gardens and sat on a bench talking. They talked for nearly two hours ignoring the wind zipping around their bodies making them sit closer together, before Billy asked her if she fancied getting into the warm for a bite to eat. She told him she was famished and frozen, so they made their way to Granger and Co. an Australian restaurant that served decent sized potions for the hungry crowd. Billy and the lads had eaten there several times before so he felt quite safe going to a place where the staff wouldn't stand in a corner staring at them and making Elizabeth feel uncomfortable.

"You do realise, you haven't asked me about my tattoos all day. We've spoken about our work, travel, places we like, but not about my ink."

"That's because it gives me an excuse to talk with you another day." Their worlds were so far apart they may as well have come from two different galaxies. As they started getting to know each other, it didn't matter to either of them. Elizabeth was nothing like he had expected a wealthy woman to be, she was sensitive, funny and bore no airs or graces.

"I care about the people I represent as MP. I want people that aren't as privileged as me to succeed in life. I want to see kids, like the ones you volunteer with, achieve their goals. I genuinely want the world and especially my social realm to be less greedy and learn to share their wealth instead of hoarding it. I know I'm fighting an unwinnable battle, but I'll keep trying."

On the next dry, sunny Sunday they spent the whole day together in Hyde Park. They started at Hyde Park Corner, making their way to the Serpentine and Princess Diana Memorial Fountain, then up to the Italian Gar dens and finally making their way back down to the Serpentine Gallery and the Albert Memorial. The park was full of people soaking up the rare fine weather of a December day. They had dinner in a small secluded Italian restaurant they just happened to walk by and fancied the look of.

"You know, Elizabeth, it's amazing and very rare for me, but I haven't noticed the stares from people I usually get. They must think us an odd couple. I also haven't felt any sense of embarrassment from you. Not once. Even when we stopped to chase those giant bubbles. It all felt so natural. Today was perfect."

She smiled. "Billy, I would never be or feel embarrassed about being with you. Why would I? You're a lovely person and a very handsome man.

They still hadn't talked about his tattoos.

After four weeks, two lunches sitting for forty-five minutes on a park bench and four dates, Billy felt totally at ease with her. He also felt he wasn't a circus freak.

As Christmas approached Lizzie explained the House of Commons and Westminster Hall would be taking their recess for the holidays and she would be returning to her seat and home in Norfolk. She told him she would be back in the New Year and they would continue seeing each other.

Billy though, thought this might be the end, of the beginning, of a wonderful relationship. Before her departure,

"Billy would you come to my flat for dinner next week. I want to see you before I leave for Norfolk."

"That would be great. I'd love to."

This was the first time he saw the inside of her flat at Thirty-two Eaton Place. He realized that she fitted here, whereas he felt like a blight on a beautiful landscape.

Her flat was like the one above, but she had made it her own. A fireplace was situated in the middle of the lounge, lit on a cold night, not that the flat was cold. No, every room had underfloor central heating, the fire place was really just a show piece. The kitchen was an L-shaped affair with white marble counters and all mod cons, a wine cooler pointed out to the lounge. On a long uninterrupted wall, bookcases and display shelves had been built into the wall with subtle back lighting. Furnishings were comfortable, chic and modern. The designers had left the old period pieces in place, which Billy approved of, as so many of these old buildings were being gutted of their historic past.

Billy had asked her once how much one of these flats cost, when she casually replied *around five million* he nearly chocked on the pizza he was eating.

She had been out and bought a Christmas tree. It was nearly as tall as the thirteen foot ceiling and was decorated in traditional greens, reds and golds. A white and gold angel sat atop looking over the occupants of the room.

"My family have all these ancient traditions at this time of year and I'm afraid I can't get out of any of them, so I thought you and I could have our own little Christmas here tonight."

She showed him to the dining table as he handed her the bottle of wine, he had bought with the help of a wine merchant he knew. His recommendation had been a red Burgundy, **2002 Domaine Faiveley**

Mercurey Clos Des Myglands Premier Cru, Billy could hardly say the name let alone remember it off by heart, although he had been trying most of the day. In the end he was honest and explained a friend had chosen it and he hoped it tasted good. Lizzie looked at the bottle and read the name perfectly in French, of course, and said she had never tried this one so she was looking forward to tasting it.

The table had been laid like a photo from *Town and Country* magazine.

"Wow, this is something", Billy declared "When did you find time to do all this, weren't you working today?"

"You've caught me out, I didn't do it. The food was ordered from the Bulgari Hotel and I asked my housekeeper to lay the table. I just opened the packets, put the food on plates and placed them in the warmer. I must admit, I'm not the best of cooks. I manage beans on toast and basic recipes, and I can cook a mean Dawat, an Ethiopian dish, but a full Christmas dinner, umm, I would fail miserably."

"Well it looks like we are going to critique the Bulgari Hotel's kitchen tonight, although you really didn't have to go to so much trouble. I would have been happy with your beans on toast or your 'do you what' dish, whatever that it might be."

She laughed her infectious laugh and Billy's heart soared as it always did. It was at that moment he knew he was going to get his heart broken.

"Come on let's eat and get that lovely bottle of wine of yours open."

After dinner they sat with their feet up in front of the fire.

"I have something for you Billy. It has a little history I'd like to explain. I spent some time with my charity work in Ethiopia, years ago, hence the Dawat recipe. A traditional way of showing someone respect and friendship is to invite them to a coffee ceremony. When I was there, I met some wonderful people who took me into their hearts and at a time when they thought I was worthy to be considered a friend, I was invited to be an honoured guest at a special ceremony."

"Every guest invited is extended the hand of friendship and welcomed into a circle that takes on familial overtones. The honour of conducting an Ethiopian coffee ceremony always falls to a young woman. That was me. I know I'm not a young dippy girl any more, but when I'm with you, you make me feel as though I'm a younger, giddier woman than I am. So here is your gift and I hope you will allow me to invite you to a coffee ceremony when I get back in the New Year."

She handed Billy a beautifully wrapped box. He hated the thought of opening it and spoiling the wrapping and told her so. It felt pretty heavy and after the story she had just told, he wondered whether it was a few kilos of coffee.

"Don't be silly, open it I can't wait to see what you think."

He unwrapped the bows and ribbons with care and folded the paper neatly after removing. There was an incredibly intricately carved wooden box. He opened the latch and lid. Inside was a strange looking pot, which he removed with care. It was black in colour with what appeared to be a hand painted design of dots and stripes. The base of the pot was rounded tapering into a long neck. The spout protruded just above the main coffee chamber. The handle seemed excessively wide and open. The box also contained six small cups minus the handles, with the same hand painted pattern. A small side chamber held six silver spoons.

Billy had never had anyone give him such a thoughtful gift, something that obviously meant something to the giver and well as the receiver. But what should he be reading into this? She had said it showed respect and friendship, but then she went on to say, when it was time to be something more familiar. What was she trying to tell him, if anything? He could be totally misreading the gesture and this was just something she has been trying to get rid of for years. *No, you stupid idiot, she's not like that, why would you even think such a thing?*

"I don't know what to say Lizzie. I'm really lost for words. It's beautiful and I've never owned anything quite like this before. It's really thoughtful and I'm looking forward to being invited to this coffee ceremony when you get back. Is it suit and black tie?" He asked, trying to lighten the intense feelings he felt.

"Do you really like it Billy? It was a time in my life that was very special to me and I would like to start sharing parts of my past, parts of my history with you. What do you think?" She asked hesitantly.

"About what?" Billy had become a bit confused at where this was heading.

"About us being maybe more than friends, silly."

"Shit, Lizzie, how do I feel about it? Bloody hell, it would make my year, no, not my year, my decade, my life. God that would make me so happy, but you and me? Well come on, Lizzie, we're not exactly Cover magazines ideal couple. We would face a lot of resistance you know that don't you?"

"I don't care if we're not other people's ideal, I think you're my ideal and I'd like to see where we go. How about you?"

He moved over to her and was about to taste her lips for the very first time. "You know this will end in heartbreak for me don't you Lizzie? So be careful when you drop the axe and give me fair warning."

He kissed her passionately and she responded. That night they savoured each other and rested in each other's arms until the inevitable morning light broke through. When she woke, he was propped on this el bow looking down at her.

She could feel crust in the corner of her eyes and her mouth was as dry as a bone. Realization dawned after she yawned and saw he was staring at her.

"Oh, my God, I didn't remove my makeup last night, I bet I have mascara smudged all over my eyes and you're propped there looking at me. Fine way to start an affair, not."

He smiled at her.

"What?"

"I just can't believe how lucky I am."

"You have got to be kidding, I must look a mess. I promise next time we stay together I will set my alarm to wake early so that I can pop into the bathroom, do my hair, add some makeup and sneak back into bed. That way you will only see the Miss Jekyll me and not the Miss Hyde."

"Miss Jekyll and Miss Hyde are both perfect for me."

"Right, well, I'll kiss you good morning when I've brushed my teeth, meanwhile if you would like to find the coffee machine in the kitchen, it's on the breakfast bar next to the toaster. In the cupboard above it, you will find some Tassimo capsules, just put water in the container at the back and switch it on, I'll be out by the time the water's hot and will do the rest."

She removed herself from below the sheets and stood in front of him naked. Billy looked her up and down, it was the first time he had seen her in all her glory and he could swear he could see a halo behind her head. She was perfect. She hadn't actually told him her age yet, but he placed her around mid-thirties. She had a curvy body, as a women's body, in his opinion anyway, should be, he couldn't stand the new thin-as-a-rake, huge boobs and enormous arse, with fat pouting lips of some of the women he saw now-a-days. Magazines that promoted such images should be banned.

Photoshopped pictures tweeted to look real, with normal boys and girls trying to mimic those images, which naturally, couldn't be done unless someone injected fats and chemicals into their bodies.

This led to a whole load of problems such as disfigurement,

infections, low self-esteem and sometimes suicide. He had witnessed it first hand at the kid's charities. He had become involved some years back. A friend of his had a son that committed suicide due to bullying and it had prompted him to find somewhere he could possibly help struggling children.

Lizzie on the other hand, especially given her background and the fact that she could afford any treatment she wanted, seemed to have let nature age her without faking anything. He knew her full breasts were her own as they weren't as perky as they probably were when she was a girl. When he held them in his hands last night, they were soft, a pillow to bury his face in. She had a lovely oval, backside that he held onto as they made love, a gorgeous Venus lying below a soft tummy that carried a few extra pounds. Her head reached just to where his heart was, her beautiful wavy blonde hair falling around her shoulders. In all of his forty-seven years he had never felt like this. He had so many feelings welling up inside him, he didn't know what to do with them.

Coffee was made but they had run out of time to eat, and they had to say their goodbyes.

"Oh, crikey Lizzie, you swept me away so much last night I almost forgot, I got you a gift too." He handed over a small box.

She opened his gift and recognised the **Van Cleef & Arpels** box immediately. Inside was the most exquisite **Frivole** gold earrings shaped as flowers.

"Do you like them?"

"I love them, they are gorgeous."

"You Elizabeth Dowels-Hudson are gorgeous."

Billy left knowing the next three weeks were going to drag, and he believed, Lizzie was feeling much the same.

Chapter Three

"What time is Derrick and Jenny arriving Mum?" Billy called from the lounge.

"They think they'll arrive about tea time around five or six. Why have you got something planned?"

"No, just asking, I thought I'd take them down to the pub for a quick one this evening, not for long, just a pint or two. What time will Lesley and Sofia arrive tomorrow, does she need collecting from the train station?"

Mum walked into the lounge from the kitchen. "I can't be doing with all this shouting. No, she said she has a friend that is going to give her a lift back from Bristol. He lives in Richmond so it's sort of on his way, just a small diversion. She doesn't know what time she'll get in; it depends on traffic I suppose. She said she will ring us when she's about an hour out, that should give me time to prepare something for her to eat when she gets home. How's your dad? Does he need anything? Do you need anything John?" she called over as he sat in his armchair, but Dad was off in Lala land.

"He's alright, I'll get him something when he comes back to planet earth." He kissed his Mum's forehead and she turned to go back to the kitchen.

Billy went over to his father and sat in the chair next to him. He told him about his day so far, how he had had to go to work after he had left Elizabeth and how he found it nearly impossible to concentrate on what any one was saying to him, everything sounded like blah, blah blah. He hadn't told anyone about Lizzie yet, except Pops, but only when Dad wasn't really with them.

He had a feeling his Mum knew something was going on. He had been out a lot more of late he had been acting a lot chirpier. He wondered whether his mum had picked up on the fact he had come home today with a box in his hands and gone straight up to his room without a word. This was very strange behaviour for Billy, he always sought out his father in the lounge for a quick kiss and then he would find her in the kitchen for her daily hug and kiss. Still, he was sure she would wait for him to tell her when the time was right.

He was dying to tell someone and had planned on revealing his secret to Derrick over a pint at the pub hoping that Jenny would say she wanted to stay at home, which she may well do to unpack their things. He was going to tell him he was in love and ask his advice on what to do. Given who Lizzie was and who he was, he wasn't sure whether they had a future and believed he was letting himself in for a big fall.

Billy turned on the telly and started flicking through the channels. The News was showing some sort of riot, *flick*, washing powder advert, *flick*, soap opera, *flick*, celebrity live show. Nothing was on so he turned it off.

"I'm going to have a shower, Pop, I'll be back shortly. Mum I'm off for a shower, Dads fine, I'll be about half an hour."

He made his way to his bedroom, which he used to share with Derrick growing up. He remembered the farting competitions they would have, and if Mum or Dad walked in,

"This room smells like the back end of a gorilla", they would moan.

"How do you know what the back end of a gorilla smells like, Mum, Dad?"

Neither of them having smelt the arse of any animal.

Instead of two single beds, the room now housed an extra-long double bed, which had cost him a packet, to accommodate his six-foot two height. He had gotten fed up with hanging his feet over the end of the bed whilst his head was pushed up against the wall.

He could afford it. After coming back from his travels, he had set about getting a teaching job. Everything would be great over the phone and the headmasters would spout enthusiastically about meeting him and what the school had to offer, but basically the doors were closed in his face once they saw him. Of course, good excuses were always made, someone more qualified, someone with more experience, someone more suited to the position, they felt he was over qualified for the position. He always knew it was the tattoos and there weren't even very many, back then.

Once he had faced enough rejections, he decided to learn a trade and decided on construction.

He could have taken a Master Building, Planning and Construction Management course and used credits he had obtained, towards a new degree, but he realised he would face the same discriminations in management as he did as a teacher. He opted for a skills course. He did well, studying was easy for him, he'd spent seven years doing it previously, not counting his school years and like riding a bike, he retain what he'd learnt in the past. He knew how to condense his study down to the essential information and passed with flying colours, then he spoke with Pops.

"Dad, I have a favour to ask. I've spoken to a bank for a loan to start my own business. However, as I have no track record, they have asked for a cosignatory on the loan. I've got all the paperwork. I've done my forecasts, growth plans, budgets. The bank is happy to go ahead. Will you stand as cosignatory, so that I can get stated?"

"Let me take a look at your figures Son. If I agree with the bank, I'll do it willingly."

Right Way Construction, was a two man show, to start, but over the next fifteen years, it had developed into a fifty-employee one, with several projects on the go at any given time. Billy employed a manager at the front of the business. Noel was the 'face' that went with the presentations and quotations. Noel would always have his foreman with him, Billy and over the years the two had come to read each other like a book, so if Billy thought anything was amiss, he could discretely signal it to Noel and vice versa.

He had offered to buy Mum and Dad a newer, bigger house, but they weren't interested.

"We bought this place when we wed. The walls of this house have memories soaked into them from long before you three arrived. We can look at a patch of a wall, door or floor and remember, that is where something happened. We want to stay with those memories until we're gone. It's a lovely thought Billy, but no."

Billy could have bought a house of his own to live in, but he chose to remain at home with Mum and Dad and especially now Pops was ill, he was needed there more than ever.

He had invested in property and had an agent renting them out, but he really didn't take that much notice.

"You seem to be running smoothly, you're my agents', so I'll leave all this in your capable hands."

He also had a small place in Spain, in a coastal town called Sotogrande, not too far from Marbella. He would fly there two or three times a year, depending on work, sometimes taking Dorrie and John if they felt like a break, maybe a couple of mates for a few rounds of golf in the sunshine instead of rain and when the mood took him, alone to read a few good books in peace. He enjoyed his visits, but after making the mistake of going one August, concluded he could never live in that sort of heat. He was amazed how the locals managed to continue functioning, all he wanted to do was sit indoors, naked except his boxers with the air-condition set to maximum.

Billy sat on the edge of his bed, his body wet, hair dripping from the shower. He stood and looked at himself in the mirror, the towel wrapped around his middle. *I'm still in good shape for my age, work hasn't let me become flaccid and not being a big beer drinker helps. Luckily, I haven't developed a protruding beer gut like so many men my age, even many younger guys have a gut on them. I'm OK. Alright I haven't got a six pack and my stomach isn't as flat as it would be if I went to a gym but overall, not bad.*

He dropped the towel and looked at his penis, he cupped his testicles in his hand. *These have dropped a bit, not as round and firm as they used to be, but still functioning well, so is this,* he touched his penis. He hadn't had any complaints in that department, but then again, he hadn't really been in a relationship long enough for complaints to creep in.

The longest had been Susan, an accountant who worked in the office before they grew big enough to work with an accounting and consulting firm. They were together five years and everyone thought they would marry. Shit, he thought they would marry, but it wasn't to be. Maybe her instincts told her he wasn't in love with her, that he was basically just going along with what was expected, by her and everyone around them.

She broke up with him in Sotogrande. She asked him if they were going to get engaged and set a date for a wedding.

His response of "Yeah, whatever you want, just tell me how you want to do it", may have shown a less than enthusiastic acknowledgement. She had told him she didn't want to get married just to get divorced ten years later and that she felt she deserved to have someone that truly loved her. Marriage she said "was hard enough without just one person being up for it." He was sad, but not heart broken and that was the problem she had seen.

He realised he still had his hand on his balls. After having another quick look at things and deciding he had nothing to moan about, he gave his stomach a quick slap and got dressed.

Dad was still looking at a blank TV screen and as soon as he sat on the sofa, he heard the beep of a car horn outside.

"Derrick and Jenny are here Dad, I'll let them in." He rose and went to the front door. "I've got it Mum", he called to the kitchen from where some really delightful smells wafted which set his tummy to grumble with hunger.

Jenny stood at the door, whilst in the background Derrick was collecting things from the boot and placing them by the back wheel. Billy gave Jenny a hug which lifted her off her feet.

"Take it easy Billy, we've only been gone two months. Put me down and go and help Derrick, he's got all the Christmas presents and they need to go under the tree. Has Lesley and Sofia arrived yet?"

"No, they'll be arriving tomorrow. A friend is driving her apparently", he looked at Jenny with a suspicious look. "Not sure what this guy is about, friend or more."

"Well, university isn't just for working or studying" said Jenny and winked.

"He'd better not be", said Billy.

"He'd better not be what?" Asked Derrick, who had come up behind, arms full of boxes and two carry bags in his hand.

"I'll tell you inside. I'll get your suitcase."

"Who'd better not be what?" he whispered to Jenny. "Lesley appears to have a beau" she replied.

"Oh shit, he'll be in for a grilling when he visits."

"He's bringing Lee and Sofia tomorrow, apparently driving her home from Bristol. This could be an interesting Christmas." She kissed her husband's cheek and went inside.

"I thought Sofia was going to see her dad this Christmas."

"It seems not, you know Carlos, he's probably come up with yet another excuse. Poor child, you'd think her own father would want to see her as much as possible. Maybe he has too many *señoritas* keeping him occupied. I'm so glad Lee got rid of him eventually."

"Yeah it only took four affairs for her to do it. She should have divorced him after the first, then she would have had a better chance of making a new life, with a decent bloke."

"Come off it Derrick she's done great on her own. Not every woman born needs a man around them."

"Well, I'm glad you're one of the ones that does" he said and patted her backside.

"Well, so far yes, but beware…"

"Hi Dorrie, John it's us."

Jenny pop her head around the door of the lounge and saw John sitting in his chair. "Hi Dad." She went over and kissed his head "How are you? It's Jenny."

He looked up from where he had been sitting alone for the last... how long? He couldn't remember.

"Hi Jenny darling. I'm fine and you? Is Derrick with you?" He was back, for how long nobody knew, but for the moment he was coherent.

"Yes, he's just saying hi to Billy and Mum. Do you want a cup of tea?"

"Oh, I'd love one, I'm parched. Ask Dorrie if she has any carrot cake left, would you? Thanks Petal."

"Will do."

"I've left your dad in the lounge, go and speak with him Derrick. He's coherent at the moment so go and chat with him while you can, and you Billy. I'll help Mum make a pot of tea. He said he's parched."

Derrick and Billy went to speak with their father.

"How's he doing Mum?" Jenny asked.

"Well, you know, he comes and goes. Maybe a bit more often than before, but Doctor Maklin told us it would be like this. He's fine on the whole, gets a bit frustrated with us when he can't remember something. Brenda is a Godsend; she handles him so well when he gets irritable and usually manages to settle him down. Health wise he's fine, he's had a bit of a lingering cough this winter, but he always gets a winter cough. We'll keep an eye on it."

"And, how are you? Are you looking after yourself, getting out and about, keeping up your strength?"

"Oh yes, I'm fine. I've got Brenda, so I'm managing to go to my clubs and bingo and I've got Billy at night, who basically takes over everything but the cooking, when he gets home. He's brilliant with John, chats with him for hours. Well, you know Billy, nothings too much for him for anyone, let alone family."

"Yes, I know. He's wonderful, you're lucky to have them all. I hear Lesley is coming home with a boyfriend."

"Well, we don't actually know that yet. She said her friend Fetu was bringing her home by car. Apparently, his family lives in Richmond and he is going to visit them, so he has offered her a lift. She did say she'd like me to meet him. I didn't tell Billy that part in case he read too much into it. She did sound excited about him when she was talking about him though. You never know now whether people are friends, boy or girl friends, lovers or one-night stands, they all seem to merge into one. Defining a relationship doesn't seem to be as it used to be."

"And Billy, is he seeing anyone?"

"Billy, I wish he were. He leaves for work, comes home, sits with

Dad, goes to his charities and out for a pint or a game of golf with the boys and the rest of the time he's keeping me and Dad company. He needs a good kick up the bum the boy does."

"Well hardly a boy Mum. I suppose it is difficult for him. We know what new people are like around him. But, don't worry, there's a really special person out there looking for him, just as he's looking for her. Your right though, he won't meet her sitting at home or going to work, he needs to get out socially more."

"Take this through Jenny and I'll get the cake." Dorrie handed Jenny a tray set with the pot of tea, cups, saucers, sugar and milk.

"I don't know why you don't just switch to tea bags Dorrie; they're so much easier." Dorrie smiled.

Jenny set the tray on the coffee table in front of the sofa and poured the tea. Dorrie brought up the rear with carrot cake.

"Now don't you lot eat too much; dinner will be ready at six and I don't want to be wasting good food.

They chatted and caught up on news taking the opportunity to speak with Dad. He had been diagnosed a little over a year ago.

"Do you two want to pop to the pub for a quick drink?" Billy asked.

Derrick looked at Jenny

"You two go, I'll stay and chat with Mum if it's alright. We were so busy at the end of term and then getting ready to come here, I'm pretty worn out, I'd rather just sit here and chat. But you go with Billy, Derrick."

"Are you sure?"

"Yes, I need to unpack anyway. Where are we staying Dorrie?"

"You're in Lee's room. She said she and Sofia will take the pull out in the back lounge for the three days you're here, then they'll go upstairs."

"Great. Do you want a clean shirt Derrick?"

"Not thanks pet, this is fine. We'll just have a couple of pints, I'm pretty done in too."

"We don't have to go, if you're not up for it bro", Billy injected.

"No, it's fine, I'm not that done in, a couple a pints will be good."

After dinner and stacking the dishwasher Derrick said,

"OK, grab your things and we'll make a move. We won't be long."

The men put on their warm coats and made their way into the cold. Winter so far had been kind and Billy had managed to keep working all through, but the last couple of weeks had seen temperatures drop dramatically.

The ten-minute walk from Park View Gardens to the Royal Feathers at the end of Bedford Road saw the men walk in rubbing their hands to encourage circulation.

"Hello you two. Haven't seen you for a while Derrick" came the call from Christine, the landlady. "You here for long, how's Jenny?"

"Just three days, then we are visiting Jenny's folks. How are things with you Chris, Charlie around?"

"He'll be up in a second, he's just changing a barrel."

She didn't ask what they would have, she knew. They had all grown up together, gone to the same school and when she took over the pub from her parents, Billy and Derrick made sure they gave their custom. She placed a pint of Guinness and a pint of light and bitter on the bar.

Go sit over by the fire and get warm, I'll send Charlie over to say hello when he gets up here.

Billy and Derrick made their way to the fire place one of the many attractions in the pub.

The Feathers, as the Royal Feathers was known by the locals, was one of those pubs that managed not to get swallowed up by a big brewery. Chris's parents had the pub before they asked Chris if she wanted to take it over when they decided to move over to France and retire. Charlie was a car mechanic at the time and had his own garage. Another of the small businesses that were struggling, at that time, to survive the hunger of the corporate Machine, who were buying, putting their company brand and then franchising everything they could lay their hands on. That was back in the nineteen eighties.

Chris had grown up in the pub and knew the trade inside and out, but when they first took over Charlie had to go through the learning curve of not drinking all the profits. After the first couple of years Chris gave him an ultimatum to stop drinking or he had to leave. It was tough going for him, but he eventually kicked the drink and the pub went from good to excellent when he found a passion for cooking.

An old sixteenth century Coaching Inn, the Feathers, was apparently one of the first inns to have a wall enclosed coal fireplace when England's woodlands disappeared due to the demands of shipbuilding. It occupied a huge part of the wall and dominated the middle space of the pub. It was because of this feature Chris and Charlie had decided to renovate the interior, into a replica of the original inn. Billy's firm did the work. The result was like stepping back in time, but with comfortable furnishings and modern appliances.

The *Guardian* did a feature on it once as one of the top ten pubs in England, after that, Chris and Charlie were inundated with offers for features in loads of specialist magazines and tourist guides. They declined all, stating they didn't want the pub to become a mere tourist attraction, but wanted it for their locals to enjoy. If they did ever decide to retire it would be worth a fortune.

Charlie had built a small restaurant to sit thirty in one of the back rooms and was proud to display his National Chef of the Year award. Eating there was purely by reservation and now-a-days had a waiting list of at least two months, so if you wanted to celebrate a special occasion, you had to know and book well in advance, unless you were a regular client. He always kept a table empty and available for a local customer. To the side of the building was the beer garden which they had spent many a summer day in, when it wasn't raining. The people here were like family.

They sat on one of the two sofas placed around the fire.

"So how are things Derrick, still having run ins with the headmaster?"

"Not really, I've learned to keep my mouth shut. He's due to retire next year, I think we're all just hoping he doesn't stay on after retirement and we get a more progressive head in. If he does, Jenny and I have spoken and I think I'll take early retirement myself. We'd like to do a bit of travelling and Jenny would like to take her writing to the next level, but never has the time. There's an early retirement scheme on the go which is not that much lower than when I hit sixty-five so with our private pensions, money from the scheme and maybe a bit of private coaching, we'll get by fine and you never know, Jenny may become the next J.K. Rowling and keep me in luxury for the rest of my life. How about you, anything new?"

"Well actually there is something I wanted your opinion on, but you can't tell anyone, not Mum or Jenny."

"Sounds intriguing, anything the matter?"

"The opposite, I've met someone and I think I'm in love."

"You've what?" blurted Derrick "Well blow me down, that was the last thing I expected to hear. What's she like? Tell me more and why on earth do you want my opinion? Is there something wrong with her?"

"Again, the opposite, she's amazing, beautiful, intelligent, sexy, kind, loving."

"So, what's the problem? Sounds great to me."

"She's mega rich, an MP in Parliament and landed gentry."

"Yeah, come on, what's really the problem?"

"No, honestly, those are the problems. She says it doesn't matter, that she doesn't care, but I don't think she's looking at the bigger picture."

"Oh, shit bro, you really do let yourself in for it don't you. You know this could end in misery don't you?"

"I know, I know. She and I are great together. We get the usual odd looks and giggles when we are out, but they don't bother us. Elizabeth seems not to notice. The thing is, I think I love her. The problem is going to be her family and possibly her constituents. She comes from a town surrounded by villages and the inhabitants, her voters. Many rely on the good will of her father and his estate for their income. If we become really serious, I can imagine what the gutter press will do and that could affect her job. Maybe for her sake I ought to stop it now, before we both get hurt. That's what my mind tells me to do. She's gone back home for Christmas and my head keeps telling me to write her a letter and break it off, but my heart just won't let me. I mean what's the worst that could happen, we're both adults, we both know our feelings and minds, why should we give a shit about what others think?"

"Because and I think you know it Billy, this relationship could have you both loosing so much. Her, her career and livelihood, let alone what her family will say when they meet you. Has she said they are open-minded like her or upper-class superior twats?"

"Oh, come Derrick, I don't know what they're like, they may actually be open-minded for all I know, although the feeling I get from Lizzie, is they are not.

"Have you spoken to her about your fears? How long have you known her? Have you asked her whether she has thought about the consequences of this relationship? You want my opinion? Well I think the two of you both need to sit down and make a list of pro's and con's and see if it's worth pursuing, but I personally think this will end badly. Sorry Billy but I do."

***

The car horn outside announced the arrival of Lee, Sofia and friend or more after much family speculation. It was left to Mum to open the door and let them in. Lee swung her arms around her Mum then after her kisses she moved onto all the other family members. Fetu stayed back outside the front door until the fuss wore down just enough for him to gently cough his presence.

Lee caught it, "Oh Fetu, Fetu sorry. Come in, come on it is freezing outside."

The fuss stopped and everyone looked back towards the front door with a welcome on their lips that died mid-air. There stood a tall man with jet black hair pulled tight across his head, looped into a ponytail with a mass of curls cascading down his back. A strikingly good-looking man with finely built features, a slightly flattened nose and light brown skin.

Jenny logged him at about thirty-two years of age. A wide grin appeared on his face that exposed incredibly white teeth. He extended his hand to the first person which was Mum.

"Hello, I've heard so much about you, I'm Fetu."

Mum looked up at the tall man, smiled and declared "Well my boy, I'll shake your hand, but here we normally hug." She went to him and gave him his hug, her arms encircling around his body. "My goodness you're nearly as tall as Billy." She released him and let the others take their turns, with a hug from Jenny and handshakes from Derrick and Billy, although Billy's hand shake held the mans grip for just a little too long while he tried to inspect Fetu.

"Right let's get into the lounge everyone, we can't stand here blocking the hallway all day" said Mum.

Billy turned and led the party into the lounge.

"I'm going to make tea, sit yourselves down and I won't be a second. Do you drink tea Fetu?" Mum asked.

"Yes please, Mrs. Johnson"

"Oh, I don't get called Mrs. Johnson here lad. Just call me Dorrie like the rest."

"Yes please, Dorrie" he said giving her that amazing smile.

"I'll come with you Mum", announced Lee.

"So, will I." followed Jenny, she was totally intrigued to hear who this magnificent creature was.

Fetu sat down on the sofa, Dad made his way to his chair, Derrick decided to sit on the sofa, Sofia went to the back room having hardly lifted her face from her mobile phone and Billy decided to sit opposite Fetu ready for the grilling.

"Well" started Billy "How do you know our Lesley then?"

"We're at the same University, I'm studying medicine. We met at a lecture she was giving."

"And I hear you live in Richmond, good of you to come all the way to Grays to give her a lift. It's a bit out of your way isn't it?"

"Oh, it's fine. My parents won't actually arrive home until late this evening. They are both working, so I have time to kill."

Derrick interrupted the conversation as Billy's tone wasn't the friendliest.

"Do you like it, the university I mean? I hear Bristol is excellent for medicine, has a great rugby team as well."

"True, I'm actually in Bristol University League, we train every Mon day and Wednesday. Terrific bunch of blokes. This year we're fielding a first team and a 9's development team. We have quite a lot of BUCS fixtures and rolling substitutions which means I get plenty of play practice. I won't make the first team, too old in the tooth for that."

The chat had turned normal, much to the relief of Fetu. In the kitchen Mum and Jenny immediately wanted to know more.

"So, who is he and how come he is so gorgeous?" Asked Jenny

"He is rather hot, isn't he? Well, he's thirty-three years old so yes Jenny, twelve years younger than I am. I was giving a lecture jointly with Dr. Najeeb, a well-known doctor who has all these websites and easy study videos and things. Once I'd done my bit and the podium was handed to Dr. Najeeb, I sat and he took the seat next to me. I don't remember much about the lecture, I was too conscious of him and every time I tried to take a peek, he seemed to be looking at me and kept giving me that smile of his.

At the end of the lecture we both left but as he stood up, he said he had for gotten to introduce himself, which he did and asked me my name. About a week later he was waiting outside one of my classes and asked me out for a drink. That was it. We've been seeing each other for the past, what three months? I think. I didn't mention him when I was home last time because we had only had two dates and there wasn't anything to tell, but well now, we seem to be pretty serious and so I thought it was time a let you guys meet him. But only briefly because I didn't want Derrick or Billy giving him the three degree over a full weekend or even a night, so I just told him this time he could meet you all for an hour or so."

"Is he English?" Mum asked.

"Sort of, he was born here, but his parents are from Samoa and the family still have a lot of ties there. He was an Architect for a few years but he found he hated the job, so he has returned to University as a mature student and is actually hoping to be accepted into her Majesty's Royal Physicians then return to Samoa to practice."

"I don't think you should tell the boys that part, for the time being anyway."

"Oh, no, we are well off anything like that yet, we just really get on well together. Oh, for goodness sake I'm not thinking of running off to Samoa with him", she laughed at the thought.

"For certain we wouldn't like to see you go to Samoa to live if it gets serious." Jenny said.

"Well I'm glad to hear that."

"Now let's take these things through to the living room and let's get those boys watered and fed. I'll take these sandwiches through and Jenny you take the cake, I'm sure Fetu must be hungry after the journey."

"I'll go and get Sofia off that mobile and out of the back room. It's time she came and joined the family. She's in love with a new boyfriend."

"Yes, you do that, tell her, her grandma needs to see her."

The three women made their way into the others to find everyone generally relaxed and talking about rugby. Derrick was well up on just about any sport and not just men's sports but women's as well and could keep a conversation going for hours on the subject.

When the girls arrived and everyone had their sandwiches talk changed more general. Lee talked about how her work was going and Sofia talked about her studies, Jenny and Derrick about their jobs and things happening in Surbiton. Dad had drifted off to Lala land again but still sat there eating and drinking whatever was handed to him.

Billy talked about the job in Eaton Place, and how with the cold they were finishing some inside work, but not about Elizabeth.

"So, what do your parents do Fetu, that they have to work late?" Asked Jenny.

"Well, my father is a doctor, I guess I'm following in his footsteps at long last, but I'd probably like to take a different path than him." Lee shot him a look to go no further on the subject which he picked up on, they had already talked about what could and couldn't be said just yet to her brothers. "Yes, Dads a surgeon, which I find a bit boring, a bit like a glorified butcher in my mind. I think I'd like to specialise in an illness, Cancer, Diabetes, Alzheimer's. I hope you don't mind me mentioning Alzheimer's, Lee has told me John suffers with it. I'm not sure yet either way. My Mum, well, she is an artist. She exhibits, basically all over the world and when she's not travelling, she paints at her studio, which is attached to our house in Richmond. I have another brother and sister, both older, Aleki, my brother, lives in New York with his family, he's a teacher like you Derrick. My sister Aonani lives in New Malden with her family, she's a GP. Aonani will be bringing her two daughters and husband up for the family Christmas. So, it's great, Aleki tries to get over whenever he can and Mum always pops in to see him if she's in New York. Apart from that the rest of my family still live in Samoa." He didn't mention one day he wanted to return.

"How lovely you have a close family, it's so important, especially nowadays, when everything is so difficult", said Mum.

Billy was wondering how old the toy boy was.

"Well, it's been great getting to meet you all, but I think I had better make a move, I'm not sure how the traffic will be this close to Christmas crossing London on the ring road." He stood, as did everyone to say good bye, hands were shaken again and hugs were given by the girls. Lee went with him to the front door and returned fifteen minutes later.

"That was a long goodbye for a friend." said Billy.

Lee winked at him and smiled, "A little more than a friend Billy."

"Ah, I see, he seems a bit young for you Lee."

"Not at all Billy, he is introducing all sorts of new things to me. Ex citing things, I feel like a young woman again and his tattoos, I imagine they are just like yours in certain places." She giggled

She knew she was teasing him but it was true. She and Fetu were doing all sorts of things she never thought she would. They went skydiving, windsurfing, hiking at least twice a month, walked every day. He had even said the next thing they were going to try was bungy jumping. She loved it all.

Chapter Four

Christmas with the family was great, and New Year's Eve was seen in at the Feathers. The following day was quiet for everyone, relaxing at home before setting back to work.

He had tried to phone Elizabeth at midnight on New Year's Eve but her line was constantly engaged. He thought about phoning her a five a.m. when lines were clear, but decided she wouldn't appreciate him calling if she hadn't long gone to bed. They spoke on New Year's Day.

"Hi there beautiful, how are the celebrations going?"

"Oh, the usual stuff, lots of dinners, too much wine and then too much whine from the company. My parent's friends drive me nuts, always moaning about stupid irrelevant things, I have to bite my tongue most of the time. And yours, how are things going there?"

"Great, I caught up with my brother and Jenny for a couple of days before they went off to her parents for the New Year. My sister Lee was here with my niece Sofia and the big news is my sister brought her toy boy for us to meet. Actually, he's not that much younger than her, I think about eight or nine years but still. He looks like some sort of Samoan God or warrior, long hair all the way down his back. I think Jenny and Mum are totally smitten. He seems alright, but I can't see anything coming of it, he's a student and she's a lecturer, there's too many differences."

"Ah, like us then", she said.

"No. Not at all like us. We've got loads of things in common, the right age gap for a start."

"You cheeky devil, how old do you think I am and what on earth is the right age gap, may I ask? I'm not that close to your age."

"It's different our way around, the man should be older. I miss you" Billy told her.

"I miss you too, oh so much. By the way it's very sexist of you to think women shouldn't date men younger than themselves but it's alright for men."

"I didn't mean..."

"I know what you meant Billy Johnson and it's wasn't good." She changed subject and went on. "I've keep thinking about the last night we spent together and I keep getting aroused at all the wrong times. Mother thought I was coming down with 'flu because I shivered, but it was the memory of how you made me feel."

"Me too and I can't wait to do it again, at least two or three times. When are you coming back to the city?"

"Not for a least another week I'm afraid. I have some work to do here in the Norwich office, but it won't be too long and then we'll be together again. You said Lee's boyfriend is Samoan, did you ask him about his Tatau?"

"His what?"

"His Tatau, surely Billy, what does it sound like?

"I don't know."

"Tatau, is the original word for tattoo. Tattoo came back with the first Europeans when they returned from the islands inhabited by the Polynesians, but they mispronounced the word Tatau which became tattoo. If he is Samoan, and he has chosen to, he may have started his Pe'a years ago, any time from eighteen when a boy is deemed a man. I thought you would have known about the Polynesian tattoos. They're very fashionable now; lots of celebrities have them, especially sports celebrities and of course film stars, the butch male ones mostly. I wonder if he has one."

"According to Lee, yes he does. Elizabeth, you never cease to amaze me, how do you know so much about ink. I know about Polynesian tattoos, seen quite a lot of them, but I thought they mostly came from New Zealand."

Billy actually knew a lot about Polynesian and Kiri Tuhi history, but loved to hear the woman he was falling in love with talk about his passion, she knew a lot and enjoyed showing her knowledge.

He continued "I thought they all became fashionable with the Maori tattoos on the Kiwi rugby teams when all the women swooned."

"I told you when we first met, I wanted to look at your tattoos and now that we are intimate, I expect you to lie still while I start examining them all. You can tell me the story of every single one, not just the ones on your neck and head. You can tell me all their history, which means you will have to lay quietly naked on my bed, often and for long periods of time." He heard a slight giggle.

"I somehow doubt I will lay still for long if I'm on your bed and have you close by", he told her.

"I'm looking forward to it", she laughed. "Listen I have to go, but call me again tomorrow if you can."

They said their farewells and when Billy stood there with his mobile in hand, he knew he was in real trouble because there was no way on this Earth, he was going to tell her it was over to save them from future heart break.

They were a week away from finishing the building work on Eaton Place when she came back to the city. They would be moving onto a job they had taken on in Twickenham. Elizabeth's house was just about ready for the interior team to go in and do their magic. Billy was dreading the move. There would be no opportunity for him to move across into the city to see her during lunch times, the traffic would deem it impossible. He briefly thought about renting a bedsit or small flat in the city so that he could go straight there after finishing work, but dismissed it as quickly as the thought came. Mum and Dad needed him at home.

Twickenham was situated on the west side of London, Grays on the east and Lizzie in the city. He could see he was either going to be spending a lot of time in his car, or he would have to try and work out a commuting system, which would be a whole lot quicker than driving. He had worked with his team for many years, but looked at forthcoming contracts to see if any were in the centre of London so he could switch teams. He knew it was a bad idea, that it took a long time to develop a good team and at present they were all working like clockwork, it wasn't a good idea to put a spanner in the works.

***

The first night they were together on her return they spent the night at her flat. He got Dad ready for bed before he left and when he knew he wouldn't make it home that night phoned Dorrie to let her know not to worry.

"I told my brother about you" he told Lizzie as she stood in the kitchen in a white T-shirt and, knickers. They had just finished making love for the second time and were hungry for something.

"You did? And what did you tell your brother?"

"I told him I had met the girl of my dreams and that I loved her more than I could ever imagine and that one day I'm going to make her my wife."

Elizabeth's hand stopped mid-air above the scrambled eggs she was making.

"You told him what?"

Billy realised that he had just spoken his true feelings out loud and not just in his head.

"Sorry Lizzie, I didn't mean to say that, it just came out. I know it's all too soon and I don't want to frighten you off. I meant the first two things, but well marriage, that was a bit hasty even for me. It's just, you've swept me off my feet. I don't know whether I'm coming or going and it gets even worse when I'm not near you."

"Does that mean you wouldn't consider marriage?"

"No, no, not at all, but well let's be honest no matter how deeply we feel about each other, there are major problems ahead of us if we get too serious. Don't you agree?"

She turned the heat down on the cooker and faced him.

"Do you believe if two people love each other like neither have loved before, they could possibly surmount those problems" She asked seriously.

"Well, I come from a real harsh world and sometimes reality doesn't give us all that we want in life. I have fallen in love with you Lizzie, I can't believe it at my age, I had given up hope of ever feeling what I feel for you. You and I are from totally different worlds, I can see so many problems arising from your job, your family, your whole world in fact and sometimes those forces are very strong. I would give my life rather than have you suffer because of me Lizzie, I really mean that."

"I know you do Billy, but you have to know, that I too had given up all hope of meeting the man I would fall head over heels for and you are him. I feel as strongly as you do and I don't want to give you up. I don't know why but I felt an instant connection, even before I got to know you. Since I've known you, I learned you are intelligent, educated, honest, the kindest person I have ever met and sexy, oh so sexy. My family won't approve, I can assure you and they will have their reasons, but it will not matter to us. I really don't care about what my friends are going to think, if they don't love you for making me happy, then they were never true friends any way and I can live without them. I love you too Billy and if at some point in the future we want to get married then we bloody well will."

Their lips touched just across the breakfast bar as the smoke alarm started bleeping.

"Barbequed eggs?" She asked.

Billy went around and lifted her off the floor into his arms to carry her into the bedroom.

"I'm not longer hungry for food."

"Let me turn off the cooker."

***

February saw nothing but rain and more rain. Billy and Elizabeth managed to get a couple of weekends away together renting country cottages. The weather was never an issue as they would walk when they could and the rest of their time was spent getting to know each other and sitting quietly reading, talking and making love.

During one of those weekends Elizabeth asked the question

"So, tell me about your tattoos Billy. How did it all start?"

"It was never going to be what it turned into" he told her, "It started when I was eighteen and I wanted my biological parents to be part of me. They had been gone six years at the time and I was beginning to forget how they looked. I asked Dorrie and John if they would mind me getting a tattoo with their faces. I didn't want them to feel I didn't like being adopted and explained I just felt I wanted them to be part of me. They agreed, so I sat down with a notepad and started to draw their faces from photos we had that had come along with our personal possessions from our old house. I came up with a design and took it along to the nearest studio. Donald had the studio before, his son Matt, my friend, took over. Donald sat me down and gave me a bit of a talking to and explained that once I had a tattoo there was no going back and they weren't like a picture hung in a house that you could easily sell or swap; that this would be a lifelong attachment to my body and I had to understand that. After talking to me, I think he knew it was something I wanted and accepted that it would mark me for life and so he did it. That's this one." He showed her his first tattoo, his parents faces within angels wings encircling his left shoulder, over his breast and down to his heart.

"When I was nineteen and heading off to University a very good friend of mine died driving his motorbike into a cemetery wall of all bloody places. At the time he had been drinking and my parents were killed by a drunken driver, and it brought back a lot of submerged feelings about my parents' death I found myself designing a picture to remind me that drinking and driving don't go together. It was really a spur of the moment thing to take the drawing to Donald and ask him to turn into my second tat too. That's this one." He showed her a tattoo of a motorbike crashing into a cross with the name Lewis woven around the bike. "At University, whenever me or anyone I knew was on the piss and thought about getting behind a wheel I'd either look at the tattoo or show them it and relay the story to discourage them."

"I found drawing designs, of events in my life, helped me either celebrate or commiserate them, which kept them with me. I used to look at the drawings and I don't know why, but they helped make me happy. One day I was looking at my parents' tattoo and thought I would like one to re member Dorrie and John, so I designed something and had that done. I don't know really, but people who saw some of my designs suggested I start selling to tattoo studios as a way of making extra cash for my studies, which I did. Not the personal drawings, but others. I can't really say why I started putting my drawings on me, I guess maybe just being around studios quite a bit let me see the beauty of having your history live with you throughout your life."

He talked on "The Maori have Manawa lines, which is the word for heart and represents your life, your journey and your time spent on Earth; it just seemed to strike me and I started putting my '**Manawa**' on my skin, her on my stomach. Once I had finished with my version of my Manawa, I started looking at **Korus** which represents people and groups of people that come into your life and maybe influence it in some way, it represents..."

"New life" said Elizabeth. "Because of the spiralling shapes, I believe the resemblance comes from the shoots of a fern plant found in New Zealand."

"That's right, new life, new beginnings. When you add each new koru, you are adding important people in your life journey. I suppose it became a bit of an obsession and I suppose if I ever got in front of a psychiatrist, they would probably tell me I can't let things go, which I might add has been suggested on more than one occasion."

"What, that you need to let things go or that you need to see a psychiatrist?" Elizabeth asked with a smile.

"The second, no both" Billy replied. "I think by the time I got to my neck and head I was totally insane about showing my life in pictures; so obsessed, I didn't think of the consequences. I was too involved in myself and what I wanted to say. The man speaking to you now, is not the man I am, I don't talk to people, and I can't explain my wants, needs or anything like that to people and I guess this was my way of communicating those things. If I had met you Lizzie, when I was younger, I'm sure it wouldn't have gone this far, but I didn't and I can't change the past. I hope, when I die someone can find somewhere to donate my skin. I know it sounds macabre but for me it would be like being a Vincent van Gogh, a nutter in life but an artist in death."

"That's beautiful."

"It's insane really, I looked into it some years ago and there's this guy in Tokyo, a pathologist, his name is or was... Dr. Fukushi and he started a museum of skin art. I don't know whether the guy is still alive or whether the museum has been burnt down by the local villagers, but I can see my skin being there."

"Wow, that's crazy, but I do see your and point of view and how he got interested in it as well. I mean, who would want to lose all this beauty and the fact that your tattoos are originals, you never know, you may make me a very rich widow once you kick the bucket and after my parents disinherit me"

They laughed, but the fact that Lizzie had seen herself with him when he died sealed the deal, he decided to propose.

Chapter Five

April saw the rain and cold ease. Billy by now, had quite a few of his things at Lizzies flat and was there as often as he could. They had managed to make a loose routine, changeable at the last minute due to any work hic ups, which happened more with Lizzie than Billy.

April also saw an opportunity for Lizzie to introduce Billy to some of her family and friends, when an invitation arrived.

Mr. & Mrs Tom and Nancy Flores-Hythe
and
Mr. & Mrs Duncan and Bridget Byrne

Request the honour of your company at the marriage of their children

Talia Flores-Hythe & Stephen Byrne

27th May 2012 / 11.00 am / Saint Augustine Church / Brookesley

We invite you to share in our joy and request your presence.
The wedding supper will take place in the orchard field
at Brantley Park Estate at 20.00
R.S.V.P.

"My friend Talia is getting married Billy; I've known for a year it was coming up but the official invite has arrived. Will you come with me?"

They knew the time had arrived for them to start letting other people into their cosy, secret world and both were dreading the outcome. Billy knew his family and friends would adore Lizzie and love her nearly as much as he did, he also knew Lizzies family would hate him and from what he had heard about them would try to interfere and separate them. He felt he could deal with everything they threw at him. He had nothing to lose and everything to gain, but he was deeply worried about how it would affect Lizzie. How on Earth could anyone choose between their family or the person they loved? The choice should never have to be made.

> R.S.V.P.
> Hi Talia and Stephen
> Thank you for inviting me to your wedding.
> I will be attending and have marked the date on my calendar
> Is it at all possible to bring a plus one? My boyfriend Billy Johnson.
> I really look forward to seeing you both on the 27th May
> Love as always
> Lizzie

"Well, that's done", Lizzie declared with a smile and flourish, "we are going to a wedding. You will love Talia she is the sweetest of women. This will be her second wedding; I do hope this one works out for her. We've been friends forever. I can't wait for you to meet her."

"Dare I ask if any of your family will be going?" Billy asked.

"Oh, I dare say so, her parents and mine are very good friends, I would think she has invited my whole family."

"Is that going to be a problem? I don't want to go ruining your friend's wedding with any conflict or bad feeling."

"Don't be daft. For a start my parents would never make a scene in public, they are definitely stiffer upper lip and all that. They will be shocked to see you for the first time at a social event, but it's better this way, then Daddy can't go off and make a scene."

"Is that why you have invited me along, so that you can reveal me to your family without them making a scene?"

"No, not at all, I'm inviting you because I want you by my side. The fact that my family will just have to behave is a bonus."

"Look Lizzie I don't want to stop anyone from enjoying this wedding, I don't think it's a good way to start off with your parents, if they're likely to be miserable all day."

"Billy, if my parents want to be in a mood all day, that will be their problem, not yours' nor mine. Being bigots has its price. Now that is all there is to it. We are going to enjoy our day. Talia and Stephen will enjoy their day and as far as I'm concerned the others can enjoy it or not."

"Well, OK, if you say so. I'd better go buy myself a nice suit."

R.S.V.P.

Hi Lizzie and Billy
Thank you for accepting our invitation.

Absolutely fine about the plus one, we can't wait to meet him. It's about time you had a man in your life. With that in mind I wondered whether you would both like to come and stay with Stephen and I for a weekend before the wedding? I could do with your help shopping for some outfits to take on my honeymoon. I don't think my tie-dye clothes will be suitable in the Bahamas.

The weekend would have to be the first weekend of May as after that things are really going to get too busy for me. You know mother, she is going all out as usual.

I can't wait until the wedding to meet your mystery man. I've asked around and nobody has any idea you are dating, not even Phillip and he's your cam paign manager, he's always hanging around you. I think he is intrigued as I am. I take it you haven't introduced him to your parents yet because they certainly haven't said anything to mine. I can't wait to see you and him.

Will you drive to Norfolk or get the train? If you are coming by train, we can collect you from the station, or I can ask Mumsy to send a driver, she won't mind her driver bringing you to my place. What do you think?

Love as always
Talia and Stephen xx

Lizzie grabbed her mobile and wrote a text:

Hi Talia,
We will come to you on the 1st of May, which is a Friday and return on the Sunday. We will be driving. We'll come straight to your flat. Love you XX PS: My man is a bit different, a beautiful different.

"I've accepted an invitation to go to Talia's for the first weekend of May. I've accepted for both of us Billy so don't you think about making any excuses not to come."

"Well, with everything moving like it is, I suppose the bride and groom have a right to know me in advance so that they know where to hide me from all the posh people."

"Billy, you have to stop putting yourself down all the time. You are not a monster, you are beautiful and anyway, when you're in a suit you can hardly see your tattoos, so as long as you're not intending on stripping, I can't see a problem. You really do need to start loving yourself more."

"I do love myself and I have many people that love me, it's just that I don't think your polo crowd will be some of them. OK, well as I'm about to be exposed to your friends and family, I think it's about time you met mine. I'm going to phone everyone and see if they can get to Mums to meet you, hopefully this weekend."

"This weekend? That's four days away, a bit quick, I need to get ready."

"Get ready for what? You're fine as you are. They're not going to roast you naked over a spit fire and Lizzie 'you need to love yourself more'", he laughed.

Later that night when he went home, he found Mum sitting in the lounge, Dad had already been put to bed by the new night nurse Billy had employed. With not being around much anymore he had found someone to come in for a couple of hours every evening to deal with Dad's needs. Although Mum was twelve years younger than Dad, she was nearly seventy and couldn't manage him at times.

"Hi Mum, how are things tonight? Did Brian get Dad to bed OK?"

"Oh, yes, everything is fine, he's a lovely boy that Brian. We had a super chat about his wife and kids."

"That's great, err Mum I'd like to have a talk to you about something."

"Oh my, that sounds serious, I hope everything is alright."

"Yeah, it's actually great, I need to speak to you about someone I've met and I'd like the family to meet her."

"My goodness, it's about time. I've been wondering when you would get around to letting us meet her."

"What, you know?"

"Of course, I know, I'm your mother for heaven's sake. Coming in, getting showered, dressed up and smelling like a perfume parlour, then leaving and not coming back until late, if at all. I've known for a while but I have been waiting for you to tell me."

"I'm in love Mum and I intend on proposing to her. Her name is Lizzie and she's incredible, smart, funny, beautiful, you're all going to love her."

"Oh, Billy, I'm so very happy for you at long last. So when can we meet her?"

"I'd like to contact Derrick and Lesley to see if they could make it up here for the weekend. I like her to meet everyone. Would that be alright with you?"

"You know I never miss the opportunity to have you kids around me; that would be fine. Lunch, dinner, tea?"

"I thought I would bring her here to meet first and I want to have a chat with Charlie at the Royal Feather's to see if he could accommodate us on the spare table for a meal."

"Well that would be a wonderful treat for us all, wouldn't it?"

"I hope so."

"Lizzie", said Dorrie, "what a sweet name, is it short for Elizabeth?"

"Yes, Elizabeth Dowles-Hudson. I'm going to phone Lesley and Derrick to see if they can make it."

"Mm Elizabeth Dowles-Hudson" Dorrie repeated and thought how posh it sounded.

"Hi Billy this is a late call isn't it?"

"Yes, sorry sis, I just wanted to have a quick word to see if you could make it home this weekend?"

"What's wrong is Dad OK? Has something happened to Mum?"

"No, nothing like that. I've met a girl and I've been seeing her for quite a while now. She's coming to meet Mum and Dad at the weekend, I wondered if you could make it so that she could meet you and Sofia too."

"Oh, Billy, that's wonderful news, I'm so happy for you. What's her name?"

"Elizabeth, but I call her Lizzie."

"Hold the line just a second I need to speak with Sofia and Fetu."

There was a pause. "Me and Fetu can make it, but Sofia is off away this weekend but she said she would try and contact us via Messenger Live or WhatsApp so that she can say hello. Will you and Elizabeth be staying at Mums? Is Derrick and Jenny coming?"

"I'm going to phone Derrick after I've spoken with you, but I guess they will come, it's not far. Derrick already knows about her. I spoke with him at Christmas to get his advice. I think he'll want to meet her."

"OK, well that's great, me and Fetu can have my old room; Derrick and Jenny can have the back room seeing I took it at Christmas."

"Right, that's fine. I won't chat now; I want to phone Derrick before he goes to bed. See you what Friday or Saturday?"

"Make is Saturday, it's a long drive after a day at work. And Billy I'm so pleased for you, I can't wait to meet her. She must be very special if you want her to meet Mum and Dad":

"Yes, Lee she is."

The phone went dead or so Lesley thought. He could hear what sounded like screaming and jumping on Lesley's end of the call. He wasn't really sure what was going on at first until it became apparent when she started singing:

"Billy's got a girlfriend, Billy's got a girlfriend, Billy's got a girlfriend, she started singing. Sofia stood up from the sofa,

"You are mad Mum", and walked off to her room. Lesley continued with her singing and dancing.

"I take it this is good news" said Fetu.

"Such good news darling, such good news."

Shaking his head and chuckling to himself his call to Derrick brought up the same questions, about if anything had happened.

"I'm bringing Lizzie to meet Mum and Dad. I thought you and Jenny would like to meet her too. I'm going to speak with Charlie about having dinner in the Feather's, neutral ground so as to speak. Can you come?"

"The Lizzie? Wow bro, so you have decided to stick with it and go for it huh. Count us in, I want to see the girl that has convinced my brother to jump off the fence."

"Lee said you and Jenny have the back room this time because she had it at Christmas, are you alright with that or do you want me to book at room in a B & B?"

"Back room is fine. We can only stay overnight; I have a football match Sunday afternoon."

"You're playing?"

"No, those days are well gone, my under sixteens are playing."

"OK Derrick, I'll see you Saturday."

"OK Billy, Saturday. Thank goodness I can tell Jenny you have a girl friend at long last."

Billy could only imagine what exactly Derrick was telling Jenny.

Since he already knew about Billy's mystery woman, he imagined Jenny was intrigued as apart from Susan she'd never seen Billy with a woman and would be itching to know who had captured his heart. Had Derrick already realized that Billy wanted more than just a girlfriend, that he wanted Lizzie to be his wife? His brother was smart but he wasn't sure.

***

"Hey Jenny" called Derrick up the stairs, I have some very interesting news for you."

Jenny was already in bed, reading.

"Really, at this time of night, who was it?"

Derrick started making his way to the bedroom. Inside he sat on the edge of the bed.

"Billy's got a girlfriend and he wants us to meet her this weekend."

"You are joking aren't you?"

"Nope, dead serious. He told me about her at Christmas, but swore me to keep it to myself until he decided whether it was going to go anywhere. Apparently, she and her family are mega rich and own all this land around the country, so he wasn't sure whether anything would come of it. I can tell you this, he was in love at Christmas, so if he is now going to bring her home, I think he is going to take it further."

"What do you mean take it further?"

"Well, if I know Billy and I do, I think he is thinking about marriage."

"No way"

"Yes way, my darling. He wouldn't bother about us all meeting her if he wasn't thinking about it. By the way Lee is bringing Fetu and we are sleeping in the back room."

"Ooh I love intrigues" said Jenny, "now turn the lights off downstairs and come and give me a cuddle."

"I'll be two minutes, who could resist an offer like that."

With the downstairs secured, lights turned off; Derrick went back upstairs for his cuddle. All of Billy's family lay in their beds wondering about Billy's girlfriend.

***

"Let's go out tonight" suggested Billy

"But we are going to your Mum and Dads tomorrow."

"So?"

"Well, I need to make sure we have everything before we leave."

"Lizzie, stop fretting, for goodness sake they are ordinary people. They are going to love you."

"I know darling, it's just that I want to make a good impression."

"You will just by being yourself, now let's pop out for a drink and some fresh air."

"OK, let me grab my jacket."

***

Dorrie had been cooking and cleaning since Thursday ready to meet

Elizabeth. The house was spotless, the bedrooms were all made up for the kids and she had cooked so many cakes and goodies you would think it was the Royal Jubilee. She had spent most of the morning making sure Dad looked smart, even making him put on a tie which he kept loosening and looking through the curtains to see when they arrived. All of Dorries' neighbours were doing the same with their curtains as Dorrie had told everyone she saw during the week that Billy was bringing a girl home. Well, she couldn't be a girl, Billy was forty-seven, so she hoped not a young girl any way. She was just about to look through the curtains yet again, when she heard Billy's car drive into the driveway. She immediately took off her apron, patted herself down, took the apron and hung it on the back of the kitchen door and got to the front door just as Billy was getting some bags out of the boot.

A lady stood by the passenger door; about five feet seven with long blond hair, which she had tied up at the back of her head, with what looked like two pretty chopsticks sticking out of a rolled bun. She stood straight and held herself well. Dorrie put her at about thirty-eight, she was very smartly dressed in a nice blue and green floral shirt and a green silk shirt. She was holding a lovely blue and green checked jacket which matched perfectly with her outfit, even her handbag and shoes matched. My goodness, the woman matches her name.

***

Billy saw Dorrie at the door and put down the bags. He moved over to Elizabeth and placed a reassuring hand on the small of her back to encourage her forward.

Dorrie stood with her arms outstretched.

"Ah, Billy, how lovely you have brought your friend home", she said as she went to the lady and gave her a hug.

"Welcome, welcome, it's so lovely to see you. Elizabeth isn't it?" The woman spoke "Yes, that's right, but you should call me Lizzie." Came the reply.

"Lizzie it will be then. Come on inside. Billy you pick up the bags."

"What about my hug." Moaned Billy.

"You, you big baby, can have one when we are inside."

Dorrie gave a quick glance around the street to see who of her neighbours were watching at least three curtains were moved aside. All her friends in the street adored Billy, he was always willing to help them out with a bit of gardening or some small repairs and when she had told them about Lizzie, they were all so pleased to hear it.

Once inside Dorrie ushered them into the lounge. Dad stood from his chair and held out his hand to Lizzie. Lizzie took it and realised once he had hold of her, he was pulling her in for another hug.

Billy went over to rescue her, took his father's hand and gave him a hug.

"OK Dad you can put her down now." He kissed his dad as was customary.

"This is Lizzie, my girlfriend Lizzie."

"Hello Lizzie, nice to meet you girl. It's about time this boy of mine brought someone home. Now you sit yourself down and get comfortable and let me get a look at you."

Elizabeth sat on the sofa. "Billy has told me so much about you both and the rest of the family. I must say, he has been so very lucky to be adopted by such lovely people. So many kids from children's homes or orphanages ended up in dreadful situations, but obviously Billy and his siblings have won the jackpot here."

"Why that's a lovely thing to say, thank you dear. Would you like a cup of tea and some cake Lizzie?" Asked Dorrie.

"I would really appreciate a nice cup of tea Mrs. Johnson, can I help?"

"No, you sit where you are, me and Billy will get it. Now what sort of cake do you like? I've got chocolate, lemon, carrot or fruit cake."

"Crickey Mum, how many people are you expecting this weekend?" Piped in Billy.

"Your brother and sisters will be here shortly, I just wanted to make sure everyone had what they wanted. Fetu is coming as well, so at least there will be plenty to go around."

"Mum you do my head in, you must have been baking all week."

"I don't mind, I like baking and your dad likes cake with his tea, you know that."

"Sit there, Lizzie, I'll just go and give Mum a hand. I promise I won't leave you alone too long."

She smiled up at Billy, "Don't worry, your dad will keep me entertained."

Once Mum had him in the kitchen, he knew she would have questions.

"Well, well, lad she is lovely and speaks with such a nice voice, sounds like the queen's handmaiden and dressed so lovely too, she seems like a real find."

"She is Mum and whilst she isn't the queen's handmaiden, I think her family are friends of the royals."

"Oh, you do make me laugh Billy, you say some daft things sometimes. I'll put a bit of each of the cakes out and then everyone can take what they want."

When Billy returned to the lounge, he held a tray full of different cakes and biscuits in one hand and a pot of tea in the other. Just as he was setting them on the table, he heard Derricks horn hoot lightly giving a signal he and Jenny had arrived.

"I'll get it Mum" he called.

"Hi you two, how was traffic?"

"Fine, fine" said Jenny as she hugged him "Where is she then?" she whispered quietly.

"In the lounge" he whispered back jokingly. "Oh you" she said

They moved into the lounge just as Lizzie was getting to her feet.

"Hello I'm Jenny, Derricks wife and you must be Elizabeth. It's so nice to finally hear about you. My husband knew at Christmas but omitted to tell me, so I've only just found out you exist. Welcome to the family."

She moved over to Lizzie and gave her a huge hug. "It's so nice to know that someone has, at long last, got my brother-in-law to date seriously. I was beginning to give up hope for him. Oh, I know he's not much to look at, but underneath that skin is a true gentleman, and what a skin", she said laughing out loud.

"Hello Jenny, please call me Lizzie. It's so nice to meet you all as well, I've heard so much about you all and to finally be here meeting you is wonderful."

"Oh, my Billy, where did you find Lizzie in *Town and County* magazine? What a lovely speaking voice you have. Some of the accents my students have would make you cringe, they do me."

"Excuse my wife" interrupted Derrick, "I'm Derrick the long sufferer that has to listen to Jenny's chatter, but she means well" he gave her another quick hug before directing a question to Billy. "I take it Lesley and Fetu haven't arrived yet."

"They will be here by lunch; Bristol is a bit of a hike. Look sit down everyone, I hope you have empty stomachs as Mum has baked enough for an army."

Billy noticed that everyone was talking as though Lizzie had been in his family all her life.

Lesley arrived with Fetu and they all had lunch around a large extendable table in the dining room. His mum had only made a light lunch of salads, cheese, hams and homemade pickles, all home grown from a friend's allotment, except the cheese and ham.

Lizzie looked at the gathered company and told them what a pleasure it was to be sitting around such a diverse bunch of people. "You are all very, very different and yet all so much alike in your easy banter and jokes. I was so nervous about meeting you, but as it turns out I had nothing to fear and only the warmest of welcomes."

Billy had indeed arranged for them to dine that evening at the Royal Feather's, with food to die for. After dinner and during a pause before dessert, Lesley got out a tablet and connected with her daughter Sofia. They made a space in the middle of the table and as everyone spoke to Sofia, the tablet was moved around so that Sofia could see who she was speaking to. Then it came to Lizzie's turn to speak with her,

"Hi there, Lizzie, so, you are the one that has got this family going crazy with curiosity. Well, It is really cool to see you and you must be a pretty special person if my uncle has fallen for you. There are not many in this world that he lets close, but then again there are not many in this world that want to get close, they don't take the time to find out he is the kindest, most trustworthy, gentle person I know. Is that what you wanted me to say Billy? Oh, and can you ask uncle Billy whether he will be paying my fee by cheque or transfer?"

A roll of laughter went up around the table. The other diners all looked to see what was going on. Billy stood and placed the tablet at the end of the table and asked Sofia if she could see everyone?

When she affirmed she could, Billy clinked his glass.

"I have something I would like to say." The whole restaurant went quiet. "My brother, sister and I lost our birth parents when we were very young, but I think God had a plan for us. He brought us into the life of John and Dorrie Johnson, who not only adopted one of us, but all three. I think my brother and sister would agree with me that we have been blessed to be known as their children."

"Here, here" said the company.

"I haven't finished. I have lived with people not really knowing how to take me, because of my tattoos, but recently I met a lady, and she is truly a lady, that from the first moment, even before I had spoken to her, I was smitten. When I did start talking to this lady" he looks at Lizzie "she not only treated me as a normal human being, but according to her, and I only have her word for it, fell in love with me as a man despite the appearance of my skin. You have made my life wonderful Lizzie and in front of all the people I love, and yes you strangers in the background there, I would like you to honour me and accept me to be your husband?"

A gasped went up around the room. Billy placed his hand in his pocket and pulled out a small ring box. He made his way over to Lizzie, knelt on one knee and said "Elizabeth Dowels-Hudson, will you make me the happiest man alive and marry me?" He opened the box to show a blinding oval cut two carat diamond ring with tiny diamonds embedded around the band.

During the speech, Charlie had quickly let Chris know what was going on and along with Chris and Charlie as many of the locals that could fit through the door had done so and were waiting for the reply. You would have heard a pin drop until Lizzie said

"Oh, my goodness Billy, I would love to be your wife and I happen to love your skin."

A roar went up from everyone, strangers, locals and family, tears of joy were flowing.

Chris looked at Charlie tears streaming down her face. "Go and get the champagne Charlie. This is a night for a celebration" and he did.

Billy took a quick glance in his brother's direction. Although Derrick looked happy, Billy wondered how he really felt.

Derrick leaned over to Jenny, "I told you so."

Chapter Six

The drive to Norfolk was pretty long after getting stuck behind traffic on the A11. The M11 was fine up until Saffron Walden, but the A11 proved to be frustrating. Every time they would overtake a slow vehicle, they would get stuck behind another, just a little further up the road.

That evening they arrived at Talia's house about six, exhausted and tired. Lizzie had said Talia was funky and as she bounded out onto the street to greet them, Billy understood why, when a billowing rainbow charged at them. On her head she had a green and purple scarf wrapped like a turban, red hair escaping from every fold, then down to a loose fitting, pink, purple and green multi coloured tie-dye T-shirt, baggy brown Aladdin trousers with elastic at the ankles and blue and grey flip flops. Billy knew she was the same age as Lizzie, they had been childhood friends, confidants, as they worked their way through their privileged private education. They had shared their girlie secrets and now Lizzie had decided to share her latest secret, maybe to gauge what reactions to expect at the wedding.

"Oh, you are different aren't you" she said as she approached Billy, "after all Lizzie's years back and forth to Africa, I was convinced she had met an African man, but you're not, your... well your... What are you exactly?" Are you a fascist skinhead?

"Talia, really, where are your manners" a voice said behind her.

Billy looked at Talia "Well, you tell me Talia, do you think so little of your friend Lizzie, that you could believe she would go out with such a person? What am I indeed, I've been called many things in my time, maybe I'm the boogie man?" he winked in her direction.

"Actually, he's the most wonderful man in the world" piped in Lizzie.

"I'm sorry Billy, that was totally out of order of me. It's just you see so much hate in the media now and no, my friend Lizzie would only date a really special man. What you are, is tired by the looks of you. Let's show you two your room so you can settle."

"Hello I'm Stephen and you of course are Billy. Nice to meet you

Billy. I will apologise for my fiancé, sometimes she speaks before her brain knows what it's saying."

"Yes, yes, of course, do come. We've made a spare room up for you, the two of you look done in. Relax for an hour before dinner."

The troupe entered into the foyer of the flats and took the lift to the penthouse. The apartment was very much like Talia, a mix match of all sorts of decorations, colours and nick knacks and it looked totally lived in, the sort of place, your eccentric aunt would live in.

The walls were covered in paintings of all different styles and sizes, along with wall hangings, cushions scattered the floors and sofas. Sequin curtains hung at the windows, it was a total assault on vison and senses.

Talia noticed the look on Billy's face

"Cool isn't it?"

"It certainly says a lot, I'm not sure what it's saying but, yeah it's cool."

"That's exactly it. It says something about everything. Why only state one thing when there are so many good things to shout about?" She giggled in a high girlie tone. "Come on I'll show you your room."

They followed Talia into a bedroom which was the complete opposite to the lounge, minimalist in four shades of grey, a much more relaxing atmosphere than the previous.

"It's really kind of you to invite us this weekend; I've been waiting to meet some of Lizzie's friends."

"It's great to have you. I can't say I've been waiting to meet you as we didn't know you existed until recently, your Lizzie's big secret. Have you known each other long?"

"We met in November, when I started some work at her flat."

"Eaton Place? Lovely building and so quiet given it's in the heart of the city. Do you live in the city?"

Before he could answer Lizzie came up from behind.

"Are you grilling my man?"

"Not at all darling, just trying to find out a little bit about him. After all he is dating my best friend."

"Don't worry Tally", Lizzie's childhood name for her friend, "I promise we will give you lots of details at dinner. Now can we have a shower and freshen up, the trip has made us both rather sticky."

"Absolutely darling, dinner at eight-thirty. Relax a little."

When Talia had left Lizzie looked at Billy

"She's quite something isn't she?"

"She certainly is, but she seems nice."

"She is nice. She takes a little getting used to with all her darlings, and sweeties, puppets and I can't remember how many more little endearments she uses, but she's good hearted and one of the most open-minded people I know. Do you fancy washing my back?"

"You bet I do."

***

Dinner was as mixed as Talia, the table was laid with all manner of things to eat.

"We're having a tapas night, a little bit of Spain, oh, and there are a few bits from Greece and I've made a few relishes from India. Help your selves. Red or white wine?"

"Red for me" replied Billy.

"Yes, for me too" said Lizzie.

"OK everyone on the red. Would you do the honours Stephen darling?"

Between the Tzatziki, Samosas, Jamon de Serrano, Mantequo cheese, spinach with chickpeas, ensaladia, squid, octopus and three bottles of red wine, Talia, Stephen and Billy got to know a bit about each other.

Billy and Lizzie had decided not to tell them about the engagement, they felt Lizzies parents needed to know first and Lizzie didn't want to take any lime light from Tally. She knew if she said anything Tally wouldn't be able to keep it a secret and she wanted to tell her parents. She decided she would introduce Billy, after the wedding. Her parents would see Billy at the wed ding, get used to the idea that she had brought someone along. She then hoped to get to the family home for a weekend with Billy and she would tell them exactly what was going on. In the interim period she could drop hints about her relationship being serious, slowly get them used to the idea. At least that was what she was hoping would happen.

After dinner Billy wandered around looking at the paintings, some portrayal, others cubist, or landscapes.

"You certainly have a variety of paintings here Talia. Did you paint some yourself?"

He heard her laugh "Oh you are adorable sweetie; I wish I had. I have absolutely no talent what so ever, Stephen will tell you, the only thing I'm really good at is speaking with people, isn't that so darling?"

"Talking too much to people sometimes, my love."

Talia laughed "Oh you are silly, sweetie. No, one of the three cub ist's was done by Lyubov Popova, she was a Russian artist. That's the one depicting what looks like knights in armour but it's actually called Daily Muse. The one with the violin is a Georges Braque, he was French and died in 1963. The one with the women is a modern painting by Robert Yaeger, he is a British artist. Georges Braque was actually the forerunner of cubism; Pablo Picasso was greatly influenced by him.

She moved closer to Billy. "Now this one is by Giorgiones, his Sleeping Venus, Daddy gave me this one from the house and..."

Stephen cleared his throat with a light cough, beginning to feel just a little uncomfortable for Billy.

"I don't think Billy is here to have a lesson in art my love, needless to say, they are all painted by quite prominent artists from around the world. Talia's father is a great art lover and Talia is following in his footsteps, but she can be a bit curative at times."

Billy was beginning to realise he was way out of his depth. The nearest he had ever gotten to buying paintings were prints for his rented properties.

Lizzie and Stephen had been clearing the table and stacking the dishwasher when tally brought up the next day.

"OK, so what time do you want to make a move tomorrow? Shall we start off in the town to see what delights they have? There are quite a few small independent boutiques we can wander around. Lady B Loves is one, Ginger and there's Milly J Shoes. There's also Jarrold, and John Lewis. If we don't find what I want in town we can head somewhere else. I know Stephen wants to get some bits for the honeymoon as well, so you two can wander off if you get bored being with us girls."

"Well, let's just wake up at our own pace and then we can walk into the town. If you girls weigh us poor blokes down with bags, we can get a cab back" suggested Stephen.

"Good idea" said Lizzie "and now I'm off to bed, I'm exhausted are you coming Billy?"

"I think I'll go to bed too. Stephen are you coming?" Asked Talia

"I'm just going to have a small brandy; will you join me Billy?"

"Sure, why not, I'll be in, in a minute Lizzie?"

The girls took themselves away and Stephen went and poured two generous glasses.

"So, this is your first taste of Lizzie's life Billy? I hope Talia didn't go too overboard about the paintings? She gets a bit carried away with art."

"Yes, first venture, but you have both been great. I'm a bit of an artist myself in my own fashion, as you can see" he pointed to his exposed ink.

"Hard not to notice, how far does it go."

"Most of my body, if I were honest all of my body. There's a couple of gaps left but not many."

"Painful?"

"You get used to it."

"Has Lizzie told you much about her family?"

"Not overly much, her father is a Lord; her mother was a rich heiress and became a lady when she married Lord Hudson. She has a sister in Scot land with two kids. I know about her job and I know she has done a lot of charity work in the past in Africa. Not too many intimate details about her family, but I know she is really worried about how they will treat me when we meet."

"Yes, her father can be a bit of a bastard, he's a hard man, especially to outsiders. Elizabeth is the golden-eyed child. He had great expectations for her. She was engaged once to a chap of nobility, which her father loved, but he left her very suddenly to run off with someone else. Her father made sure the chap suffered. Personally, I think he made sure the poor man struggled to make decent contacts for work and his business after that. I think Omar put the word around that if people did business with Harley, they would stop doing business with Omar and Omar is the better bet. After it happened that's when Lizzie decided to get involved with charities that would take her abroad."

Billy didn't mention that Lizzie hadn't told him she had been previously engaged.

"Well, I won't be leaving Lizzie for anyone or anything, so hopefully I will not attract Omar's wrath."

"I just want you to be aware that this world can be harsh. It all looks pretty from the outside, but on the inside people can be very bigoted and nasty. I hope you're ready for it. I struggle and I'm a pure bred, but a poor one and sometimes that's as bad as being an outsider. These people have a way of making you feel inferior, when most people are far more superior than many of them. Maybe that's what they worry about. Anyway, good luck with it all. Lizzie is a lovely lady, you're lucky to have her. She is one of the good ones. Right I'm off to bed. I'll see you in the morning when we both become pack mules."

"Thanks Stephen, thanks for your honesty."

"Billy, I'll have your back as much as I can, good night."

"Good night."

Billy made his way to the bedroom where Lizzie was fast asleep. He slipped in beside her and gave her a protective hug.

***

After three hours shopping the men were beginning to realise, they would need a taxi back, in fact they may have to split up and take two. It was nice to see Lizzie enjoying herself with her friend, this was her natural setting, out shopping, price no bother and not a care in the world. The men had found a bench to park themselves on while the girls went into Lady B Loves. After forty-five minutes they came out again loaded-up with another assortment of bags. Both Lizzie and Tally came and sat on the men's laps and landed a great big kiss on their mouths.

"Lizzie, Lizzie is that you? What on earth are you doing here" Came a voice.

Lizzie stopped dead, while Talia jumped to her feet.

"Lady Bethany, Lord Hudson" voiced Talia in surprise. What are you doing here? I mean…How nice to see you. You know Stephen, we are all just out shopping. I asked Lizzie if she would come and visit and lend me a hand to choose things for the honeymoon." The reasoning was falling on deaf ears.

Lizzie got to her feet, "Mummy, Daddy, I didn't expect to see you in town on a Saturday.

"Obviously not" came her father's voice. "What are you doing making a show of yourself in public like this? And who —turning to look at Billy— is this person you are making the display with?"

Billy got to his feet and held out his hand.

"Hello Sir, I'm Billy, Billy Johnson. It's a great pleasure to finally meet you. Sorry about the show, the ladies are a bit excited about their shopping success." After presenting his hand after introducing himself he realised it was left without response in mid-air.

"Yes, Daddy, this is my friend from London, Billy. Mummy, how are you? Sorry I didn't let you both know I was coming, but I knew with the shopping trip I would never be able to find time to pop home. Are you well father?"

"Well, I might be if my daughter wasn't acting like a harlot in the middle of the town on a busy Saturday afternoon."

"Now Sir", interjected Billy, "I think that is uncalled for."

"Do you sir, I would ask you not to interject your opinion on how I interact with my daughter."

Billy went to say something, but Lizzie stepped in

"Leave it Billy", she looked at her mother and father and said the one thing that would shut them up. "father, now, I don't want to make a scene here in public, and start raising my voice, for your benefit, so I am going to leave now with my friends. Sorry Mummy if this has upset you. Maybe I should have just let you know I was visiting Tally, but I'll get in touch once I get back to London. Now you two have a good weekend." She picked up her bags, put her arm through Billy's and said. "Let's go", then proceeded to walk away. As they did so Billy could hear her repeating Shit, shit, shit.

The shopping trip was over; the troupe went directly to the taxi rank. Billy, was sure all four of them were thinking the same thing. As first meetings go, that couldn't have gone worse.

Chapter Seven

Talia opened the door to the flat whilst Billy and Stephen struggled through with all the shopping. Nobody had said anything about the encounter with Lizzie's parents on the short journey home, but as soon as the door was closed behind them Talia said

"Bloody hell, I need a drink after that. Anyone else going to join me?"

"Make mine a double" came Lizzie's voice. "Mine too" said Billy.

"Stephen?"

"Just fill the glass."

"I'm so sorry about that Billy. My father can be an ignorant bastard sometimes. I can't believe the way he treated you. Don't think I didn't notice he didn't take your hand, that's just downright bad manners. He makes me so damn mad at times."

"Don't worry about it, I guess it was a bit of a shock. He wasn't expecting to see you for a start. I'm just worried we haven't exactly got off on the right foot."

"I don't think he has a right foot with Lizzie, if he's not in control of everything in her life" said Talia.

"He's not in control of my life" came back Lizzie.

"Oh, come on Lizzie, you're an MP because he refused to keep supporting you with your charity unless you agreed to come back to England, I mean that was outright blackmail."

"I like being an MP."

"Yes, I know you do darling, but it was never your choice, it was your father's and Phillip was chosen by your father, you wanted Mark Stanley, but your father knew he wouldn't be able to control Mark as well as Phillip, so he managed to get Phillip embedded with you. He stopped you from getting involved with the Aids campaign because he thought it would be bad for your image, the stuff with Harley."

At the mention of Harley, Lizzie threw Talia a look that told her not to go there.

"All I'm saying is he hates anything in your life he can't control and with Billy he probably knows he will have no control over him, he doesn't know Billy or the things Billy wants in life, he doesn't really have contacts in his world and that means he won't have control over you and he will not like that one little bit."

"You make it sound as though I haven't a mind of my own and that I don't do the things I want. I do, I represent a whole town of people in parliament, I look after things that are important to them, all sorts of things that are my choice."

"I know you do darling and you are wonderful at it, but let's be honest all the things you do, are done with his approval. You don't rock his boat, but with Billy he thinks you may capsize it. Your father would have met, judged and condemned Billy in the first thirty seconds of seeing him. You know I'm right."

"Well, anyway, lets drop the subject. I'm not going to let him ruin our weekend. Shall we go dancing tonight, I fancy letting off steam?" Lizzie asked.

***

The two men had stayed out of the conversation quietly drinking their whiskies. For Billy it had shed a little light onto Lizzies father and her life. He realised he didn't know as much about her as he thought. Everyone agreed they would like a night out.

Sunday saw them dine for lunch in Wymondham at a small country pub. Billy and Lizzie had packed their things for the return journey to Lon don before they left for lunch, as the village was partly on their way. For the rest of the weekend conversation reverted back to chatter about holidays, work and trivia. Stephen as it turned out was an insurance under writer for special and financial risks at ACE Europe. His great grandfather had lost the family fortune, but as he had stated before, he was a pure bred and having his name allowed him some privileges and acceptance in Talia' and Lizzie's world. He freely admitted it was his name that allowed him to be marrying one of the richest heiresses in England.

Arriving back in the city Lizzie asked Billy,

"Will you stay the night?"

"No, I'll go straight home. It's late and I want to check on Mum and Dad before the working week starts."

Billy knew Lizzie probably had a lot to think about regarding her parent's reaction to him as well as what Talia had revealed.

***

On Tuesday, Lizzie phoned Billy and asked him to go to her flat later that evening. Earlier she had, along with the usual mail, a letter. She had recognised immediately as from her father. The family crest emblazoned on the envelope. She wanted Billy to be with her when she opened it. She had thrown it aside to read when she didn't need to concentrate on work. She knew it was going to upset her.

When Billy arrived at eight on the dot, she had just finished her shower and was readying herself for work the next day. Billy could tell immediately she was nervous. He went to her and took her in his arms.

"Lizzie, it's a letter, nothing more. Whatever he has written, we will deal with it together." He glanced at the letter on the breakfast bar and thought they had better read it and get it over and done with. Without a word, she simply nodded. Billy took her hand and led her to the sofa where they sat as close together as possible. He lifted the flap on the back of the envelope and took out a crisp white sheet of paper. Unfolding it, he held it up so they could read.

Dear Elizabeth,

It is with a heavy heart I write to you after your display of disrespect towards your dear mother and myself, in public, this past weekend.

I feel compelled to point out the stress you have caused. Your mother was quite shaken by the time we returned home and neither of us enjoyed our luncheon with the Hamilton's, which we had both been looking forward to for some time. I'm sure our disposition reflected on our company.

I have over the years tolerated all of your whims and tried to guide you through to a suitable and acceptable position in life. To now place that direction in jeopardy for a silly romance which would be beneath you and your stature is completely irresponsible of you and might I say, selfish.

You are a privileged member of this country; your ancestors having held this position for centuries. I will not have that ancestry mocked.

You are no longer a young girl; you are a mature woman that has family and public responsibilities. I ask you now to think about those responsibilities and come to your senses in this matter before I am compelled to take action.

Your loving father.
Omar

Billy watched Lizzie closely has she folded her hands in her lap and lowered her head. He wasn't sure what to do. Her father's response was expected, nothing new was told in the letter. Billy had hoped that her parents would surprise him somehow, respond like how his parents had to Lizzie. Putting an arm around her shoulder, he pulled her closer. In a quiet voice she said,

"I feel like I'm going to throw up."

"Would you like a glass of water?" He asked beginning to rise.

"No, I just can't believe them. I mean I can. I knew exactly how they would respond, but still..."

Tally's word's echoed in Billy's mind: "All the things you do are done with his approval. You don't rock his boat..." Now was the time to find out how Lizzie truly felt about him. Would she dare go against her parent's wishes, for him? He loved Lizzie with all his heart, but at the same time, didn't want her to lose everything.

Before he knew it, Lizzie ripped the letter from his hand grabbed a pen that sat on the table before them. He watched as she flipped the sheet over and quickly sketched the family crest on the top right-hand corner.

Dear loving Father,
This is bullshit. Go to hell.
Your loving daughter.

On Thursday another letter had arrive with a different family crest. That of Lizzie's sister. Lizzie gave it to him to read.

Darling Lizzie,
What is going on? I've had Daddy on the phone telling me you are going out with a skin head. What on earth darling? If the press gets hold of it, they will have a field day.

Do let me know, Mummy and Daddy are so upset. Tell me your side of the story.

Daddy said you were 'snogging' outside Jerrold's, please tell me this isn't true. It's not like you.

Mummy said Daddy is livid with the way you wrote to him. You know if you do that sort of thing, it just makes him worse than he already is. Why do you have to antagonise him?

Mummy is arguing with him over you now too and she is getting very upset about the situation. Mummy said you should have handled

things better.
Love you darling. Penelope XX

Dear Penelope,
Don't get sucked into Daddy's paranoia. I was not snogging I just landed a kiss on his mouth.
Billy is not a skinhead, well he is, but not in the way you think. He shaves his head so that people can see his head tattoo and that again is not how it sounds.
He is the sweetest person I have ever met and far more educated than just about everyone I know, including Daddy.
Don't let Daddy drive a wedge between us. Love you
Lizzie xx

***

A week after her later the doorbell rang. Billy was in the shower.

Lizzie opened the door to find Phillip, her campaign manager standing there. He barged past her.

"What the hell are you playing at Lizzie, a skinhead for Christ sake, my God anything but a bloody skinhead. Have you gone out of your mind? Do you realize what this will do to your career? I mean once the press gets hold of this, that's it, your career as an MP will be over no one will vote for you in the next elections. You can forget support from the party if you don't get elected again. And what will you do then? What is it menopause? Hot flushes frying your brain?"

Billy emerged from the bedroom, he heard Lizzie saying, "I see you've been speaking with Daddy. Sorry Phillip but my private life is my private life."

Billy walked over. "Can I ask what's going on here?"

"Ah, so here is the culprit" he looked at Billy "Do you know what you have done. You've ruined her and her career. I know you from somewhere. Where do I know you from, you seem familiar?"

"You're the twat that dealt with the building quote on Eaton Place."

The penny dropped

"You're... you're the foreman from the builders."

"That's right" said Billy. "What of it?"

"Do you know what will happen to her. She has a public life. That's what politics are all about, serving the public. You and Lizzie are public domain. You have to stop this at once. Think about all the other people's jobs you're putting in jeopardy."

"Like whose?" injected Lizzie.

"Like mine for a start. Once you lose the next election, no other candidate with have faith in my abilities to manage a campaign, not if I can't keep a middle-aged woman in control."

"So, this is about you, not me. Get out Phillip before I lose my temper and fire you."

"You can't fire me Lizzie, it's only with your father's donations that your even an MP and he donates nicely. He would only have to have a few words in the right ears and you'll be out. It's his donations that pay my wage."

Billy was about to lose his cool. "Now do as you were told by the lady, get out before I kick you out, and I won't put you in the elevator I'll kick your arse down every step in the building."

"Right, I bet you're used to doing that." Billy clenched his fist

"I'm warning you now. Leave."

"You haven't heard the last of this. You don't realise who her father is, he could destroy you. Now that I know who you are, we could make sure you never work another construction job in the city. No, not the city, the country."

"Piss off." Billy got hold of Phillips collar and basically lifted him out side the door. With the door shut, Billy turned to Lizzie.

"Are you alright?"

She burst into tears.

"Oh Billy, why are people like this?"

He wrapped his arms around her,

"Don't worry, we'll sort it out. I'll go and speak with your parents. Make them realise how they are hurting you."

"Oh, Daddy knows. He knows exactly what he is doing."

Billy wondered how he could sort this mess out. *Maybe I should just let her go.*

The next day he phoned Derrick and told him what had happened and about the letters.

"So soon? Derrick said "I thought it would take longer for them to react."

Billy told him about the weekend at Talia's.

"OK, so the cat was out of the bag then. I don't know Billy. Do you think they can damage the business? You've worked a lot of years to build it."

"I don't give a fuck about the business Derrick. I'm worried about Lizzie and her job."

"Well bro, you do need to worry about the business, for a start Mum and Dad would never manage on their pensions with the home help you give them and everything. And you, what would you do at your age. It would be hard to find another decent job."

"We would all manage on the rentals income if worse came to worse" Billy replied.

"You have mortgages on those properties. Look, the old fart may not be able to touch you. Nobody really listens to the likes of him. I don't think he can do much to you. Lizzie on the other hand, it sounds as though he has real influence on her career. What does she say about it all?"

"She says she wants to walk away from them."

"Well, that's an option; you can support the two of you very well in deed, if she's willing to give up her family and friends, maybe that's the way to go."

"I don't want her to have to make that choice. I want her to be able to be with me and have her family, friends and yes her job, she loves it."

"There's hard choices that need to be made here Billy; all I can say is follow your heart."

"Yeah, you're right. I need to think. Thanks for letting me sound off."

"No problem, I'm here whenever you need me."

Chapter Eight

Talia's wedding gown was a masterpiece. A ballroom silhouette of white satin emblazoned with crystals, the fitted bodice tapering to a full skirt and royal train. At the back of the neck was a crystal necklace and be low she had decided to be daring with an open V back down to the skirt, which accentuated her tanned skin and tiny waist. Luckily, she had the height and small hips to accommodate the billowing skirt. She looked every bit the princess.

Billy didn't have a clue about dresses, but the one currently on Talia… even he could appreciate. *I wonder if Lizzie would want to wear something like that to our wedding? If we get that far.*

Billy wore his Armani suit, a white cotton shirt patterned with a silk which made the shirt pop. He had lifted the collar and wore a white silk scarf with a small silk handkerchief in his breast pocket. He had toned down his tattoos for the occasion, them showing on the front of his neck, hands and faintly on his head. He has decided a few weeks ago not to shave his head and had a thin layer of dark hair which disguised the head tattoo.

Lizzie had decided to wear a cream satin knee length dress printed with different shades of pink flowers and light brown leaves. The dress had a tie belt which created a bow at the front. A short, waist length jacket in the same shade as the flowers, matching slingback shoes with a small bow on the front, a headband with three taffeta flowers and matching handbag completed the outfit.

Billy thought they looked beautiful together and they were certainly turning heads. He didn't know whether through curiosity about who she had on her arm, or, for the picture the two of them made. Lizzie was also wearing her engagement ring in full view, although Billy had told her not to push things. She still hadn't announced her engagement to her family. She had insisted that now would be as good a time as ever to let people know.

Billy knew many of her childhood friends and celebrities were guests, this was one of the biggest society weddings of the year. Lizzie and Billy were standing outside the church when her parents, sister, brother-in-law and nephews Stewart who was five and Anthony who was seven arrived. Of course, the children were unaware of the family feud taking place and ran up to Lizzie with their arms out stretched. She gave them a hug as her father and mother passed without a word. Penelope came up and took the boys by the hand.

"Hello Penelope, this is Billy"

Penelope's husband John McBride brought up the rear.

"Hello Lizzie, Hello Billy, it's nice to meet you." She held out her hand which Billy took and noticed she had offered her fingers only as though he might kiss her ring.

John held out his hand and shook Billy's without a word.

"We had better go in and get seated" announced John and ushered his family away.

"Can we sit with Aunty Lizzie?" Asked Anthony.

"No Anthony, we have all been allotted seats and I don't think Aunty Lizzie is sitting near us."

"Oh, I want to sit with Lizzie" piped Anthony again.

"Well you cannot, so move. I'll see you two later" she said to Lizzie and Billy.

Before Penelope could get away Lizzie asked "Why isn't the family sitting together?" It would be normal for us all to be together."

"I have no idea Lizzie; you would have to ask Talia that. It's nothing to do with me."

"Is it something to do with Daddy?."

"I don't know Lizzie, I really don't."

Of course, it's something to do with her father. I'm beginning to realise what a petty old man he is. I wonder where he has managed to get us moved to? They found out when they entered. They had been seated not quite at the back, but near enough to be with guests that were not close friends of the bride or groom and placed in the middle of the pew so that Lizzie couldn't get a good view of the couple on their special day.

"You, arsehole." Lizzie said under her breathe.

Billy looked in her direction and took her hand. He gave it a gentle squeeze and winked at her, she smiled back. He was not going to let this ruin their day, they would be able to see Tally after the wedding.

When Stephen and Tally went back to the church registry room, the guests filed out for the throwing of rice and seeds which the birds would clean up once everyone had left.

Lizzie pulled Billy along and managed to catch up with Tally and Stephen once the rice had been thrown and people were milling around for the photos to be taken.

"You look wonderful Tally, you really do and so happy, I'm so happy for you."

"Thank you darling, it is all rather wonderful isn't it. I'm sorry about the seating, but Daddy insisted and I really didn't want to cause a fuss on to day of all days. I knew you would understand."

"It's fine Tally, don't worry about it at all. We knew it wouldn't have been your doing and you were right not to make a fuss. This day is about you and Stephen. I'll let you get on and I'll see you at the reception, hope fully Daddy hasn't sat us outside the tent for tonight."

Tally laughed

"I'll see you later, the old fuddy duddies won't stay long. I expect they will all leave after the toasts and once the band starts playing. They will probably make their way into the drawing room or go home. We can spend time together then. Where's Billy by the way?"

Lizzie realised she was no longer holding Billy's hand. He had wandered off to the side and was speaking with Stephen.

"I did tell you. These people can be really petty sometimes. I hope Lizzie isn't too upset. It was so awkward when Talia's father came and told us he had changed the seating in the church, neither of us really knew what to say to him. We thought it best just to let it go."

"It's not a problem, Lizzie and I understand. Congratulations by the way I hope you and Tally will be really happy together."

"There you two are. I have to drag my husband away now. The photographer is waiting, we'll see you later" Tally blew a kiss.

"Shall we go back to the hotel and rest a bit? I can then change into my outfit for tonight."

"Don't you want to stay and say hello to your friends?"

"No, I'll catch up with the important ones later, it will be a more relaxed atmosphere."

"OK, if you're sure. On a side note, can I make love to you in just your headband and shoes?"

"You silly bugger, yes you can."

Back at the hotel Billy asked

"Are you alright?"

"Yes, totally, Daddy is playing his games to provoke a reaction and we are not going to give him one. I'm determined to enjoy Tally's wedding, have fun at the reception and let my friends know I'm engaged to the most wonderful, and sexy, in that suit, guy around. He can kiss our arses."

They made love as promised and relaxed before the evenings event.

**

The evening meal was delicious, as was expected. The main toasts were made after which a microphone was handed around for Tally and Stephen's friends to say a few words. When passed to Lizzie, she spoke about the childhood antics the two would get up to, then the holidays abroad together and finally she spoke about their friendship as adults and when, even though she had known Stephen growing up, it wasn't until he stated dating Talia she realised what a great match they were. After the speeches people started moving around the tables, catching up with old friends that hadn't been seen for a while. It was during this time Lizzie's engagement ring was noticed by some passer-by and she would introduce Billy as her fiancé.

They both knew damned well that word would spread and gossip would be exchanged, but thankfully everyone was being discrete, as they should be at a wedding.

Unfortunately, Phillip appeared and had to get his threepenny worth into the conversation. Billy was away in the gents and as he re turned, he could see the twat standing at the table talking to Lizzie who was visibly getting upset. He was in no mood to have this git either upset Lizzie, Tally or Stephen.

He came up behind Phillip, placed his hand around the man's shoulder and told the gathered company he just needed Phillip for a moment to discuss a work issue. Phillip, was about to object when he felt the grip around his shoulder tighten to such an extent a pain shot through his shoulder blade. Billy moved him to the entry of the tent.

"Phillip Hawthorn, isn't it?" Well Mr. Phillip Hawthorn, I'm giving you due notice. You will not say another word to Lizzie. If you have anything to discuss with her about her work, you can do it in the office on Monday. I want you to keep a wide, wide berth from us for the rest of the even ing. If I see you anywhere near her, I will come and get you, bring you back out here and break your miserable arm. Do I make myself clear?"

"Phillip through the pain in his shoulder, gripped his teeth and said

"This isn't finished you know. I have the backing of Lord Hudson and the rest of Lizzie's family. By the end I will also have the support of her friends, and between us, we will stop this relationship." He felt his knees buckling. "Now let me go."

Billy released his grip and as he turned away, he looked back and shot an imaginary gun at Phillip.

"You've been warned, Phillip, stay away."

It was the last they saw of Phillip for the rest of the weekend.

On Sunday Lizzie phoned her home, and the housekeeper Mrs. Douglas answered.

"Hello Mrs Douglas, could I speak with my mother please." Billy smiled and gave a nod at Lizzie letting her know she could do this.

"Ah, Miss Elizabeth, yes just a moment, I'll take the phone to her.

She's in the breakfast room with Mrs. McBride and the children." Lizzie place the receiver in her other hand and took Billy's hand for strength.

"Hello, mother."

"Hello, Elizabeth."

"You looked lovely at the wedding yesterday, I loved the blue you wore."

"Thank you. How can I help you?" She said coolly.

"Billy and I are going back to London today and I would like us to pop home and speak with you and Daddy about the situation we find ourselves in."

"I don't think that is a good idea, Elizabeth. As you know we have your sister and the children here, and I really don't think it's the right time to discuss the issue, not with the children here."

"Oh, come on Mummy, Mrs Douglas will look after the children when we talk and I'd like Penelope and John there anyway. I have some news."

"You mean the news of the ring you were wearing yesterday? I hardly think it is news now, do you? You placed us in a very difficult position yesterday. People coming up to us saying how pleased we must be that at long last you were engaged. Can you imagine, especially the first person, as we had no idea and had to hear it second hand. By the fourth person your father was so outraged, we had to leave. I thought he would have a heart attack if we stayed much longer. I don't know what this man has done to you, but you certainly are not acting like our daughter. I don't know what ideas he has put into your head and neither does anyone else. Your sister agrees with me, we should never had heard about this the way we did."

"Well after Daddy and Penelope's letters, and Phillip Hawthorn showing up at my door, threatening me and my job, what did you expect?

I could hardly call you and say, Oh, by the way, I'm engaged to Billy', now could I? Really, we do need to speak. I love Billy Mummy and I want you all to be as happy as I am."

"Your father will never accept it Elizabeth, you know that don't you? We are planning a garden tea with the children this afternoon at three. If you wish to come by and try to speak with your father, you can, but I don't hold out much hope that he will speak with you, especially if you bring Billy."

"Well, I think I need to try."

"If that is your wish. I will not tell Omar you are coming, but I will let Penelope know so that it's not a shock to her and John. We will expect you at three."

"Thank you Mummy, I'll see you later."

"Well?" Billy asked but half dreading the answers, whichever way it had gone.

"We can go, but we are not going to get a friendly reception. They heard about the engagement through the grapevine yesterday."

"I told you not to wear the ring, it has just made things worse."

"I suppose I did act a bit like a bull in a China shop, but it's done now and it's time we face them and told them how happy we are."

***

Billy drove to Brookesley Manor, and as they approached the entrance gate, he started getting a bad feeling in the pit of his stomach. Lizzie pushed a code into a security box on a side pillar and the gates automatically opened. The drive was lined with trees for what must have been half a mile, then opened to display cultivated hedges in the shape of half ovals.

He could see that not one shoot escaped its confines of symmetry. Omar must have host of gardeners tending the gardens, but of course he did! Billy didn't see the house until they followed the drive to the left when it appeared before him. He didn't know from which century it was, but he could imagine Elizabeth I visiting. He'd made a joke to his Mum that Lizzie probably knew the queen, a joke that he now realised was more than likely a truth.

"Here we go", said Lizzie with a deep breath, in a rather subdued tone.

Billy said nothing and wasn't sure what he had agreed to let themselves in for. His instinct was to run. They approached a circle of landscape with a display of coloured flowers in the form of the family crest embedded in a circle of grass. He counted twenty windows on each floor of the manor; there were what looked to be three storeys. Either side of the building were what one could only describe as wings, orientation wise, he couldn't decide whether they were west, east or south. Looking at the shadows created by the sun, he thought east and west. Lizzie told him just to park outside the front entrance as the grounds were not open to the public today.

The pentagon entrance protruded from what was the centre of the building, it's massive wooden doors the focal point. Lizzie was nonchalant and casually said "They will be in the gardens; we won't go through the house."

It seemed to take an age to circumvent the property to the gardens, Billy noticed the roofs of an unknown number of outbuildings, of which one he assumed to be some sort of botanical dome-shaped greenhouse, another that looked like stables, the rest he had no idea. He was trying desperately to think of good reasons he could present to these people as to why they should accept him and came up with a fat zero. Once they managed to get to the back of the house, they had the additional walk back to the centre property. It did cross his mind that going through the house would have been a shorter route and that maybe Lizzie was delaying what was to come.

As they approached a group of people, he saw two women sitting in lawn chairs, a table in between and another in front of them. Tea had been set on the larger of the two tables. Two men were playing football with the two young boys he had seen at the wedding, Anthony and Stewart he re membered.

The two boys were the first to glimpse Lizzie

"Aunty Lizzie" shouted one and then the other, running towards them.

The two men stopped in their tracks.

"Come here boys" called the older lady.

But they were already in Lizzie's arms. She swung first one then the other into the air. With their feet back on the ground they looked at the strange man, the one they had seen yesterday.

"Hello" said the youngest "I am Stewart, Stewart Carlson McBride."

"And I am Anthony John McBride" said the other. Billy held out his hand "Hello and I'm Billy Johnson." Their mother had come up behind them

"Come on now boys, Mrs. Douglas is going to take you to the kitchen for ice-cream."

They both looked up at Lizzie, but the thought of ice-cream was just a little more enticing. Mrs. Douglas stood a little way behind Penelope and took the boys off. Once they were safely out of sight Omar strutted over.

"What are YOU doing here Elizabeth?"

"I have come to talk father. This situation is ridiculous. I want you all to meet Billy and get to know him."

"It certainly is ridiculous," he replied, "to be congratulated on my daughter's engagement by strangers was totally ridiculous. I hold nothing against you personally Sir" he continued, "but you do see that this relationship of yours with my daughter is totally unacceptable?"

"I'm sorry about this situation Lord Hudson", replied Billy," but I want you to know that I truly love your daughter. I would have wanted to speak with you all privately and personally about marrying her, but it seems things just got out of hand, and the opportunity hasn't arisen to do so. Forgive me for that. However, having said that, Lizzie and I are in love. I will do everything in my power for the rest of my life to make her happy, and I know she could be very happy with me. I will make sure of it and we would really like your blessing."

"A magnanimous speech, Mr. Johnson, however, after knowing my daughter and seeing her struggles to find a place in our society and you having known her all of five minutes, I suggest I know my daughter better than you. She has grown up with this" he waved his hand around the scene "and the society this belongs to. She is my heir and the heir to all this; she has a responsibility to continue and safeguard it. I have no sons, so this passes to Elizabeth. Do you really expect me to believe, as her husband you could step into this and continue it for the next generation? I think not, Mr. Johnson, I think not. I can say no more on the subject, I will say no more on the subject. If this relationship continues, she will be left with nothing. She will be out of my will."

"My God, I never really understood until now. This has nothing to do with Lizzie. This is all about you. Who will continue your interests, who can live up to your name, who will continue the way you deem fit? You're not actually interested in your daughter's happiness, only in your own. You could be totally correct about one thing, I may not belong to this society as you call it, but times have changed, living and thinking the way you do is antiquated. Royalty are marrying commoners, as I'm sure you think I'm one and look at the disasters that occur when your kind are forced into suitable marriages, such as Prince Charles and Lady Diana. I bet half of your society are TV and sports' personalities because your society is changing, but you Sir, are not changing with it. Come on, Lizzie, we are leaving, before I knock this pompous arse on his arse."

Billy could tell that Lizzie was gobsmacked; he was surprised he'd had the guts to speak to someone who deemed himself so high and mighty, especially given it was Lizzie's father.

Before they made it back to the car, Lizzie pulled Billy to a halt. "I'm so proud of you, for sticking up for yourself, for sticking up for me against my father. I don't think anyone has ever spoken to him like that before. I hope you know this will probably make things worse. Daddy will be even more angry and try to create as much havoc as he can."

Billy held her hand before saying, "Well, we'll be ready for him, won't we?" As Lizzie continued to the car, she realized Billy wasn't moving. "Do you want to leave with me, Lizzie?"

"Yes", she replied.

Although Billy had been brave about the encounter, he really did see Omar's point of view. He could never see himself living in a place like that or running it and the estate, or ordering household staff around. None of it sat with him at all. But what was the alternative? Lizzie give up her in heritance, live with him in a four-bedroom detached house? And what about her work? What would she do as an alternative? Come and work for him in the company typing up quotations, doing bookkeeping? Oh, Lizzie, this is all wrong.

Billy was home for a while, getting some things together in his bedroom. Mum was downstairs baking for the local church Bizarre. He heard a car pull up into the drive. Heading to the window, he glanced out, unsure of who the car belonged to. Downstairs, his mum quickly washed her hands caked in flour and looked out the curtains. There sat an old Bentley, emerg ing from which were people she didn't know. As Billy made his way to the top of the stairs, the doorbell rang. Glancing around the corner, he watched as his mum opened the door.

"Hello" she said hesitantly.

"Oh, hello, you must be Lizzie's parents. How nice, do come in, please, come in and make yourselves comfortable." Billy had no clue how Mum knew who the people were, although they did exude an air about them as though they were royalty, and unfortunately, had to deal with the local peasants.

She ushered them into the lounge as Billy watched in the shadows, wondering how they were going to treat his mum.

"I'm Dorrie and this is my husband John. Can I offer you tea?"

They all remained standing. *What the heck are they doing here?*

"Please, don't bother, Mrs Johnson, this is not a social call. We have come to you to speak about Lizzie and your son."

"Oh God, what's happened, are they OK?" *She must have forgotten I was home.*

"I'm sure they are fine", said the younger man.

"Let me introduce myself, my name is Phillip Hawthorn and this is Lord Hudson, Lady Dowels-Hudson, Penelope McBride and John McBride. I'm Elizabeth's campaign manager and these are her family. We are here to talk about the situation we find ourselves in, as I'm sure you can appreciate."

Dorrie didn't appreciate anything and didn't really know what was going on.

"I'm sorry, you have me at a loss."

"We have come to speak about how unacceptable the relationship between your son and Elizabeth is."

Dorries' hackles were beginning to rise as she realised these people were not here to be pleasant.

"Unacceptable?" she said "Why, there's no problem, we think Lizzie is lovely."

"No, not unacceptable for Lizzie, for your son" piped in Lord Hudson.

"My son? Why, my son is accepted everywhere he goes. Everybody I know loves Billy. What's the problem?"

"Well," Phillip started to say, but Omar cut him short.

"My dear lady, I'm sure you and your family are splendid people; however, you must see that this relationship my daughter has with your son is nothing but, well, doomed and could harm both of them. I met your son recently, for the second time. I have to say, my daughter's position really will not accept her marrying him. He is a splendid chap, I'm sure, but his prominence as a suitable spouse for my daughter, is to say, the best, undesirable."

Dorries' heart was beginning to beat rapidly and swear words were racing through her mind. Billy could tell his mum wanted to explode, to tell these people what she thought of them, but she held herself back. Billy knew he wouldn't have been able to.

"My son is undesirable? To who? Lizzie finds him very desirable I would imagine, otherwise she wouldn't have agreed to marry him."

"Well, that is the point, isn't it? Desire and suitability are two different things. I have told them both, if she persists with this relationship, she will no longer be part of our family."

"How dreadful of you, to condemn your own daughter, just because she loves someone you don't. What an awful way of behaving. I'm sorry, but Lizzie is and will always be welcome in my family. She makes my unsuit able son happy. I now have to ask you to leave." Billy smiled, loving his mum even more, if that were possible.

"But this is" started the younger man.

"Please leave or I will call the police to remove you"

Dorrie spread her arms wide and ushered them out the door. She bent over, hands to her knees to breath as the door closed. "Oh, my poor Billy."

"Who was that?" Asked John

"Nobody, just Jehovah Witnesses" she relied.

He could strangle the bastards, upsetting his mum like that, mind you, she held her own. Pompous bloody bastards. Before he could work herself up any further, Billy stepped out. Dorrie turned with start, hand clutching her chest. "Oh my, Billy, I forgot you were here. Why didn't you come out when *those people* were talking about you in such a horrible way?"

"I knew you could handle them. Don't be worried, Mum. I'll get this figured out; I'm not sure how yet, but I'll think of something.

"How will I protect you?" She asked, her worry seeping out to encompass him.

"I'm a grown man. I appreciate your help, but this is my battle." He bent down and hugged his mum, knowing she would always be there for him.

Chapter Nine

Billy and Lizzie knew things were about to get worse. Tally contacted them telling them she had been summoned to Lizzies' home by Omar.

"Ask her if she knows why?"

"Have you any idea why?" Lizzie repeated down the receiver. "Just one second, I'm putting you on speaker, so that Billy can hear.

"I have no idea. I just got a message asking if I could go and meet with him and your mother. What should I do? Should I say I'm going out of town?"

Billy responded. "I know it would put you in an awkward position, Talia, but would you go and let Lizzie know what they want?"

"Without hesitation" she replied. "I'm disgusted with the way they are treating the two of you. It's so bloody petty."

Three days later Lizzie answered her phone. She put it on speaker once again, for Billy to listen.

"Hi Lizzie, well basically they are trying to come up with ideas on how to separate you two. Mr. Despicable was there, Phillip. They didn't say much. Phillip hasn't been able to dig any dirt so far on you Billy. Obviously, a work in progress, but he has a PI looking into you. Your father had an idea but didn't enlighten us. It has something to do with the Flower show, which I gather you are going to on the 5th, so look out for strange happenings."

Billy looked at Lizzie and mouthed, 'What's a flower show'? Shaking her head, their attention went back to Talia.

"Thank you, Tally, I knew he would start planning something. I'll keep my ears and eyes open. Really, thank you."

"No problem, darling, it's all rather exciting being a spy."

They all laughed and Billy stood to let the two women chat about the honeymoon.

Before long, Lizzie was hanging up her phone and redirecting her attention to Billy.

Billy knew Lizzie was glad she had Talia on their side. She explained how important the flower show was. She was on Whitsun recess from the commons until the 11th of June, a time when MP's took the opportunity to be seen at public events and meet potential new voters, officiations and participation in all manner of festivals which was a good way of getting your name into the local papers so that the constituents could see you were in terested in local and traditional events.

"Chelsea Flower Show is one of these events. Norwich submitted our entry for the event and I was asked to officially open their garden. Brookesley Manor gardeners played a big part in the creation and my father played a big part in donating the fauna and flowers."

Billy grabbed the mail the next day and brought it to Lizzie, noticing one envelope said something about the flower show, or so he assumed.

Lizzie opened the seal and removed the letter. *Due to unforeseen circumstances we regret to inform you…* "Blah, blah. Daddy, you rotten sod." Talia had said her father had something planned for the flower show and this was obviously it. Over the next few days, three more letters arrived cancelling her place to officiate.

"Well they can't stop me from going" she said smirking at Billy. "Do you think you could get time off to come with me?"

"The 5th? I don't see why not."

They looking at the Arthritis Research garden designed by Tom Hoblyn, when Lizzie heard a long lost, but familiar voice

"Elizabeth, is that you?"

She turned to see Harley Buxley and his mother Lady Buxley. She hesitated.

"Hello Harley, Lady Buxley, how nice to see you here" she said in a rather cool monotoned voice. "I didn't know you liked gardens Harley."

"Mother has been on at me for ages to bring her this year. As you know father died a few years ago and mother keeps complaining she has no one to accompany her, so here I am."

"That's kind of you" she turned to leave. Her heart had started racing and she could feel anger rising from the pit of her stomach. She looked up at Billy and smiled. "Billy, the is Harley, Harley Billy, my fiancé. The two shook hands. "Harley and I were good friends when we were younger."

Billy looked at the good-looking bloke in front of him. *'**Were** good friends? From the look of Lizzie, she no longer considers this man a friend.'*

Harley looked at Billy. "Do you mind if I just have a quick word with Lizzie in private? I will not keep her but a moment or two."

'Who the heck speaks like that anymore? Another jerk like Hawthorn.' Billy mused. Billy looked at Lizzie. She nodded to him. "I'll just be over here Lizzie."

Harley turned to his mother, "I will only be a moment mother, I would just like a word with Elizabeth." His mother nodded.

"Goodbye, my dear," she said to Lizzie.

"Lizzie, please, I want to speak to you. I want to say how sorry I am about what happened. I was under so much pressure. Father was so ill and I..."

"You what Harley? There is no excuse for what you did. Do you seriously think you can just walk up to me and apologise and everything will be fine?"

"Lizzie, it was so many years ago. I was never good enough for you anyway. I was young, too young and stupid. Oh, God I was so stupid. You look wonderful Lizzie. Please let me say I'm sorry, even if you don't forgive me, just let me say it."

"You've said it, Harley, job done, now go back to your mother. I'm meeting friends for tea and I have to go."

She turned and left. She felt flushed. He had aged well she thought, given all that she had heard over the years, but she learned to stop listening some years back. She remembered how he had totally broken her heart and how long it had taken her to find her self-esteem again. The sympathetic looks people gave her and the whispering in the ears when she at tended a party alone. Well, he made his choice, which turned out to be a fiasco and she made a career. She now felt herself the fortunate one.

She went back over to Billy. "Who was the ponce?" He asked.

"I'll tell you about him later. He's nobody, just someone I know from my past.

"Is he the guy you were engaged to?"

"You know?"

"It was mentioned in passing."

"I'm sorry. I didn't tell you myself. It's not something I think about any more. At the time I was really hurt, but I got over it. Now that I have met you, I'm glad it did happen, otherwise we may never had met. Well, I have to go and meet the girls. Are you sure you don't want to come? I'm sure they won't eat you."

"No, I've got to get back. I'll pop by tonight. Around nine p.m. Do you want me to bring anything?"

"No, I'll pick some things up on the way home. I'll see you later."

She kissed him goodbye and started walking to meet her friends.

She was meeting Penny and Daisy for afternoon tea. She took a stroll through Hyde Park and remembered the day she spent there with Billy. It eased her anger a bit at seeing Harley.

Billy arrived in the city a little before nine. Lizzie had picked up a pizza. "How did it go with the girls?"

"Depends on how you look at it. Only one showed up to start with, the other. Well, who knows? I tell you what Billy. I'm glad my family are rejecting us. If they didn't, I wouldn't be finding out many shitheads I had in my life.

"That bad?"

"This is how it went."

She told him what had happened. Only one friend showed, Daisy, making an excuse for the other, Penny. They spoke about the wedding, then the friend asked if Lizzie intended on going to some anniversary of the missing friend Penny. It was suggested that if she planned on attending with Billy, they wouldn't be welcome.

"I told her I wouldn't want to make anyone uncomfortable. Daisy, told me she thought it was all so stupid, but that some of the parents weren't taking it very well. After having seen Harley at the flower show, I was ready to go to the pub rather than have tea. Bless her heart, Daisey came with me."

'And so, it starts' thought Billy.

***

Billy sat at his new laptop. He spent so many evenings at Eaton Place now he had decided to buy one to leave at Lizzie's so that he could do some work when there. He and Noel would look through Construction News and other construction publications looking for higher end and larger projects being opened for quotations.

He opened Google search, typed in History Brookesley Manor, Nor folk, UK. Links filled the page, and he clicked on the first. "Top Ten Privately Owned Estates in England', he read.

Inherited by the Hudson family in 1566. Construction of the current manor took the lifespan of two different Hudson earls and various architects to complete. The 2nd earl commissioned the services of Vanbrugh, to design the plans. His designs reflected a Baroque style, with two wings on each side of the structure.

Construction was started at the west end, with the west wing being completed between 1704 and 1706. Other finished areas included the east end of the garden entrance, the Central Block, and the east end of the gar den front entrance. The finishing touches included an exuberant amount of baroque qualities, such as cherubs, urns, coronets, and Roman Doric pilas ters.

The 3rd earl was responsible for the completion of the East Wing. The rooms of Hudson Manor were completed in different stages over the years and the overall completion did not occur until 1814. The estate covers 1,500 acres.

Unfortunately, a large portion of the house was destroyed during a fire in 1942. The fire started as a chimney fire in the southeast corner of the west wing and spread throughout the building. The east side of the house was all but destroyed. Restoration work on the east wing commenced in 1969, completion in 1989.

The house is a stunning surviving example of English Baroque architecture and the home became iconic due to its role in the TV series and later film adaptation of For Pure Motives. Other than the incredible rehabilitation after the house fire, today the surrounding village of Brookesley is owned by the estate. Many of the staff members who work at the manor, which total thirty-six, live in the village. The family also own fourteen other properties some which include offices, workshops, livery businesses, shops, and gar ages. The estate is relied upon for two village schools, attached playing fields, garden allotments, village halls, and mooring rights on the River Yare.

Billy needed to get the opinion of some people from Lizzie's side of society. The only two he could think of were Stephen and Tally or maybe he could find a number for Penelope, but he wanted to speak to them separately. He phoned Stephen first. They met in the city one evening after work. Outlining his concerns, he asked him for his honest opinion.

"I don't know Billy. I do know you probably won't win with Omar. This is a very old family. I mean these people have been figures in English history for centuries. You see, it's nothing to do with love, desire or any of the things normal people consider, it's to do with contract and inherency. Do you know how much it, cost's per year to run their home? Between two and three million and that's just the manor. Some money comes from commercial investments, insurance, banking, all manner of things, but the rest comes from family fortunes. Lord Omar and his family were broke, well nearly, when he married Bethany Dowels, but she brought a fortune with her. It meant Omar could restore the property which had been damaged by fire, back in the fifties I think."

"Forties, I read it on the internet."

"OK, forties, it also meant Omar could start investing again and build up his own family fortune, something he couldn't do previously. It's now very healthy, but when Bethany and Omar are dead, who will manage or bring more fortune to the family? This is the only thing Omar will be thinking of. These types of estates are few and far between nowadays, most have either been turned into hotels, flats, or offices. The new rich are film stars with a sense of grandeur, sports personalities, but they have no history and Omar and the few truly noble families with history, are hysterically trying to prevent it from dying out. He only has daughters, Penelope has married into the McBride fortune, most of their interests, except for a few homes scattered in England, are in Scotland. That leaves Lizzie and then you come along. Even without looking the way you do, even if you had turned up, with pure white skin, well dressed, successful, you still would have faced the same rejection, unless that is, you had a fortune. Do you have one? I'm not talking about a few hundred thousand or even a million, but many millions. If you have that, there are probably ways to get Omar on your side."

"So, do I just walk away?"

"I can't answer that for you. The thing with Lizzie, is she isn't like most women of her standing, she never has been. The three of us actually grew up seeing each other quite a bit. I know that she would willingly give all the prominence up for love. I think, given the right circumstances she could be happy living like normal healthy people and doing normal healthy things. It would mean her being disowned by her father, but their relationship has been strained for years. She would miss her mother, her sister and her nephews. Some of her friends would keep in touch, but most would dis appear, not because they would stop liking her, but because they would start moving in different circles. She would have to stop buying couture de signer names, but I don't think that would be a problem. What can I say? I think she's a woman with her head screwed on the right way, but I can't say I know. As kids we just played around. I've known her better since I started going out with Tally five years ago, but then again, we haven't really had in depth chats or anything."

"You've been a great help anyway, Stephen. You've helped me see how Omar is thinking and what's at stake for him and their family history.

You've given insight into things I need to consider."

"You know, my family history goes back as far and even further than the Dowels or the Hudson's. When my father died, we were living in one of the estate houses. The big house had been closed for years, due to tax debts, not enough money to fix the crumbling walls and leaking roofs. It was sold to pay the debts to a development company. It is now several housing estates, the manor house long gone and to be truthful, it is sad that a big part of history disappears with these great houses. When I spoke with Tom about marrying Talia, I was sat down and asked to come up with a plan to secure her future and to restore some of my family money. He told me he would invest in me, if I had a viable plan. That's what it's like, my friend, contracts and money. The only person that can tell you truly what to do, is Lizzie. You really do need to sit down with her and talk."

"I thought I might talk to Tally, but I think you've said it as it is.

"I think Tally can be a bit of a romantic, and see's you and Lizzie as the protagonists in one of her sweet romance novels where you, the hero, will overcome the mean antagonist. I don't think she will be thinking about the realities."

"I think you're right. Do you want another?"

"Go on, one more before I go home to my bride."

***

The lights were on in the flat, so Billy knew Lizzie was somewhere.
"Lizzie, where are you?"

He went to the bedroom, not there or in the bathroom; he went to the spare room, no. She must have gone out for something. He turned on the T.V. and tried to listen to the news. Surely, she would have said something had she known.

The key in the lock caught his attention. He turned off the T.V.

"Oh, hello, you're here."

"Yes, just arrived."

She came over and kissed him fully on the lips; he couldn't help but respond. She walked to the kitchen and unpacked her goods, placing them in cupboards and fridge.

"When you finish, we need to talk. In fact, I think we need to talk about several things."

"That doesn't sound very good", she responded, "Has something happened?"

"Yes, it has, come and sit down."

"What is it?"

The key in the lock caught his attention. He turned off the T.V.

"Oh, hello, you're here."

"Yes, just arrived."

She came over and kissed him fully on the lips, he couldn't help but respond. She walked to the kitchen and unpacked her goods, placing them in cupboards and fridge.

"When you finish, we need to talk. In fact, I think we need to talk about several things."

"That doesn't sound very good." She responded, "Has something happened?"

"Yes, it has, come and sit down."

"What is it?"

"I've been meaning to tell that my parents had a visit from your family and Phillip the other day asking them to agree that you and I together are totally unsuited."

He could tell from the expression on her face that she hadn't known. *Thank goodness.*

"Oh, Billy, I'm so sorry, what on Earth were they thinking? How did they know where to go?

"Probably through that arsehole Phillip, he would have my business address on the contract and quotation for this place. I suppose it's pretty easy to have found my home address if you know where and how to look. If I ever set eyes on him again, I'll smash his fucking face in. Involving my folks like this, especially with Dad's health issues, it's downright bloody disgusting."

"Well, I suppose they didn't know your Dad was ill."

"Are you defending them, for fuck sake?"

"No, I'm not, I'm just saying that...Oh, forget it, this is all getting out of hand."

"I don't want to forget it Lizzie and you're right, it is all getting out of hand, and it's getting out of hand from your side, not mine. My family is totally on board with us. Did Tally not know they were going to do it? I thought she was your spy in the other camp."

"Well I can't ask Tally to be around every time my family decide to scheme up something, that would be ridiculous."

"This whole thing is ridiculous", he replied

Lizzie was going on the defence, just as Billy already was.

"They are trying, in their own warped way, to protect me, Billy. I know it's wrong but you don't know these people. Not just my parents the whole lot of them."

"I know, I don't know these people, and to be honest, I don't want to."

"I'm one of those people! You will have to know them, especially if we get married."

"If? If we get married?"

"I didn't mean if, I meant when, it was just a slip of the tongue."

"I think we ought to call it a night. I think we need to think long and hard about what we are doing here. I'm going back home."

"Call it a night or call it a day? Is that what you really mean?

"No, I meant call it a night. I can't be here feeling like this. I'll phone you tomorrow."

He left, closing the door just a bit too harshly.

Chapter Ten

Lizzie had never felt so enraged in her life. She remembered her friend Sarah and the horrible things she went through, when after a ten year marriage to Andrew, the Duke of York, they divorced.

She got on the phone, determined to settle this. "Phillip, I want to see you and you know why. Tomorrow, my flat, ten a.m. no excuses."

She opened the door and released the entry door, after a few minutes the lift opened.

"Get in here" she told him.

He bolshily entered the flat as she closed the door.

"What the hell do you think you are doing? What god damn business do you have to go to the house of Billy's parents? How dare you interfere like that! You have done irreparable damage; I hope you realise that."

"Good, that was the point. His parents needed to know how your side of the family felt about your engagement. I'm glad if they have come around to our way of thinking."

"Oh, you stupid, stupid man, I'm not talking about having damaged me and Billy, I'm talking about having damaged our relationship, yours and mine, what I thought used to be a friendship. I'm done with you Phillip, your fired."

"As I have mentioned before, you can't fire me."

"Yes, I can and I am. I have my own funds and I will be finding myself a new campaign manager, that's if I decide to run again. Until I decide I will have nothing more to do with you, do you hear?"

"Lizzie, you need to come to your senses. Can you really see yourself, cut off from your family and friends, being the little suburban house wife? You won't have any income to support your charities or for travel or anything else you are used to. Your boyfriend might be able to buy you a nice little three up, three down home, but is that really going to be enough? You don't really know anything about him. Has he actually told you, he is not the foreman, that he owns the company? Has he told you that he has other properties, that he was engaged to marry before and that it was her that dumped him, not the other way around? What has he told you about himself? Has he told you that his sister is shacked up with a student? She could lose her position if that became public. You need to watch yourself Lizzie, because we are still looking to see what other dirt there is, to bring you to your senses."

"Get out, Phillip, and don't come back."

She opened the door for him to leave and slammed it behind him.

She hadn't known Billy owned the company, why hadn't he told her?

They'd known each other eight months. Why hadn't he said anything? Why had he continued to let her believe he was just one of the workers? Was he hiding something? She knew Fetu was a student and she didn't like the fact that Phillip had masked a threat in there against Lee, but she also thought he hadn't realised yet that the student was a fully grown man. She looked at her engagement ring and now realised how Billy could afford it. His business must be doing well. Billy only really talked about the work he was doing at any given time, the location, how the job was going, the crew. He had explained how he looked for new projects, but just took it that, that was what foremen did. What else didn't she know, she wondered?

She wondered what her father and Phillip's next move would be after she had dismissed Phillip, she also wondered what she needed to do to make his sacking official. Her first move, she assumed, would be to contact the party officials and let them know that he should no longer have access to her computer or files in the office, in fact, he shouldn't be allowed in her office. The second would be to put it in writing so that it was official. She sat at her PC and started writing.

She loaded her official headed paper.

Dear Mr. Phillip Hawthorn,

It has recently come to my notice that our interests regarding my campaign for re-election have separated in both goals and ideology.

I have, after much thought and deliberation, decided to terminate our contract forthwith.

As per our contract I now give you one months' notice, however, I think it is in our best interests, you no longer attend any forthcoming, meetings, events or activities.

Your severance pay will be deposited forthwith into your account.
I thank you for your past services.
Yours,
Elizabeth Dowels-Hudson - MP Brookesley, Norfolk

Next, she contacted her secretary and gave her the news and requested that Phillip not be permitted access to her office, or request any documentation from anyone in the office. She also asked her to change Phillips password and deny access to the present one. Everyone in the office had to give their passwords to the secretary in case of accident or failure to appear, so she could immediately change Phillips.

"Susan, I want this done as a priority. Mr. Hawthorn and I have not parted on the best of terms and I would hate to think he could do any mischief."

"I'll get on it straight away" she replied.

***

Phillip was on the phone to Omar

"Hello sir, I thought I ought to inform you Elizabeth has just fired me as her manager."

"She can't do that, you work for me, I pay your wage."

"Yes sir, I told her that, but the contract I have is with Elizabeth, not you. I have a separate contract with you as a consultant, but she has the contract as her campaign manager, which is the one she is annulling."

"We'll see about that, you just carry on as normal, Phillip, and continue as you have been looking into things."

"I did notice sir, there was another computer at Elizabeth's flat, it could belong to Johnson. I was thinking if it turns out to be his and I can gain access, I might be able to install some incriminating things on there, things that Elizabeth wouldn't like."

"Really, good thinking, how do you think you can gain access?"

"Well, when we first started working together, Elizabeth gave me a key to the flat. It was being decorated at the time, if you remember. I think she has forgotten all about it, I've never used it since that time. Maybe I could enter, with your permission sir and see if the computer is indeed Johnson's, maybe put some pornography or something on it. I'm not quite sure yet, but I would need your permission sir."

"Yes, you have it, anything to get us out of this mess."

"Sir just to clarify" Phillip turned on his mobile recorder, "I have your permission to enter Elizabeth's flat, access a computer and install something unsavoury to incriminate Billy Johnson in something your daughter will find distasteful, is that correct?"

"Yes, why are you asking me again?"

"I just don't want there to be any misunderstanding in the future sir"

"Yes, yes, I give you permission. I own the building anyway, so you are entering my premises, there's nothing illegal about that."

"No, there isn't Lord Hudson, but I believe Elizabeth has a rental contract, which would make it illegal. I think your accountants have the place as a deductible."

"Well, whatever, I'm sure, if you get caught, my lawyers will sort it out. Just make sure you don't get caught."

"Thank you, sir, I'll be back in touch."

Phillip saw pound signs running through his head, whoever's side this little play fell in favour of, he would be taken care of. He went to his computer, he wanted to extract as many files, including any unguarded comments Elizabeth has written in emails, she often vented about other MP's and her society, which could come in useful."

He logged in and entered his password. *Password invalid*. He entered it again, *Password invalid*. What the fuck! He had one more chance, digit by digit he slowly typed in his password, *Password invalid*. That bitch. OK, Elizabeth Dowels-Hudson, you want a fight? You have one. He picked up his jacket and made his way to the office, he had stuff in his desk he could collect and he could get some paper files from Elizabeth's office.

"Susan, I need to get a few things from Elizabeth's office, I won't be a moment" he said as he entered.

Susan bounced out of her chair and stood in front of Elizabeth's door.

"I'm sorry Phillip, but Elizabeth has been on the phone and told me you cannot go in."

"Get out of the way you stupid woman, Lord Hudson has told me to collect some files."

"Well, I'm truly sorry, but Lord Hudson, isn't my boss, Elizabeth is and it's worth more than my job to let you in", she stood her ground with arms stretched on either side.

He turned on his heel.

"You'll regret this Susan, be sure of it."

He stormed over to his desk and opened the drawers, empty.

"Where are my files?" he shouted.

"I'm afraid they are the property of the party and have been re moved, however we have left all your personal items, which you are welcome to collect."

There was nothing except his Filofax with all pages removed, a pen holder and his name holder. He began to doubt whether Omar would win this battle, but didn't really care, he had just secured his pension.

***

The next day, in the popular and gutter press appeared the head lines: *Beauty and the Skinhead, Down and Dirty, Downton to Down, Dowry and Dismal, Don't Do It, Sieg Heil Elizabeth.*

Recent photos of the two of them displayed underneath, along with exposés of their relationship and how both families were opposed, to the match.

The press appeared outside Lizzie's apartment and Billy's house.

"Can we have a comment? Are you in love? How does your father feel about this? If your son married her, will you be Lord and Lady Johnson? It went on and on.

Billy's didn't make the call until the third night after their last meeting.

"It's me."

"Yes, I know your number. How are you?" She was dreading the answer.

"I'm OK, and you?"

"I'm OK. I had a run in with Phillip, I've sacked him?"

"Good."

They both spoke together

"I'm sorry…" they said at the same time.

"You go first, Lizzie."

"I just wanted to say I'm sorry for what Phillip and my parents did.

I'm also sorry about getting defensive the other night. I wasn't sticking up for them. I was just trying to see their point of view. I love you, Billy, and I don't want to lose you."

"I love you too, Lizzie, you will never know how much I understand about defending your family. That was exactly what I was doing, defending mine. It's natural and right to do so, these people are our flesh and blood and have done so much for us. We should try and understand them."

"Oh, I'm so glad you think that way, I was so scared."

"I'd like us to meet."

"Yes, yes darling, please come around", she said trying to hold back the tears.

"No, Lizzie, I'd like to meet on neutral ground to have a talk."

"But we can talk here."

"I know we can, but as soon as I see you in a private setting, I'm likely to melt and take you to bed. I want to talk, seriously, about us."

"OK, anything, where, when?"

"Tomorrow, seven p.m., the Grove Café."

"Perfect, I'll see you there. Billy, I love you with all my heart."

"I love you too, see you tomorrow. Night, night."

"Yes, night, night."

Billy held his head in his hands. He knew Lizzie was crying, he had heard the sobs in her voice as she was speaking, yet there was nothing he could do for her at the moment.

Billy was there waiting when she arrived; they ordered coffees, kissed each other on both cheeks like old friends and sat.

"So, who goes first?" Lizzie asked.

"I think I should" stated Billy. "Firstly, I was so angry the other night and I took it out on you; I shouldn't have. Secondly, I understand us both be coming defensive about our families, but that isn't the issue."

"What is?"

"The issue Lizzie, is us. Our worlds just don't go together. Just like Romeo and Juliette I think this is all going to end in tragedy. Your life has been so different from mine, but it's not just that. Over the last few days, I've tried to empathise with your parents' point of view, and I get it, in fact, I think they are right. You have a birth right that needs protecting and that's all your parents are doing, trying to protect their daughter and her birth right. My parents don't need to do that, I have no history. My history, died when my parents died. I could probably research my history, but what would I find? Maybe one of my ancestors was a chamber maid to one of yours. That's not a bad thing. I also know times have changed and are still changing, but your family history is the history of England."

"Billy, stop this, you are talking rubbish. My ancestors inherited their titles, they didn't earn them. They were just handed down from generation to generation. Most of my ancestors were lechers, traitors, conspirators, all manner of things. Okay, there were a few good ones in there, but it was still all handed down."

"That's not the point Lizzie, they were..., they are, and you are important to our history, and you like your father and his father, actually have a responsibly. I see what your father is trying to do, he's trying to protect his family and home, for the future, not the past, and I really cannot see me being part of that. I'm sorry Lizzie, this is going to kill me, but we are not right together."

She grabbed his hands across the table.

"Don't say this darling, we have such a love for each other, we can get through this. I'll give it all up. I don't want the history, the status, the wealth, I want you and only you. Don't destroy us, I beg you."

"I'm sorry Lizzie, it has to be this way. I also can't put myself or my family through the media. They don't deserve to read all the crap. Now let me take you home."

With tears streaming down her face, she wiped her hand across both cheeks.

"No, I'll make my own way back. This isn't finished Billy. I'm here and I will be waiting here when you want me. I'm not going anywhere until you come to your senses and come and get me. I'm your end of story!"

"Lizzie."

"No, I'm going now, as I've said I'll be here waiting." She rose and left.

Billy paid the bill and walked the streets of the city with a pain so deep in his chest he was finding it hard to breathe. He hoped he'd made the right decision, but didn't know how he was going to live with it, and without Lizzie.

***

Lizzie, on the other hand, was deciding to give everything up. She would not stand for re-election, she would disinherit her inherency, she would cut off her family and friends before she gave them the satisfaction of winning. They had just destroyed her happiness, and she wanted nothing more to do with them.

She contacted her lawyer

"I want to disinherit my family."

"You what?"

"You heard me. I no longer want to be my father's heir."

"But, Elizabeth, be sensible, you can't possibly be thinking..."

"I'm not thinking, I want it done. I want you to tell me what I have in my own right, from my grandparents on my fathers' side and my mothers' side. If my parents can stop me from inheriting what has been bequeathed to me and I want to know how much this will cost. My father will not be paying your bills, I will"

"I'll get onto it."

"Good, I want it done at the soonest possible opportunity."

She put down the phone. If I'm poor, he can't deny me.

The media fury died down as July progressed and then August. Elizabeth continued her appoints and appearances at Royal Henley

Regatta, Royal International Agricultural Show, Royal Tournament, East Anglian Medieval Fayre, World Crabbing Championships and Suffolk Dog Day. At three of these events she bumped into Harley and his mother.

"You do seem to be getting around this year Harley, this isn't your normal style."

"My normal style, as you call it, has changed over the years. After my business failed and my divorce, I guess I had to grow up and look at where my decisions had landed me. I now live in London and visit mother often. I'm an architect and have my own studio in White City, I enjoy it and on occasions it affords me some travel, we recently completed a small hotel in France."

"I'm happy for you Harley, I'm glad to hear things are beginning to work out for you."

"Lizzie, after the summer, do you think when you're back in the city, I could take you for lunch, or dinner. Just as friends, I'd like us to be friends."

"I don't think so Harley, I'm kind of involved with someone."

"Nothing romantic, just lunch, as I said, as friends. We all need a friend now and again; I'd like to be yours."

"I'll think about it."

"That's all I can ask for, I must go, mother will be wanting some tea. Hope to see you soon."

"Yes, bye Harley."

She felt pleased she no longer felt pain at the thought of him. Maybe they could be friends again.

Thinking about the appearances she had made this summer, there was one she was not looking forward to, the Regatta of St Olaves Marina to Lowestoft an eight-and-a-half-mile race to the sea along the River Waveney. This was the last big social event of the summer before returning to work and her father was patron so the whole family would be there. Penelope would bring the boys and stay for a week or two at the manor, John visiting when his work allowed, although he always made it for the race itself. Tally always took part; sailing was one of her passions, one she shared with Stephen who would be crewing with her. Many of Elizabeth's friends and social partners would be attending either to socialise or sail. The day before the race Saturday the 24th would be the trade exhibition held in the marina with the race commencing on Sunday the 25th of August, but before that date arrived, she was hoping to have some news from her lawyers.

This had been the first year Elizabeth had not spent the summer at the manor, she would normally be seen out and about with members of her family at all events. She wasn't quite sure how she felt about it. On the one hand she was happy to be independent of her obligations to attend her mothers and fathers events, but she did miss the house and spending time in the gardens, she also missed her sister and nephews, who would visit twice during the school holidays.

She had rented an Airbnb house for three months. Tally had offered her a place to stay, but she had decided if she was going to be independent, she needed to start by not relying on friends either. It was a nice little house, two bedrooms and a bathroom upstairs, a kitchen and lounge with patio doors leading to a manageable back garden, in the village of Stoke Holy Cross. It was a quiet place; not too far from the A140 Ipswich Road. She had enjoyed meeting the villagers and often ate at the Wildebeest or Stoke Mill. There were a couple of nice pubs along Long Lane that she would walk to of an evening if she was fed up with her own company.

August came along with a letter from her lawyers.

Dear Elizabeth Dowels-Hudson,

Further to your enquiry, please find within, details on how to refuse you inheritance.

The first step is to draw up a disclaimer. The disclaimer must apply to the whole gift. You will not be able to select which parts of the gift you want and which parts you do not want.

The beneficiary must not have received any of the gift already. Disclaiming your inheritance means that you never become the legal owner and you have no rights to the assets and will not have any rights to the assets in the future, it goes back into the residuary estate to be distributed between the other beneficiaries. The beneficiary that refuses the inheritance cannot choose who their section will be distributed to. In order to fulfil your request, we must:

Put the disclaimer in writing.

Deliver the disclaimer to the person in control of the estate – usually the executor or trustee.

Do not accept any benefit from the property you're disclaiming.

The estimated cost of representing your interest in this matter will be in the region of two-thousand pounds.

As regards to any inheritance you have been bequeathed by your

grandparents, these will remain intact as long as the last testimony stated the gift should be passed directly to you and not the estate, to be passed to you in the future.
Please advise your instructions. Mark Stanford
Stanford, Bentley and Brown Solicitors

She replied by email.

Dear Mark,
Please go ahead and draw up the disclaimer. Let me know when it is ready to sign and I will travel to the city for a few days.
Yours,
Elizabeth Dowels-Hudson

Chapter Eleven

Billy was going crazy. He'd been around to the flat to see if he could get a glimpse of Lizzie, many times, but she seemed to be away. She would have gone to the family home for the summer. *Where she should be*. He thought about going into the flat, just to sleep a night in the bed, to smell her presence, even if she wasn't there. He didn't, but he still went every few days to see if he could see her from a distance. He would stand on the opposite side of the road, hoping every time a person walked into the street, or the entrance door opened, it would be her. One night he saw the lights were on and waited around for nearly two hours. The entrance door opened, but it wasn't Lizzie. It was that bastard Phillip. He made a move to go and punch the guys lights out, but after two steps, thought better of it. Lizzie, had obviously reinstated the guy, which meant one thing, she'd gone back to her family and friends. He looked up at the window again, but the lights were switched off.

Everything was subdued at home, Mum trying to compensate by making too many cakes and his favourite desserts, Dad when he was coherent, asking if he was alright and patting him on the back. Derrick, Jenny and Lee calling every other day to ask how things were going. They suggested he take a holiday, but he didn't want to get away, he wanted to be with Lizzie, but he couldn't. He couldn't ask her to give up all she had for him.

He knew she should be coming back to the city soon for the resumption of Parliament, so he took to standing outside her flat more often. Luck would have it he saw the lights on again one night and noticed her pass the window, her silhouette outlined against the curtains. The curtains moved and he watched her open the window to let in the evening air and glance along the street, then she was gone. He stood for a while hoping to get another glimpse, then turned to leave. He heard her call his name half way along Eaton Place.

"Billy, is that you?"

He stopped and turned

"No one but, the big bad boy."

"Don't be silly, how are you?" She asked hesitantly.

"Fucking awful and you, are you doing OK?"

"About the same as you I suspect. I've been busy in Norfolk doing my yearly appearances and such like. I was seeing Tally and Stephen quite a bit, but then they went off to Greece for summer holidays. They have a place there and they love sailing, so they spend a few weeks sailing when they can. They are due back this weekend actually, there's a big regatta at St Olaves they are taking part."

He had let her talk, he wanted her to talk as long as possible, he missed the sound of her voice.

"That's great, I'm glad everything is working out for you. I'd best go."

"Don't go Billy, please. Come in and have a nightcap with me or a glass of wine. Everything isn't working out for me, the opposite without you in my life. Please come up and talk."

"No Lizzie, it's not a good idea." He turned and left.

Billy glanced back as he reached the corner and watched as she made her way back to the flat. Now that he thought about it, he still had to get his computer. He wondered if he should get it now, or better yet just have her mail it to him; there was no way he could do a simple grab and go. Deciding to man up, he headed to her building. This was Lizzie, his Lizzie.

He used his key to enter the lobby and made his way to her front door. *This is a stupid idea. Oh, just do it man.*

He buzzed the doorbell.

She opened the door. Billy looked at her and her obvious unhappiness. He had her in his arms, kissing her face, neck and lips. "I can't live without you Lizzie, I just can't."

She was kissing him back as they fell towards the bedroom, removing their clothes as they went. Lizzie started laughed with joy. They made passionate love until the night sky started lightening ready for the sunrise, then they slept, the sleep of contented lovers.

Billy awoke at eleven to find Lizzie in the kitchen making scrambled eggs on toast.

"Go and sit down, darling, there's coffee on the table." Lizzie told him. "We are going to talk."

She came over with two plates of eggs and some slices of bacon, placed one in front of him and the other opposite. She sat and picked up her knife and fork and told him to eat first, and then they would talk. Billy ran his hand over his head. Had Lizzie noticed his new growth? His hair was slowly starting to come in, and he wondered if Lizzie would like it more if it covered his tattoo, which would draw less attention. You could still see the tattoo, but it was far less prominent that before.

He was ravenous after last night's activities and apparently Lizzie was too; they both devoured their breakfasts without saying a word. Billy poured them both a second coffee.

"Before you start, Billy, there's a few things I need to bring you up to date on. Firstly, I have denounced my inheritance."

"You've done WHAT!?" Billy started.

"Let me finish, let me tell you the whole picture. My solicitors have drawn up a disclaimer to my inheritance from my parents. This is in order to keep the estate intact for someone else to inherit. I'm assuming Daddy will say Penelope, or my nephews. By the time Daddy and Mummy die, the boys will be men and they would be ideal candidates to inherit. However, it's not up to me. I have an inheritance from both grandparents on both sides. Nothing like Brookesley Manor, but it means I won't be poor. I signed the documents yesterday. That's why I'm here. I have one more engagement in Norfolk before I return for the autumn session."

Billy went to speak

"There's more. I have decided not to run for the conservatives next year. I haven't decided whether I will run as an independent or whether I will do something totally different. Whatever I do, it will need to be a paid position and it will be something of my choosing, nobody else's. I will be giving my father notice on this property. I rent it from him, you see, some sort of tax benefit for him, but I've decided to find my own place and become totally independent of my father. The trustees of the estate will probably receive my solicitors' letter sometime next week. I have no idea what my family's reaction will be. I suspect good riddance. I do know Daddy's lawyers will scramble to protect the estate, but it will take time until it is all finalised. Once it is all done and dusted, I'm hoping we can pick up where we left off, if we haven't already done that. I want to be your wife, Billy, more than anything else, if you'll still have me?"

Wow this is a lot to take in. He thought about what she had said and told her what he was thinking.

"I would be the happiest man alive to take up where we left off, but I don't want to wait until everything is finalised. I can't live without you for another minute. I'm not worried about you being poor. I've never really got around to telling you, maybe because I just never thought about it, or it never really came up, but I'm not just a foreman, I'm the owner of Right

Way Construction and it's quite a sizable operation now a days. I'm not sure of the details, I leave most of that to Noel Jenkins. Noel is the face of the business, the guy I was with when we quoted for the job."

"Yes, I remember him, comes across as very professional."

"That's exactly right and he is. It was when I took Noel on, the business started to blossom and has gone from strength to strength. Anyway, over the years I've made investments in properties, which are handled by property agents. Again, I'm not sure of the ins and outs, you know it's just not my thing, but what I mean to say is, I'm not poor either and when we marry, I will look after you and make sure you have everything you want or need."

"I have no doubt about that. I did actually know about you owning the company. Phillip told me when he was trying to stir trouble between us. He is totally out of the picture now and can no longer bother us."

Billy remembered the night he had seen Phillip leave; that must have been the night he had told Lizzie.

"I do have this one appearance I have to make, at the regatta, I have promised Tally and Stephen I will cheer them on. Before I ask you a question, I have to warn you that my father is patron of this event, and my whole family will be there, including Penelope and the boys. I don't know whether Daddy will know about the disclaimer by then or not because it's next week. Will you come with me?"

"Of course, I will and this time, I won't let any of the cronies wind me up. You are my girl and you're staying my girl."

They spent the afternoon together and then she had to leave for Norfolk. Billy arrived home whistling.

"What's got into you?" asked Mum.

"Lizzie and I are back on and nothing will stop us this time."

"I'm so glad to hear that Son, maybe we can get back to normal now. We all hated seeing you so miserable."

Billy and Lizzie spoke at least twice a day and one night whilst speaking late into the night, they fell asleep with their mobiles against their ears.

Billy was travelling to Norfolk Friday. Lizzie had arranged for them to meet up with Stephen and Tally early to grab a bite to eat. When the race started on Sunday Billy and Lizzie would cheer them off, then they would drive to the river bank at Joe's Hole where on wishers had permission from the farmer to use his dirt track to the river. Once they saw Tally's boat pass, they would make their way to Somerleyton Swing Bridge. The regatta organisers had arranged for the bridge to be opened by the Broads Control, for the yachts to navigate. After cheering them on again they would make their way to Waveney River Centre and repeat the action, then a quick dash to Oulton Broad for the end of the race at the yacht station. At each point of the race, others would be cheering their crew on so it was important to get, in and then onto the next point as quickly as possible. Some crews would deliberately place slow moving cars along the road in order to slow down other crews' supporters, not very sportsman like, but a bit of fun, the slow car would always pull over and let them pass after a few minutes.

Saturday was exhibition day, a day when families would wander around the exhibition tents. The usual array of country venders would be there selling homemade preserves, pies, cakes and sweets. The fun stands, like Captain Overboard, had some brave fellow dress up as Captain Hook, sit on a plank and wait for someone to hit the bullseyes, which made the plank give way and immerse the captain in the *drink*. Torpedo Battleship Bismarck, a shooting gallery were the rifles were made to look like torpedoes, Hook a Yacht, where the kids could try and hook a plastic yacht moving around in circles in a huge water container.

For the adults an array of yachts would be on dry dock for would be clients and the merely curious to be shown around by an experienced sales person who would speed up the walk for the ones they recognised as just curious, but took much greater care of the ones they knew could be in the market to part with some serious money. On commission it only took a few yachts a year, to sell and they would have earned a decent salary.

A popular competition amongst the sailors was the 'Chart Your Course', where contestants were given a from and to location, a nautical chart, a trip planner, and a distance calculator in degrees, the idea being they had to mark the locations of harbours, bridges, sea markers and light houses along their given route. This was not a competition for the faint hearted or the newbie sailor. This was serious stuff and had a trophy prize. The winner held this for six months, had their name engraved upon the winner's plaque and then the trophy was displayed in the members nautical club for a further six months until the following year's competition took place. A very coveted prize, the competitors practicing most of the year to take part.

It would also be the day Lizzie's family would be there and the first time she would have seen them since that dreadful day after the wedding. Had told Billy on the drive over, how she was hoping that their paths would not cross. She knew most of her society friends would be there, and she guessed that word would spread to her parents, that she was there with him. Billy just hoped they had the same avoidance strategy as hers. She had told him she would have loved to see the boys, John and Penelope, and even her mother, but that would have to come another day.

When Lizzie told Billy, Tally had two boats; he wasn't sure how to show enough interest without overdoing it as he didn't know anything about yachts, or boats for that matter.

"The one in Greece is where she harbours an eighty-foot cruising sloop. It is a Greek island pleasure yacht that Tally and I have spent many a lazy, luxurious holiday on. It's a beautiful, sleek, vessel shaped like an elongated V with a near centre double beam housing an on-board sail handling system for the main sail." Billy was lost. Besides the fact she was talking about a yacht, all the unknown terminology went over his head. Smiling, he nodded his head for her to continue.

"Well, it has a glass wrapped fly bridge near the cockpit and an extended beach deck space with six sunbeds, a jacuzzi and covered lounge area near the cockpit, a combined living space of one-hundred-fifty metres. Our accommodation consisted of three cabins, the master suite, a twin suite and another twin suite with two pullman beds for the crew. If Tally didn't feel like sailing, the yacht was powered a Caterpillar C32, 560hp engine.

"I remember in our teenager and early twenties, the Greek boys and men, all believing they could get us naive young English girls to fall in love with them. That was never going to happen under the watchful eye of the captain and crew, who, under strict instructions from our parents, were told to let us have fun, but nothing was to get out of hand."

"So, it's really big?" Billy wasn't sure what else he could say. The yacht sounded interesting but, again, he didn't know anything about yachts.

Lizzie smiled and shook her head back and forth. "You are something, you know that? You will have to become a sailor for when we go on holiday with Tally and Stephen. I'm sure they will invite us. Do you swim? I've never asked you."

"I happen to be an excellent swimmer, yes."

Lizzie smiled at him. "I'm glad to hear that."

"The one other yacht, the one she and Stephen will be sailing tomorrow, is normally harboured in Hope Cove, Devon, but it has been trans ported here for the race. This is a smaller, basic version of the Greek boat. This is for Tally to sail. It hasn't got any sail handling system, and it also only had one sleeping cabin."

Billy felt Lizzie tossing in her sleep Friday night, and twice he awoke to find her looking at the ceiling.

"What's wrong?"

"I'm having imaginary confrontations with my family, friends and constituents. I'm wondering how do I get people to see beyond your tattoos, and see the man I know?"

Billy appeared the next morning, in casual tan coloured chinos, a grey shirt worn under a basil coloured jumper, the collar of his shirt pulled up, as he often wore it now. He told her he discovered it looked classier up than down, something he discovered at the wedding.

"You do look good and classy", she said reaching for his hand.

Lizzie wore a red wraparound, V-neck shirt, with a red-and-white horizontal-striped skirt and flat red shoes.

"As do you, but I'd like to add in that you also look beautiful." They left to meet Tally and Stephen at the 'Chart Your Course' tent. Billy learned that Tally had entered for the first-time last year, but didn't figure in the winners, so this year she had entered again, hoping to improve on her standing.

"Tally said once she has her chart done, we will be free to do whatever we want, without her mind being half on the competition."

Tally was sat in her booth when they entered the tent, head down, ruler and pencil in hand drawing on her chart. They watched her as she alternated between the degree calculator, a map, the chart, pencil and ruler. Stephen approached them from the right.

"I saw you come in", he whispered.

"How's she doing?" Billy whispered back.

Stephen inclined his head for them to go outside.

"I think she's doing OK; she certainly seems to be busy charting something."

"How long has she been at it?" Billy continued

"About twenty minutes, I would say. During practise at home, she can take between thirty and forty-five minutes, so it shouldn't be long now."

"Shall we go back in?" Asked Lizzie

"Give it a bit longer, it's so bloody stuffy in there."

They waited a while before entering again and waited another ten minutes until they saw Tally push the finished bell on her table. A red light lit on the side of her cubicle. A woman in white trousers, blue and white striped polo shirt and blue jacket with the club insignia on the breast pocket went and turned off the light. She said something to Tally and patted her on the back, collected Tally's tools and chart and walked away in a very officially important manner.

When Tally's head lifted, looking around for them, Billy saw Lizzie raised her hand waving to catch Tally's eye. She came over.

"Phew, that was a tough one."

"What route did you get?" Asked Stephen.

"You're not going to believe this, but I got the Cyclades. I couldn't believe my luck. I took my time charting some of the lesser known sea markers, ones that are easily missed. My route was Piraeus to Kea, Syros, Mykonos, Paros, Serifos, Cape Sunion and back to Piraeus. I nearly jumped for joy when I opened my envelope."

"Do you know the route?" Asked Billy

"Oh, Crickey, yes my darling, like the back of my hand. I sail there every year. That's where we have just come back from, we practically did that route ourselves just weeks ago as we were meeting friends in Paros." She gave a little clap. "I may be in with a chance this year."

"Well, here's fingers crossed", he said.

"What time is it? Do you think it's too early for a cider or shandy? I'm so thirsty from the dry heat in that tent."

"Never too early for me", said Stephen. "It's eleven-thirty, not far off lunch time."

They all laughed and made their way to the beer tent. After two ciders which went straight to Lizzie and Tally's heads, they headed of for the fun stalls. Tally and Lizzie both wanted to sink the Bismarck. "For the sake of our nation", Tally declared. Tally succeeded. Lizzie didn't.

"Oh, don't worry darling, let's go and get Hook off his perch."

They all brought tickets and were handed six hand-sized cotton pads filled with some heavy substance of an unknown entity. The task was to hit the bullseye of the target with enough force to release the mechanism keeping the plank in place. Tally went first, two pads hitting the twenty-five ring, one missed altogether, two hitting the fifty ring and the last one, everyone swore hit the bullseye ring, but with insufficient force. Stephen was up next, four times consecutively hitting the fifty circle; two on target, one of which everyone thought was going to release the spring, but didn't. Lizzie's turn was next, managing to hit the target all six times but not the bullseye. Billy walked up to the plate, the first hit the fifty. The second hit the bullseye but failed to trigger the spring. On the third he felt he had the idea now of what was needed, either that or the game was loaded against them. He pulled his arm back over his shoulder, adjusted his feet and let swing with his arm. It hit dead centre and immediately the spring released, down went Hook into the water. A cheer went up from the friends and some on lookers. Hook emerged spluttering and laughing. He grabbed his hat which was floating behind him and placed the sodden component with its dripping feather upon his head, made his way to the steps and climbed. In the back ground someone had reset the spring.

"Anyone else want to try, me hearty's?" he questioned the crowd. "As you can see, it can be done."

"I still have three more goes" announced Billy

"Ah, me laddie, once you've got me off, that's it."

"But that's not fair", piped in Lizzie, followed by a call from Tally and Stephen.

"Not fair", they called. Stephen turned to the crowd raising his arms "Not fair", he said to them.

"Not fair" they all responded, repeating time and again.

"OK, OK", said Hook, "If you think you can get me again, have a try."

He looked at his son who stood behind the screen and mouthed. "Tighten the spring." Hook made his way back to the plank. Billy fixed his footing again, hit the target dead centre, but the spring didn't give.

"Again", called the crowd.

Hook winked at his son and gave the slightest of nods and a smile. Billy took aim again, stretched his arms skywards, lowered his shoulder and let rip.

Twang, went the spring as it released its load. Again, Hook was in the drink. The crowd had grown as passer-by's stopped to see what all the ruckus was about. Word went around – "Some guy had managed to get Hook in the water twice so far; he still has one chance left." The gathering crowded closer, moving their heads to try and see. Billy stood there tossing his last pad in the air. Hook told his son to tighten the spring even more, which his son felt was totally out of order, so he smiled, nodded at his dad and released the spring back to its original tension. Billy's last throw saw Hook off his plank once again, and an almighty roar went up from the crowd. As the friends left, onlookers patted Billy on the back and tried to shake his hand, saying,

"Well done lad, well done."

"Never happened before."

"I think I've only ever seen him dunked once before."

"It must be time for another drink", declared Stephen and time to grab a bite. How about something really naughty, pork pie, and beans, or Cornish pasty, chips and beans, sausage rolls…"

"Chips and beans" mimicked the others laughing.

As they sat at a wooden garden table outside a food tent, they heard Lizzie's name.

"Hello, Lizzie." It was Penny, the no-show for coffee, and coming up the rear was Daisy and their other halves.

Lizzie looked up and noticed Penny had a disdainful look upon her face as she scrutinised the plates of food, a small salad being the only thing she allowed herself to eat.

"Hello Penny, how are you? Sorry you couldn't make tea the other wee. But don't worry, Daisy was fun to be with. We had quite a laugh at the pub." Lizzie knew she couldn't stop herself from trying to wind Penny up. "Oh, and about the invitation to your wedding anniversary, Billy and I wouldn't miss it for the world, darling. Oh, you don't know Billy do you? I think we all said hello at Talia's wedding, but you didn't have time to chat as your mother was looking for you." She smiled sweetly. "This is Billy, Billy this is Penny. I think I've told you lots about her."

Billy vaguely recognised her from the wedding, but Lizzie had never mentioned her since. He stood and held out his hand, which was ignored; he sat back down and took a sip of his beer. He was determined not to be wound up today, although it appeared Lizzie had no such intentions for Penny. It also appeared Penny was in the same mood.

"Oh, I thought you were dating Harley again."

"Whatever gave you that idea Penny?"

"Oh, I'm so sorry, I must have misunderstood. I had heard you and Billy had split and Harley was saying the other night when we met him at the Royal Shakespeare…, we went to the royal performance of Madam Butterfly, such a beautiful opera, don't you think? Do you like opera Billy? It is Billy, yes, I've got that right of course you're Billy. Who else would you be?"

Billy was counting backwards from one hundred.

"Anyway, Harley said he had been spending some time with you at several functions of late, and after you had agreed to dine with him, he was hopeful you could rekindle your affections for each other, so I just assumed you were becoming an item once again."

Tally stood up

"You're a malicious bitch Penny! Has anyone actually told you that you are the worst kind of snob and you are the sort of person that gives us decent people a bad name, and that snide little voice of yours! How you live with her Mark is beyond me? She looked at Penny's husband."

Lizzie interrupted.

"Penny, you have misunderstood so terribly, however, it can only be expected of someone with your lack of intelligence, moral standing or decency, that you would interpret things you hear, mould them into a small ball that suits your small mind and regurgitate it as a load of bullshit. Harley and I have bumped into each other at some functions, whilst he was sucking up with his mother, to anyone he thinks could improve his social standing. However, I did not agree to dine with him. I told him, I would think about it, in order to be polite and not hurt his feelings. You wouldn't know about any concept to not hurt people's feelings, would you? I have not contacted him since and have no intentions of doing so. So, please readjust your thought pattern and be on your way. Oh, and of course Billy and I will not be attending your party as I would hate Billy have to see how trash live their lives."

The four friends turned their faces and took huge mouthfuls of chips and beans.

"Damn, that was even better than seeing Hook fall off his plank" Said Stephen.

Chapter Twelve

Excitement was high at the beginning of the day. Billy and Lizzie had watched numerous times as Talia and Stephen checked over their boat. The race started at different times depending on the category of the boat. Tally and Stephen would start at eleven.

The dinghies were the first to leave. The boats were most commonly used with a motor, but the three-sail variant consisting of mainsail, jib and spinnaker were becoming popular along the river for weekend jaunts. Although the slower of all the categories, the dinghies went first otherwise the wake from the larger boats could seriously impair their sailing control.

The second category of vessels were the sloops, this was Tally and Stephen's class and featured the standard generic two sail sloop configuration and the fractionally-rigged sloop where one of the sails lies below the top of the mast. The sloops were known for their manoeuvrability. Again, Billy wasn't sure what anyone was talking about when it came to the different aspects of boats, so he would just nod and smile.

The third class was the three sail cutters, the sails were mounted on the main mast near the stern of the boat to allow for larger sails to be used.

"Cutters are the favoured yacht for competitions as their design favours speed and agility. These, start last, as they are more able to deal with any remaining wake from the sloops. However, Stephen is an excellent sailor and so am I, even if I do say so myself. Our sailing skills will get us to first place, Tally concluded.

***

Lizzie decided not to attend the opening ceremony, to see her father standing on the rostrum giving his speech. She still didn't know whether he had received any communications from the trustees and didn't know whether she was standing in the calm before a storm, or whether things would blow over like a breeze, she was praying for the latter. She had left

Billy to find a WC when a hand grabbed her wrist and pulled her out of sight. She was so startled she barely managed to stay on her feet. Behind a tent, her mother spun her around.

"Have you gone completely mad, child? Have you lost all your senses of late? What has happened to you?

She knew just by looking at her mother's face the trustees had been in touch.

"I just want to be with the man I love, mother. I can't understand why none of you can see this, and I'm prepared to live a normal, working class life to have the man I want. I'm getting older, Mother; I'm not longer a princess in a fairy tale. I know what I want and I know who I want; I want Billy. I love him."

"Love, love… You say you are not living in a fairy tale when that is exactly what you are trying to do. Poor little misunderstood miss giving up her inheritance to be with the man she loves and it all works out fine. The family will be so shocked they accept him into their lives and we have our happy ending. Billy takes over the estate, the banking and insurance companies, the properties and doubles the family wealth. Is that what you re ally think is going to happen? Do you think I don't know about love? I was deeply, madly in love before I met and married your father. During my finishing school years in Paris, I met the love of my life, an educated man from a good family and an Englishman to boot. We spent several wonderful months together and then it was time for us to return. He wanted to stay longer, to have adventures, he said; he wanted me to stay with him and share those adventures. Do you think I wasn't tempted? The man of my dreams asking me to stay with him in Paris, live together and one day marry, see the world, experience new things together and lay in each other's arms until our hearts content. Of course, I was tempted! Very much so, but I had responsibilities, Elizabeth. When we are born into families like ours, we are born to serve, to serve the people that rely on us. Our choices are taken from us.

"We have choices within our own society and, yes, some of those choices can turn out to be idiots, but it is we, the women, that can make them better, help them manage these great estates. Oh, Elizabeth, please don't do this. You are so much like your father. You have both dug your heels in so far into the quagmire, neither of you are capable of pulling your selves out. If you do this, Elizabeth, not only will you lose everything, you will break your fathers' heart and mine along with it. It will be the end of us as a family. Please reconsider."

"Mummy, I am so sorry this has all happened, and I have tried to look at it from your point of view. I do understand you need a son-in-law who can take over from Daddy, and you're right, Billy isn't the one to do it. That is exactly why I have done what I have done. You and Daddy have two grandsons, both would be suitable heirs, and when they are of age, with the help of Penelope and John, either one of them would be totally capable of doing all the things you need done. Don't you see, Mummy, it's the perfect solution, and then, yes, I can have my happy ending. I will have my Paris and my adventures, and you will have your history and estate preserved for the future. You need to get Daddy to see this is a good thing, good for the family and good for me. Please, Mummy, help me do this. I don't want to lose my family, and maybe one day, once Daddy has his heirs in place and Billy is no longer a threat to him, we can spend time together as a family. I don't know, but I won't change my mind. I have to go, Mummy; I need to find a WC and Billy will be wondering where I am. Give my love to Penelope, John and the boys, will you?"

Lizzie left and ran to the toilet before she peed herself. She couldn't hold it like she used to, a sign of old age creeping in. Billy was waiting outside when she emerged.

***

"Hello there, I thought you had run away."

"I'll never run from you; you know that. Now let's go and find Tally before they have to start."

Lizzie passed Penelope, John and the boys on their way to the starting point. They kissed each other coolly on each cheek. John and Billy shook hands. The boys placed their arms around Lizzies legs.

"Who are you rooting for this year?" Lizzie asked.

"Well, of course we are rooting for Tally, but from a distance because Johns' nephew Rodney is sailing today, and well, family must come first. Although I'm sure you will be rushing along the route cheering her on; she won't need us. Give her my love and tell her", she lowered her voice to a whisper, "it would be great to see a girl win her class this year."

"Thanks, Penelope, I will. We'll probably run into you en-route, but don't get in our way. Is Rodney in a cutter or sloop?"

"A sloop, I'm afraid, so may the best man or woman win." They smiled at each other and went in opposite directions. Penelope was meet ing her parents at the starting gun and they were going to stand on the pier to wave Tally and Stephen off. Billy and Lizzie agreed it was a wonderful sight to see, the sails loosely flapping in the breeze, people running back and forth across the decks, crew members standing ready on the pier to way ropes and stays.

The starting bells chimed loudly over the speakers, then every boat blasted their horns, and every person whistled and yelled. They saw Stephen wave back at them as they sailed out of the marine a big grin on his face. Billy grabbed Lizzie's hand and started running to the car park.

"What do you think so far?" Lizzie shouted at him over the deafening noise.

"I think it's fantastic, now let's get to Joe's Hole", he shouted back. Other supporters were scrambling to their cars and manoeuvring out of the car park without running someone over, or bumping another car, which was a skill in itself, but they managed.

"Fun, isn't it?" Lizzie said more as a statement than a question. "It certainly is and to see some of these people letting their hair down for a change is good to see. There are some humans amongst the crowd. I saw your sister running to her car, the poor boys were being dragged off their feet."

"Yes, she can get a little bit too enthusiast at times, I feel terrible I've placed her in this position, but she seems to be coping well. I was glad to see John shook your hand again."

"He's a Scotsman, I think they are a little less consumed with themselves than Englishmen."

There must have been at least thirty cars driving down the track to

Joe's Hole a bumpy affair that rocked the car from side to side, the trick was to try and place the tyres on the upper parts of the ruts. People were already standing at the river's edge waiting for the yachts to appear, some squeezing past others to get a better view. The bank was a flat pathway running the length of the river on one side and farmers' fields on the other. Tally came into sight and Billy and Lizzie waved frantically and giving them the thumbs up sign. Once Tally had passed, Billy turned to go back to the car when he saw Anthony screaming and desperately looking for his mother and father, "Stewart, Stewart" over and over again. Billy ran over to the lad, took him by the shoulders and said

"What's happened?" Anthony looked up at the man with Aunt Lizzie, "He's fallen in the river."

Billy didn't wait for another word but grabbed Lizzie and shouted,

"Stewart has fallen in. Find John and Penelope, quick, NOW", as he ran to the water's edge.

The river was running pretty quickly with the wakes of the boats making it nearly impossible to see anything in the water. He was moving people out of the way shouting.

"A child has fallen in, scan the water." He just kept repeating it over and over.

People started realising what he was saying, stopped their waving and started scanning. A steward's boat came into view and someone ran along the path to call it inshore to stop the race. Someone called,

"What's that over there?"

Billy scanned where the man was pointing. He had already stripped off to his underpants and socks, when he spied a little head and a pair of arms holding onto a branch sticking out of the bank. Without a word, he dove into the river, swimming for the boy. The current was pushing him to the middle, and he needed to stay closer to the bank so that he could grab the lad. A wake pushed him back, but he was moving downstream too fast. He started driving himself against the current hoping to slow himself. He drifted past the boy and grabbed hold of another root sticking out of the bank about ten feet away. He held on, his arms and shoulders aching from the strain. He looked over at the five-year-old and called,

"Stewart, do you remember me with your Aunt Lizzie?"

The boy nodded; his face screwed into a terrified contortion.

"I need you to trust me Stewart. I'm going to ask you to let go in just a moment, do you understand? The boy gripped harder onto his root and shook his head."

People were running in Billy's direction, the steward's boat having blasted an emergency horn to stop the race, boats were lowering their sails and throwing anchors to stop from drifting. Penelope was in hysterics on the bank, Lizzie trying to help her calm down.

"Billy's in the water, he'll get Stewart out. Johns running to them now. They'll get him. I'm sure they'll get him."

Billy spoke to the lad again. "Stewart, when you let go of your root, you will drift towards me, can you hear me?"

The boy nodded.

"Then when you drift towards me, I will hold you and pass you to your dad on the bank. Do you understand all that?"

The boy nodded again, tears streaming down his face.

"Now, I'm going to count to three and I want you to let go.

One, two, three."

The boy didn't move.

"You have to be very brave, Stewart, now let's try again. One, two, three."

Stewart released his grip and floated down towards him, the currant drifting him out to the centre as it had Billy. Billy stretched and grabbed hold of the boy's arm as he went passed and pulled him into his chest. The water level here was about six feet down from the path. Billy could see peo ple a little way up the path looking over the edge to see where they were.

"Over here", Billy called "I have the boy."

"Over there ", the shouts started.

Billy saw an arm stretching down from the pathway, but not reaching them. He heard a shout.

"I can't reach, they're too far down. Has anyone got some rope, or a belt? Someone, come and hold my legs and I'll try to reach further."

Billy could feel his grip giving way and tried to pull them both in tighter, but a searing pain shot through his elbow.

"Hurry up, for fuck sake, someone get a hold of this boy", Billy shouted.

The arm appeared again. "Can you lift him just a couple of inches so that I can get a hold of his collar?" the voice shouted.

He hoisted the lad into his right arm and holding the band of Stewarts trousers threw him upwards, praying someone would catch him. Someone obviously did, as the boy didn't splash back down. A voice came again,

"We've got him, we've got him, he's OK. We're going to lower a belt. Can you wrap it around you hand so that we can haul you up?"

"OK, I'll try."

They lowered the belt, there was just enough to wrap around his fist once; he could see a hand holding the other end. He needed to let go of the root soon as he was sure he had dislocated his shoulder.

"OK, are you ready?"

"Go ahead, I'm ready."

Billy let go of the root; the current dragged his legs out from under his torso, pulling him into the flow. His body was trying to follow when something hit him in the hip, and he didn't know what. He heard the man shouting,

"I need some more hands over here; the current is pulling him."

More hands appeared on the belt, three or four, all trying to get a grip.

"It's no good. Billy can you grab the root again? We need something else. Hasn't that fucking stewards' boat got here yet, what's holding them up?"

Billy twisted his body so that his back was against the bank again. He stretched out his arm to get hold of the root. Where had it gone? He couldn't find it. He moved his arm back and forth, turning his head to find it, with every move the searing pain, now in his elbow and shoulder. He felt something, not the same root, a different one, thinner, but it would have to do. He grabbed it, and once he felt he had a good hold, he let go of the belt. It took all of thirty seconds for the root to come loose from its anchorage and float downstream with Billy still holding on.

He came to his senses and looked back at the bank drifting away.

He could see Lizzie standing at the edge, arms outstretched calling his name. He had to think quick, the current pushing him further and further into the middle of the river. He went under, something brushed past him, the anchor chain to one of the boats, but it was too late to get a hold. He surfaced and saw two boats further downstream, people hanging over the sides, ropes dangling into the water. If he could get close enough, he could get hold of one with his good arm.

Someone had phoned the Broads controller to close the swing bridge, which would help stop the current, but it took time. Dinghies were released from the boats and paddled out to where Billy was last seen, but nobody found him.

So, this is the day that will change my life forever. After today, everything will be different. I stood erect, suit and shirt pressed. Witnesses on both sides of the room, waiting to play their roles. I couldn't focus on my surroundings, unhearing of the crowd, sounds muffled except an odd harsh cough, sunlight shining hazily through windows made everything dream like. Was this just a dream, was I really here? No, it's just a dream, but look, here comes my bride, the love of my life, the most beautiful woman I have ever known. It's a shame her parents aren't here, but her sister, John and the boys are standing as Lizzie enters. There are Tally and Stephen; they turned out to be such good friends. They'll look after her for me. I know they will. The vicar asked her a question, she said I do. He's asking me the same and, of course, the answer is I do, I do, I do. You can let go now, Billy, *he told himself.*

Chapter Thirteen

The world had gone mad, totally and utterly mad. No one was making any sense. Penelope wouldn't stop her bloody crying and wailing, telling her how sorry she was, that this was never meant to happen. She wondered whether Tally and Stephen had won the race. *Who are all these people here? Why is this police woman asking me questions? What is she talking about?*

"Miss Dowels-Hudson, may I call you Elizabeth? We need to know who to contact regarding the accident. Mr. Johnsons' family. Are his parents alive? Can you tell me what has happened to his clothes? Does he have a wallet in his jacket? Please, Elizabeth, I need you to try and focus."

"Why am I sitting on the ground?" She asked this stranger.

"You fainted, Elizabeth."

"Why did I faint? Silly me, it must be the excitement of the race." Nobody knew how to respond.

"Let me help you to your feet Elizabeth, make you comfortable. My car is just over here."

The stranger led her through a throng of people, some weeping, others running back and forth, she wasn't sure where to or why. The woman in the blue uniform opened the back door to her car and sat Elizabeth down, leaving her legs outside. Police Officer Maria Cobb knelt down in front of Elizabeth.

"Elizabeth, do you know where you are?"

"Yes, we're at Joe's Hole, but we need to get onto the swing bridge at Somerleyton to wave Tally on."

Maria held Elizabeth's' hands.

"Elizabeth, there has been an accident. Mr. Johnson jumped into the river to save Stewart."

"But Mr. Johnson is too old, besides he has Alzheimer's."

"OK, that's good Elizabeth. Where does Mr. Johnson live exactly."

"In Grays of course, with Dorrie. Derrick, Jenny and Lesley visit a lot. They're a lovely family, always hugging, not just pretend hugs, but real ones. Billy likes hugging. Where is Billy anyway? You need to tell him; I've put his clothes in the car."

Maria looked back at her colleague.

"The clothes are in her car. Ask the sister which car it is and see if there's a wallet with his I.D. and address."

The other officer left to look for Penelope.

***

Police Officer Jeremy Nobel found her on the grass, cradling the boy that had fallen in; another young lad sat beside her and a man on his knees behind her with his hands on her shoulders.

"Excuse me, mam, I need to know which car is your sister's."

The man stood.

"I'll show you, it's not Lizzie's car, it's Billy's." The man was choking back tears until they began streaming down his face. "How did this happen? Has Billy drowned?"

"We don't know yet, Sir. We have search parties out on the river looking now to see if they can locate him. He may have been able to find something to hang onto, or caught up in a tree. You never know, he may have managed to get himself out lower down, once the current slowed and he's walking back here now, or looking for someone to tell. It's all farmers' fields around here. He'd have to walk to Somerleyton or back here which is a good hike. Don't worry, we'll find him. Now if you could show me the car?"

John walked the police officer to Billy's BMW; it was unlocked. The policeman sat in the driver's seat and opened the glove compartment. Inside was the insurance folder. He opened it and wrote down the address on the policy. In the back was the contact in-case-of-emergency card—it listed Derrick Johnson, Billy's brother.

On the back of the car was an alternative contact, stating a sister—Lesley, Bristol. He took the card with him and put the insurance folder back. On the back seat was a wad of clothes, that looked as though they had been thrown in hastily. He leaned over the seat and shook out the items. The bottom item, which was still neatly folded on the back seat, was a jacket.

He lifted it and went through the pockets, but couldn't find a wallet. He picked up the trousers and there it was in a buttoned-back pocket. He removed it and looked inside: credit cards, some cash, drivers licence address listed in Grays. He took the licence and made his way back to Maria. The husband of the crying woman had disappeared, probably gone back to his wife. As he approached, he saw Maria was still on her knees with Elizabeth. He touched her shoulder and showed her he had some I.D.'s; she nodded at him, rose to her feet and pulled him a little distance from Elizabeth. She turned her back

"Use your personal radio, out of ear shot, and call in the details. I don't know what the inspector will want to do given we haven't found any one yet. My recommendation would be to find a sympathetic officer in Grays. You never know, there might be one that knows the family, to tell them there has been an accident, but we don't know the results yet. It helps get the family used to the worst possible scenario." Maria went back to Lizzie.

***

Police Officer Cobb

"Elizabeth, we are going to find your sister and her family and take you all back to St. Olaves marina. I want you just to sit here for a moment while I go and find them."

"Don't forget to find Billy and tell him we'll meet him there." Lizzie called.

Maria shook her head. Shock had a funny way of working, protecting a fragile mind against damage when something like this happened. Maria knew that eventually, either sooner or later, something would trigger a switch and reality would set in. That would be the time for grieving. Mind you, Billy might still be alive somewhere, miracles do happen, or so she had been told. *Not often in the job though.*

***

Chief Inspector Peter Leask

Norfolk constabulary phoned through to Grays constabulary and passed over the details. Grays constabulary reported the incident to Inspector Green who went in to see Chief Inspector Peter Leask. Many officers of Grays station knew Billy Johnson through his work with local charities and charitable social events. Pete knew Billy personally as a friend and often had a pint of beer with him at the Royal Feathers.

"Oh, fuck, don't tell me this, not Billy." Pete couldn't believe the news. Of course, nothing was definite; Billy could still be alive.

"Do we contact the parents?" Asked inspector Green.

"No, for heaven's sake, not Dorrie and John. We need to contact Derrick, but not over the phone. I'll contact the chief at Surbiton. Leave it with me. Pass the word around to the other officers, will you? Let them know what's happening."

Green left. Pete got on the phone to Surbiton. He didn't know the chief there very well, but they had met at a few events for the outer-London constabularies.

"Hi Paul, this is Chief Inspector Peter Leask at Grays. I have a little bit of a situation here and I'm wondering if you can help me with it."

He outlined the family history.

"Do you have a good family relations officer and maybe a grief councillor that can go around to Derrick Johnson's house and let him know about the accident. Tell Derrick I've been in touch; he knows me and tell him he should go to his parents to be with them. We can send some officers from Grays to the family home, but the parents are a bit old and Billy's dad suffers from Alzheimer's, so it's best if he is there with them. Can you give him my personal number and tell him he can call me? It's 0679 4014 5425 Thanks for this, I owe you one."

"Don't worry about it, Pete, in fact I'll accompany the officers, I know Derrick, he's my son's football coach and you don't owe me anything. Why the bloody hell do these things happen to the wrong people?"

"Tell me about it, he jumped in to save a kid."

"Shit", said Paul.

***

Chief Inspector Paul Surbiton

It was five in the afternoon when the car pulled up outside Derrick and Jenny's house. Derrick was sat in the front room watching the high lights of Match of the Day when the doorbell rang.

"You expecting someone, Jen?" he called out.

"Nope, not me."

He stood and went to the door. He recognised Paul straight away and placed a smile upon his face. There were two officers he didn't know, a young woman of about thirty and a tall, lanky man he thought was about forty.

"Hello, Paul, what on Earth are you doing here? Another spout of burglaries in the area?"

Paul smiled, "Can we come in, Derrick?"

The hairs on Derrick's neck stood up. Sure, come on in." He made way for them to pass.

"Jen, can you come into the front room", he called.

"Yep, just give me a mo", came the reply.

"Now, Jenny, right now."

Jenny walked in from the laundry room.

"Wha—" she stopped wiping the water off her hands.

"Would you like to sit down, Jenny, Derrick? I'm afraid we have some bad news."

"Is it Dad, Mum, has something happened to one of them?"

"No, Derrick, it's Billy."

"Billy? Billy's in Norfolk this weekend; he's not even here."

Jenny was sat on the chair staring at her hands placed in her lap.

"The accident happened in Norfolk. To be honest, details are still a bit sketchy. Apparently, there was a boat race and a child fell into the river. Billy dived in to get him out. He managed to get the boy to safety, but the current took your brother downstream. They are looking for him now. Nobody knows yet what has happened. He could be stuck in a tree waiting for rescue as far as anyone knows. They have search teams and volunteers searching now, so there's no need to panic yet, but I've spoken with Peter Leask at Grays, and he thinks it would be a good idea if you could make your way to your parents' house, just in case your needed. This is his personal number so that you can keep in touch for any further updates." He handed over a slip of paper.

Everyone looked around as Jenny let out a huge wail.

"Oh, no, please God not Billy, not sweet, kind, generous Billy, of all people. This will kill Dorrie."

"They don't know anything yet, Jenny, don't jump the gun. Billy's a fantastic swimmer, you know that; he'll be all right. Fucking typical of the stupid bastard to jump in to save a kid though. Why can't he just stand back for once and let someone else be the goddamn hero?"

"Because it's not in his nature", whispered Jenny.

"Right, OK, let's think. Thanks for coming, Paul, we'll take it from here and get over to my parents. Do you know if anyone has contacted my sister?"

"I don't think so, we thought you might be best to do that. If you like we can contact Bristol and get someone around to her house, if you'd rather that is?"

"No, No, don't worry, I'll call her now, before we leave and get her up here. Thanks again, Paul, and thanks for coming around personally. I'll let you know when things are fine, which I'm sure they will be."

Derrick shook hands with Paul before showing all the officers out the door.

***

Upon entering the lounge, Derrick placed his head in his hands. "Billy, please be all right, please, please." He started crying.

Jenny came over and put her arms around him, but neither had words of comfort for the other; they were both too heartbroken. Fifteen minutes later Derrick sat on the sofa whilst Jenny was packing some things to take to Grays with them. He had sent a message to school saying he wouldn't be in due to a family emergency. Now he had to phone Lesley. The phone rang and rang. He was about to put it down when Fetu picked up

""Hello."

Someone was giggling in the background, probably Lee or Sofia.

"Hi Fetu, it's Derrick."

"Oh, hi, Derrick, do you want to speak with Lee?"

"Not just yet, mate, can I have a quick word with you first? Listen, I don't want you to react. I want you to stay calm, but Billy has been in an accident; it could be serious, but we don't know yet. Jenny and I are going to Grays to be with Mum and Dad, just in case. I'll tell Lee know the details when I speak with her, but you know what she is like; she'll dash out to her car and drive up here without thought. I need you to keep her calm, plan how the best way to get here is, safely, not driving at warp nine along the motorway. Get her to take a bit of time. See if Sofia wants to come up. Would you be able to come with her in case she needs you? Think about all this and get here when you can. Are you OK?"

"Yes, Derrick, I understand. You can rely on me. Now I'll pass you over to Lee."

Lee came to the phone.

"What's up, bro?"

Derrick broke the news, filling her in on the details he had so far. He heard Lee's wail and who must have been Sofia in the background asking what had happened. He heard the clank as the phone was released and hit the leg of the table or something, then Fetu was on again.

"Don't worry, Derrick, I will calm things here and explain to Sofia. We will get there as soon as we can. Be safe."

Derrick stood, "You ready, Jen?"

"Yep, coming."

They made their way to Grays.

"What on Earth are you two doing here and at this time of night?" Dorrie asked as she opens the door.

Jenny and Derrick had discussed how to give the news on the way and decided it best just to go to the lounge and tell the two of them together, if dad was coherent. Then Jenny would make tea while Derrick stayed with his parents filling them in on the details. Once they were told, Derrick would try and speak with Peter Leask and see if there was any more news. If not, he would ask if there were any other people in Norfolk he could contact. Just sitting around waiting was not a viable option.

"We've got some news, Mum. Can you come into the lounge and sit with Dad a minute?"

"What's happened, Lesley, Sofia, Billy, Fetu?"

"It's Billy, Mum, come and sit down, and let me tell you what we know. How's Dad, is he coherent?"

"He was about twenty minutes ago, ask him."

"Hi, Dad, how are you?"

"I'm OK, Billy, and you?"

"It's Derrick, Dad."

"Oh, Derrick, of course. Billy's in his room, probably farting."

He was semi here.

Jenny stood, "I'm going to make tea." She left without reply. Derrick took his mum's hands and told her what had happened. "Oh, my poor boy, he'll be worried about us all if he's out there on his own. He'll be getting cold as well if they don't find him soon. How will they look for him if it gets any darker? Where's Lizzie, is she with him?

They were going to a fancy boat race and to see her friends. Oh, goodness, the poor girl must be worried sick."

"I've got the phone number of Peter Leask; he said to phone him for any updates. I'm going to do that now, see if he knows anything more, meanwhile, did Billy ever give you any of Lizzie's contact details?"

"No, I can't say he has, but what about in his room?"

"You are brilliant, Mum; I'll go and have a look and phone Pete. You stay with Dad; I don't think he has taken any of this in."

Derrick went upstairs just as Jenny came back with tea, he explained what he was doing. She went and sat with Dorrie and John.

The conversation with Peter Leask didn't bear any more fruit, but Pete promised to phone through to Norwich and see if there were any developments. Meanwhile Derrick looked through Billy's things. There didn't seem to be anything, at least not with Lizzie's Norwich details. Her London address he found on the job sheet for the work they had done on her property. There was a number with the name scratched out and written beside it, Billy had written THE TWAT in large black letters. Derrick had a feeling that number wouldn't be any good, but made a note of it anyway.

He started flicking through Billy's sketch book and came across a drawing of a face with words written at the top:

The Girl at Eaton Place. Who is she?????? She is an angel. She is a diamond. She is a goddess. She is an emerald. She is a dream!!!!!!!

Derrick realised he had struck gold as all around the drawing was a number, written over and over again, in all different fonts. He typed the number into his phone. It was ringing before a woman's voice answered.

"Lizzie is that you?"

The woman on the other end recognised the voice.

"Billy is that you? Oh, thank God, where are you? Everyone is out looking for you. Where are you? We have the police here. They can come and collect you."

"It's not Billy, it's his brother, Derrick. Is that you Lizzie?"

"Oh shit, no sorry, my name's Talia. I'm a friend of Billy and Lizzie. I thought you were him; you sound just like him."

"Can I speak with Lizzie? I need to find out what's going on there."

"You could, but you wouldn't get any sense. She seems to have blocked everything out and is talking as though Billy is around here somewhere. She keeps telling us things we need to tell him when he gets back. She seems to have gone a bit crazy. We have a police officer here with us; her name's Maria. She is in contact with people at the river and is giving us feedback as to what's happening."

"And that is?" Derrick prompted.

"The last thing we heard is that the swing gate was closed to stop the current flowing; it had been opened for the race. They have been setting up ARC lights along the riverbank to keep the search going. There are about five divers in the river. All the race boats, that were upstream of where he went in, have navigated back to the marina, to save shadows and confusion. The boats downstream have to remain, so they don't disturb the water."

"And", Derrick prompted again, "any signs?"

"No, no signs yet, but the police are saying he could be out of the water or stuck in something. If he got out of the water, he could be injured somewhere. There's an army of volunteers down by the river with search lights looking."

"What time did he go in?"

"Go in?"

"Jump in the river for the child."

"I'm sorry, Derrick, I'm going to pass you over to Maria Cobb, the police officer here to explain. it's just too painful for me. I become a blubbering idiot every time I think about it."

Another woman's voice came on the phone and introduced herself as Constable Maria Cobb. He made himself known to her. She remembered Billy had a brother Derrick as his emergency contact. Derrick asked the same question he had to Talia.

"That happened at about eleven-thirty this morning, but it took Billy about forty minutes to get to the boy and get him to safety. It was about ten minutes after that when the root he was holding onto came out of the ground and floated downstream. The last sighting of Billy was at about twelve-thirty. There is still a chance, Derrick. Elizabeth has told me Billy is a good swimmer, so there is still a chance. As everyone is praying, we are hoping he is injured somewhere and we will come across him soon."

"Eight hours, it's a long time to be missing."

"It seems that way, but we have found people days after they went missing and they have recovered fully."

"What? People who have fallen in a river?"

There was silence.

"You have my phone number Constable Cobb; please contact me with any news at all. I'm with my parents; my sister is making her way home, so as soon as you know anything, anything at all, please let us know."

"I will, Derrick, but stay positive, it's not over yet. We're doing everything we possibly can, and there are so many people from all around helping and searching. Your brother is a real hero here. What he did deserves a medal."

"Thanks, but I don't want a hero or medal, I just want my brother home. His family want him home."

Derrick closed the line and wept bitter tears; he knew he had lost his younger brother. He warned Billy this relationship would end in disaster, but he never thought for one moment it would be like this, not this sort of disaster. Jenny and Dorrie looked up at him as he came into the room, saw his face and burst into tears.

"There's still a chance, Mum, there is still a chance."

But nobody really believed the words.

Billy's body was found eighteen hours later, wedged against the spring bridge.

Chapter Fourteen

The phone call came through to Maria Cobb at two O'clock precisely. They had found Billy and it was not good news. Her sergeant asked if any family members had arrived as they would be needed to identify the body. She explained the situation to him and told him Elizabeth was his fiancé and maybe she would agree. This would save the necessity of the family travel ling at this time. She was to have a word with Elizabeth. She should con firm the details with the coroner's office as soon as possible.

Maria spoke with Talia first and asked if she thought her friend would be able to do it.

"We know it's him, the tattoos and all, but he has to be officially identified before he is taken for an autopsy."

"An autopsy? Is that necessary? We know how he died, he drowned."

"I understand, I really do, but it's the law you see, accidental and unnatural deaths."

"Well, at the moment, she doesn't even accept he isn't here, so I don't know. Maybe it could be phrased as going to see Billy, rather than identify him. I really don't know. You have probably had more experience with this sort of thing than I have."

It was decided to try and the task was put to Talia.

"Hello, sweety, did you rest a little? Do you want Stephen to make you a nice cup of tea?"

"That would be lovely", Lizzie replied.

"Darling, I need to speak to you about Billy."

"Yes, they said they had found him. He doesn't know the area you see, that's why it's taken him so long to come home."

"Lizzie, darling, Billy had an accident yesterday, remember? He can't come home anymore darling. He's resting, resting with angels. Stephen, Maria and I want to take you to see Billy. You can see how peaceful he is. They need to know that they have the right Billy at the… at the… shelter, in the resting room. Do you think you can tell them, Lizzie?"

Lizzie nodded her head. "Will we have tea first?" She asked.

At the coroner's office, they were asked to stand in front of a glass window with a blue drawn curtain. A lady came out and introduced herself as Medico-Legal Death Investigator Dr. Sally Field.

"I just want to explain a little part of what we will do today and tell you why. When we retrieve a cadaver from water, there are certain changes made to the exterior. These, I think, you would know as washer woman hands, wrinkling of the skin. This mostly occurs on the feet and hands. Mr. Johnson has also suffered some post-mortem cutaneous abrasions that have resulted in what looks like bruising on much of his body. He has many tattoos on his body and we feel it may be a kinder way to identify him, by showing you some portions of his tattoos, rather full exposure of the body. Would that be acceptable to all parties?"

"Yes, I'm sure it will be", said Talia.

"Well, what we shall do is open a portion of the curtain for you to see his upper torso. His arms and hands will be obscured with sheets. We will then close that portion and expose his back region, and then same again for his legs. Before we start, I would like to ask you to describe one or two of the tattoos on Mr. Johnson.

"There's one with a griffin" Lizzie said "He told me about it one weekend. We had gone away to Cornwall. It's a tribute to his father's Irish ancestry; he had that done just as we met. Then there's his Korus coming off his Manawa Lines on his stomach, the Manawa is a series of stripes. You will see a group of dots leading off to nine squares, each one is someone important in his life. Belinda, his birth mother, Robert, his birth father, Dorrie, John, Derrick, Jenny, Lesley, Sofia and the nineth will read Elizabeth."

Elizabeth looked at Tally, tears streaming down her face.

"Can I see all of him? You can keep his hands and feet covered if you like, but I'd like to see all of him one last time."

"Yes, we can do that if you prefer. When we open the curtains, you will hear my voice, and I will ask you if you recognise the person on the gurney and to tell us his name."

Lizzie nodded. The woman disappeared back into the room behind the curtain. They heard her voice.

"Can you hear me Elizabeth? Speak into the microphone `please."

"Yes, I can hear you."

"OK, I'm going to open the curtains. Identify yourself and say your relationship to the deceased."

The curtains opened. Elizabeth looked. Billy lay there, but it wasn't

Billy. This person was grey. He had all of Billy's tattoos. His body looked like Billy's, but he seemed bigger, somehow, or was he smaller? She couldn't decide. She looked at his art, and remembered when he had told her their stories. Why he had them done. What they meant to him. She re membered the times she would point at one, and ask him what it meant, the history behind it. She remembered drawing over his skin with the tip of her nail, watching his reaction, sensing him becoming aroused. A blow hit her as she looked at his face. His lovely face, now vacant of expression. His warm lips, now cold. This was Billy, but no longer her Billy, her Billy was gone. She let out a cry as reality sunk in.

"Are you there Elizabeth? Can you hear me?

"Yes... I'm here", she replied in a quiet voice.

"Take your time. Can you state your name and relationship?"

"Elizabeth Dowels-Hudson, fiancé."

"Would you identify the person in front of you please."

"Billy Johnson."

"Thank you, visual identification completed." The microphone went silent and the curtains closed.

The doctor reappeared.

"Would you like to sit with him a while?"

"Could I?"

"Yes, I think you can do that. Speak to him and say goodbye, sometimes it can help."

Lizzie sat with him for two hours. Constable Cobb left, but gave Talia her number in case she was needed. Stephen and Tally sat in the corridor waiting for Lizzie.

***

Derrick opened the door to Lee, Fetu and Sofia at two in the morning.

Lee dashed through. "Have we heard anything yet?"

"Not yet. Lizzie's friend Talia and an officer with Lizzie are keeping us informed."

"How long has it been?"

"Too long." Replied Derrick.

Nobody slept that night not even John. They all dozed ten minutes here and there. Talia, phoned four times throughout the night, with no positive news. Dorrie wanted to know how Lizzie was bearing up.

Talia explained what Lizzie was like and that she still thought Billy was about to walk through the door.

"Be with her if the news is bad. She will need a friend. Let her know we are here and thinking of her." He remembered his, denial, when his birth parents died.

The news, that they had found Billy, came to the Johnson home, by means of Peter Leask, who drove up in plain clothes and in his own car. As soon as they saw him, they knew without being told.

Dorrie opened the door. "Come in Peter, there's no need to say anything, I think we all know, he's gone, our Billy has gone." She excused herself and went to her bedroom; she cried herself to sleep holding a pillow.

The whole household was crying.

"What's wrong?" Dad asked "Has someone died." The news was given to him whilst he could understand.

***

The funeral was in Grays. He was to be cremated. Lizzie travelled down with Billy's body to the undertakers earlier that week and went to the London flat. Tally and Stephen didn't want her to go alone, but she insisted.

"I need time to grieve alone", she told them. "You travel down with Penelope, John and the boys; that way they won't get lost. Once you are settled in the hotel, let me know and pop around to the flat. Just you and Stephen, though, I don't want to see Penelope just yet; make an excuse for me. Tell her we are eating pizza. That will keep her away."

Lizzie was finding it hard to come to terms with why Billy had died, and every time she saw or thought of Penelope's family, it reminded her. She knew it wasn't the boy's fault and that it was just a tragic accident. It did, however, cross her mind that Penelope should have left the boys with her parents at the marina, or have kept hold of them herself when they were so close to the river, or that John should have been the one to dive into the river to rescue Stewart. Then she would change track realizing that if she hadn't seen him through the window that night and asked him back up, they wouldn't be together, then he wouldn't have attended the regatta, and he wouldn't have been there to jump into the water after Stewart. It was her fault he was there; it was all her fault. But then if they hadn't spent that reunion night together, they wouldn't have spent the last few weeks together, loving each other.

Her mother had sent a letter, after Lizzie refused to talk with her, expressing her and Omar's deep regrets. Such a tragedy, and how grateful they were that Billy's sacrifice, had saved their grandchild. They would for ever be in his debt. Lizzie vomited after she had read it. *Hypocrites*. They had asked via Penelope, whether they could attend the funeral to show their respects. Lizzie told Penelope to tell them to fuck themselves. As far as she was concerned, nothing had changed. She still discharged her inheritance and wanted nothing to do with them.

Billy's service was amazing, as far as funerals could be. The hearse and family cars arrived at Park View Gardens at ten am. Two black limousines waited behind Billy's coffin. A V-shaped reef of white lilies lain atop. The neighbours all came out of their homes, dressed in black. Some would make their way to the Thurrock New Cemetery. At ten-fifteen the family, consisting of Dorrie, John, Derrick, Jenny, Lesley, Sofia, moved to the vehicles. The second car transported Fetu, Lizzie, Talia and Stephen.

Other cars joined the procession along route, one being Penelope and John.

***

Penelope was shocked at the number of people lining the streets. Their car had waited at the entrance to Park View Gardens on Orsett Road where people were standing either side of the street. Even then John thought Billy must have been very well liked, but it didn't stop there. There were people on Palmers Avenue, then again on Chadwell Road all clapping their respect as the hearse passed through. When they pulled into the cemetery gates, there must have been two hundred people or more waiting for the cars to arrive and more arriving from the streets they had been standing on. As the coffin was taken into the crematory chapel, a police guard gave salute, the solemn party made their way in with about fifty guests behind. Penelope, John and the boys sat towards the back, Penelope feeling a little bit out of place with such a show of affection.

The vicar stood on the podium.

"I have had so many requests from people wishing to pay tribute to Billy Johnson. For his kindness, his selflessness, his generosity and much more. If I allowed all the tributes to take place, I'm afraid we will all need sleeping bags." There was gentle laughter. "Instead I have asked five people to speak, but before they do, I would like to read out the names of the people that wanted to pay tribute but have not been able to speak here today. Do not worry, just your presence is a great tribute to Billy." He read out a list of thirty-seven names, some organisations, businesses, private people and charities.

The first person to speak was Dorrie, Billy's Mum. "I remember the day the three children arrived into our lives. All three have given us such joy. Billy was very special and he will be sorely missed…"

Secondly it was Billy's brother Derrick. "I am speaking on behalf of my sister, wife and niece. We composed our tribute together. Billy, Lesley and I lost our parents at a young age, and we were so blessed to find Dorrie and John." Derrick took a deep breath, keeping his gaze on the crowd, and then continued, "Billy was so sensitive and yet so brave the way he stood up against the discrimination that came his way due to his tattoos and shaved head. What those discriminators don't realize is that they lost out on so very much for not having known him. Billy was loved by everyone who got to know him, as people can see today, and was respected for his kindness and generosity…"

Lizzie came next and read a poem before she spoke.

"This is a poem, I'm sure many of you here today will know, by Mary Elizabeth Frye. I think it is fitting for Billy as it reflects how I feel and how I'm sure you all feel, that we haven't lost him, he is and will always be all around us."

> *Do not stand at my grave and weep,*
> *I am not there, I do not sleep.*
> *I am a thousand winds that blow.*
> *I am the diamond glint on snow.*
> *I am the sunlight on ripened grain.*
> *I am the gentle autumn rain.*
> *When you wake in the morning hush,*
> *I am the swift, uplifting rush*
> *Of quiet birds in circling flight.*
> *I am the soft starlight at night.*
> *Do not stand at my grave and weep.*
> *I am not there, I do not sleep.*
> *Do not stand at my grave and cry.*
> *I am not there, I did not die!*

"I haven't known Billy as long as many, in fact, all of you here today.

You are his friends, his family, his colleagues. You are the people of his life.

I became a person of his life last November. From the moment I saw him, I knew I was meeting someone incredibly special and, within moments, I knew he would be extra special for me.

"People talk about love at first sight, well, if you don't believe in it, I can attest it to be true. Sometimes the most unexpected person is the per son that will make you whole. Billy made me whole. He has given me the strength to stand up for myself and the things I believe in, a gift I will treasure for the rest of my life, but the most precious thing Billy gave me, and no it's not that huge diamond he proposed with"—small laughter went up, many had heard about the proposal at the Feathers—"it was the 295 days of love, the 7080 hours of happiness, the 424,800 minutes of being with him."

The next person to speak was Chief Inspector Peter Leask who talked about how Billy was a wonderful member of the community. Always giving help where needed, encouragement to youngsters trying to take a better path in life. How he would often drive a long and see Billy mending someone's fence, or painting their door. A true community member.

The last speaker was from the Big Brother charity, that help terminally ill children to achieve a dream. The hours Billy would spend with the children building up their spirits, the hours contacting sponsors to make the children's dreams come true. A true champion that would be sorely missed.

The service over, the gathered crowd made their way outside where they joined in with the crowd outside, crying, laughing, remembering and Billy's favourite, hugging.

***

Lizzie watched the scene in a daze. The family and some invited friends made their way back to Dorrie and John's house, others scattered, some to the Feathers where Chris and Charlie had put on a free bar and food, others to their own homes. Lizzie had asked Penelope back to the house as John had asked to meet Dorrie and John and introduce the boy Billy had rescued. When introduced, Dorrie put her arms around each and every one of them and gave them the Johnson hug.

"Now, now there. There is no need to say a word. Billy wouldn't have had it any other way. It was his choice and he did the right thing.

The cost was high, but if he stood here with us today, he would say it was worth it to see such a beautiful boy safe, back in the arms of his family."

Penelope and John left later understanding a whole lot better what Lizzie had seen in the man she loved. Why she had fought so hard to stay with him and felt a little bit envious of having not known more. They would and could never forget the man that had saved their boy.

Lizzie couldn't remember who she had spoken to, nor what they had said. The sympathy and grief overwhelming her. She said her good byes to the family, with the promise she would see them soon and phone them the next day. Tally and Stephen drove Lizzie back to the Eaton Place flat and went up for a drink. They could walk to the hotel from Lizzie's.

They spoke about memories, of things said and things done, and when Lizzie fell asleep on the sofa, Tally and Stephen laid a blanket over her and sneaked out the door.

The next day Lizzie awoke determined to change how she was living. The first step had already been made with her father. How he now sorted out the future of the estate was down to him. She sat at her computer and wrote her resignation letter as MP for Brookesley, sent it by email and placed the follow-up hard copy in an envelope. Next, she phoned an old friend in Paris and explained she needed to get away for a while and asked if she could visit.

"Ah, *mon chéri*, you can come and stay as long as you like. I will text you my new apartment address. *Ah, mon amie* it is splendid and right in the middle of life. You will love it."

Her next move was to send an email to her father's property management agents telling them she would be vacating the premises in two weeks' time. Enough time to say goodbye to the people that mattered and finish up any outstanding business. She already had her euro account in place and transferred one-hundred thousand pounds from her inheritance trust to the euro account. That should be enough for at least a year, maybe even two.

She booked her flight, laid her empty suitcases in the spare room, went out and bought some bubble-wrap to store her personal possessions and post her resignation. She popped into the Knightsbridge Hotel to catch up and say goodbye to Tally. She would be leaving for Norfolk again soon to arrange transport of the 'Spirit Tally' back down to Devon. The race was to be reorganised for another date, but this year, it would not be as before. Certainly, for Lizzie, Tally and Stephen. Some local yachts might take part, but competitors from other parts would all be wanting to get their boats back to harbour for the winter. Tally declared she would never take part in the race again, to which Lizzie responded, she must, and she must win, just to please Billy.

The three had drinks at the bar, but Lizzie didn't stay long. She told them, she was going to visit Claudette for a while, and they both thought it a good idea. Claudette, was the life and soul of a party and could help Lizzie with her sadness. She didn't tell them she had resigned, that would come later.

"Well, you know where we are. Paris is only a few miles away, so if you ever want to come to ours for a long weekend, we will be here, or better still, we will visit for a long weekend. I love Paris, especially after that foul summer smell disappears. I mean it Lizzie, if there is anything, anything at all, you want us to do, don't hesitate to ask."

"There is one thing, don't tell my parents where I have gone. I will let Penelope know, but I want to have some time alone and recover. It's our secret."

She kept in touch with the Johnson's as promised and they invited her to tea the Sunday before her flight. When she arrived, everyone was there including Lee, Sofia and Fetu.

"Well, this is a surprise. I didn't expect you all to be here, this is lovely."

"We had the will reading Friday, in fact, you and Fetu need to contact the solicitors. Billy left you both something."

"Left me something?"

"You might not think it much, you know, given what you have and everything but it might come in handy one day."

She wasn't sure whether Derrick was angry with her or not.

"Whatever, Billy left me will be treasured, I can assure you. I would have thought Billy would have told you, but I disinherited myself from my family, before Billy and I got back together."

"You did what?" came a call from Jenny, "you must be mad."

"No, not mad at all Jenny, free, at last I'm free. He didn't tell you then? Well, typical Billy, not to think it important."

"In that case it may come in handy sooner than later."

Over tea she explained the situation with her family's fortune, she also explained that she did have some inheritance from her grandparents, which consisted mostly of cash payments.

"Not enough to live on for the rest of my life, but enough to help me start anew, sometime some place."

She told how she was going to stay with her friend in Paris for a while. They all thought it a good idea, as a change of scenery would do her good; she was looking a bit off colour.

"I have some news", declared Lee, "Fetu and I are getting married." Joyous acknowledgments came from all directions except Sofia, who already knew.

"We got engaged two days ago. Losing Billy has shown us, we need to grab our happiness while we can. We have set the date for next spring and we hope you will all be there."

Everyone agreed they would. The afternoon was spent chatting, remembering Billy, asking about plans for the wedding and where it would take place. Lizzie returned back home feeling she hadn't lost a family, but gained one.

The day before her departure, she really did feel sick and wondered whether she was coming down with the flu. She made a quick appointment with her doctor, who managed to fit her in due to a cancellation.

"OK, let's see what's going on here. How long have you had symptoms?" Dr. Fleck asked.

"I haven't been feeling well for weeks, but there was a recent close death, a dear friend, and I thought it was to do with being sad. It seems to be getting worse thought, so I thought I might be getting an early flu virus. I travel tomorrow, so I could really do with something to help."

"Let's take a blood sample and a urine test to rule out a few things, those results will come back quickly. Other infections we will have to wait a few hours, but the nurse can phone you at home later with the results."

He gave her a urine cup, took some blood, took her blood pressure and did a thorough external check. He handed over her specimens to the nurse and sent her off. Dr. Fleck, might be a bit expensive, but she didn't have to see him often, although she did wonder whether she would be able to afford him in the near future.

"OK, well everything is underway. If you'd like you can wait in the reception, the receptionist can get you a coffee, or you can come back in an hour and we'll have the results."

"I'll pop back in an hour."

She walked around the shops window shopping, stopped at a small café and had a tea and bun, then made her way back. She was shown into the doctor's office after a ten-minute wait.

"Right Elizabeth, we have some results back and the good news is it isn't flu. No antibiotic for you today."

"So, do we know what it is?"

"We do, you're pregnant."

"I'm what? But that's impossible, I'm thirty-nine years of age. I can't be pregnant."

"We ran the test three times and it came back the same each time. I'd like to do an internal to make sure. I'll call in the nurse."

The nurse prepared her, and she laid back with her legs in the stirrups of the examination table. When the examination was complete, the doctor removed his gloves and told Elizabeth she could sit up.

"You're definitely pregnant, I would say about five weeks, but we need to do more tests on your blood to determine exact dates. Can you remember your last menstrual show?"

Shit before the reunion night. She left not knowing how she felt. The doctor had assured her they would run potential danger tests, but as far as he could see, as long as she stayed as healthy as she was now, there shouldn't be any problems, however, if she didn't want to go through with the pregnancy there were other options. She needed to speak with someone. She dialled the number

"Hello?"

"Dorrie are you home? It's Lizzie."

"Oh, hello Lizzie, yes I'm home."

"Can I come and see you?"

"Why of course you can, I thought you were off to Paris today."

"Tomorrow, I leave tomorrow, but I want to speak with you before I leave. I need your advice, can I come, now?"

"Yes, my dear, come around."

When Lizzie arrived, Dorrie told her to come sit in the kitchen.

"I know you want to talk, my dear, so I thought we would be better in here out of John's ear shot."

"Thanks", said Lizzie.

"Now, you tell me, what's bothering you? Are you having second thoughts about your trip?"

"No, not really, I really do feel I need to do something new. Billy told me once that I had allowed people to control my life because it was easy. He was right and I've wanted to change things for a long time. I thought I would be doing it with Billy, but now, well... now, I'm alone and I'm not sure I'm strong enough."

"Why, my dear girl, you're not alone, you have us now. I have lost my son and he was a wonderful boy and gave us all great joy, but as he has left, you arrived. That's what life is like, someone comes and others go. This world, my dear, is just one piece of a journey; none of us know what awaits us when we leave here. While *we are here*, we need to do the best we can, be the best we can, help others the best we can. Billy did all those things and more, and I'm sure he is on a beautiful journey somewhere else now. You are not alone, as you said in your poem: *I am the swift, uplifting rush. Of quiet birds in circling flight. I am the soft starlight at night.* You are not alone. There are many that walk beside us; we just can't see or touch them."

"Dorrie, I need to tell you something. This morning I found out I'm pregnant, with Billy's child, and I'm scared. I've been feeling off for a while. At first, I thought it was the stress of what was happening with my family. I found myself vomiting. I thought, I was reacting to their letters and everything. Then after we lost Billy, I thought it was my grief. It never occurred to me I could be pregnant, but once the doctor told me, it all made sense."

"Don't be scared, child, as I said, someone goes someone arrives, this is a blessing. We are here for you whenever you need us."

"I'm still going to go to Paris, but I promise I will keep in touch at least once a week to let you know how things are going. Will you tell the others for me? I guess I'll have to come back for the birth. It really would be a scandal if the child were born French, and besides, I'll be back for the wedding. Thank you, Dorrie, for everything, for all your love and support."

"Well if you need a home when you come back, you come here.

You are as much part of this family, as Billy was. Now with my grandchild on the way, this will always be your home. Can I tell John and the others? This and Lee's wedding is going to bring some much-needed happiness."

Chapter Fifteen

Lizzie warned Claudette she was arriving loaded down with luggage, and accordingly, Claudette arrived in the brightest yellow, stretched V8 Jeep Wrangler.

"Is this big enough, *mon chéri*?" She asked.

"It's certainly bright enough, I must declare."

"The 'd' in Claudette does not stand for demure, but dare", she laughed with a bright happy smile.

It was difficult to describe Claudette, as her appearance depended on her mood. Today seemed to be a 'see me day'. She stood propped up against the monstrosity of a vehicle, its huge tyres reaching her breast line, in the no-parking zone, right outside the airport entrance. Not only the jeep declared her presence, but Claudette herself did. She was dressed in yellow-and-black, striped, bumble bee tights; red polka-dot skirt; a black, totally transparent lace vest—her petit breasts shown blatantly to the world— and a bright-yellow, leather jacket with so many zips, there was hardly room to spare for the material. Upon her head she wore a large, floppy, black, bow headband, that drew her long jetblack hair away from her face. To make sure she was seen, she was wearing the brightest red lipstick on her full, wide lips and thick black lines of eyeliner around her eyes.

"You'll get a parking ticket staying here", Lizzie laughed.

"No, *policier de circulation* would dare. Come, let us load *les bagages* and be gone", she said with a flurry of hand and combination of French and English with her wonderfully theatrical accent.

As they approached the city, Lizzie started to feel she had made the right choice coming here. If there was anyone in the world that could lift her spirits, it would be Claudette. She, Tally, Claudette and two other girls, Mercedes from Spain and Roselia from Italy, had all met in the tiny village of Glion, roosting high above the city of Montreux and accessed by funicular, at the *institut of Madame de Pierrefue*. Muriel Spark must have written her final novel *The Finishing School* based on the institute *"Where parents dump their teenage children after their schooldays and before their universities or their marriages or careers."* Even in these modern times, still many parents never expected their daughters to ever have a real career, but certainly a good marriage.

During their time there, they had become known as the *fabulous five*, amongst the other girls, but those *five wildcats* amongst the staff. Madam Alarie, the headmistress, would march the five out to the hillside in front of the classroom windows, for all the other girls to see, stand them in a row and as she smiled, and gestured gracefully, towards Lake Geneva, tell them they should contemplate their misbehaviour in the face of such privilege, whilst she slapped their delicate hands with a cane and made them stand, if it was cold and miserable enough, during their luncheon and several hours after as extra punishment. This only served to bond them together even more and plot their next escapade.

"How will you manoeuvre this thing in the city?" Asked Lizzie, rather worried about some of the narrow streets in the neighbourhoods, especially ones with parking problems.

"You worry so much, *ma douce petite amie*, you must relax more."

The neighbourhood of Canal SaintMartin had become a firmly established centre of coolness, developed around the charming strolls along the nearly two-hundred-year-old waterway. Claudette had acquired eleven Rue Dieu from her second marriage, even though she was cited as the adulteress when she was caught in *infidélité* with a young model. She had agreed her ex-husband could live there until he found something more suitable. It took him three years but he was now settled with a new young wife in a new part of the city.

Claudette had sold off the upper three storeys for conversion into apartments and kept the ground and first floor which she had converted into a complete living space. Parking was atrocious so she had applied for part of the building to be made into a drive-in garage off the street. Adjacent to her was an Art gallery with offices housed above, which meant her weekend parties only disturbed a few guests staying in the hotel on the other side of the property. Entrance to the property was either through the garage which had a side door leading to the living area which was a vast open space of lounge, kitchen, dining area combined. The other entrance was through a front door on the other side of this vast space. On the first floor were six bedrooms with their own private bathroom, two of which were more like suites and had their own lounge area, kitchenette, dressing room and bathroom. There was a large interior courtyard with terracotta floor tiles, sofas, chairs, tables and ceramic-potted plants. A domed skylight let light stream down from five floors above.

Lizzie had been allotted one of the suites facing out to the street, the other being at the back of the building. It had a tiny wrought iron terrace where a pair of feet would be hard pressed to fit, but it meant the French doors could be opened to let a cool breeze flow through the rooms. Once they had unloaded the luggage and placed it upstairs, Claudette insisted Lizzie leave her unpacking until later and they go downstairs for a drink.

"There is a divine little bar just one-hundred metres along the road that serve wonderful lunchtime cocktails along with delicious treats. I will introduce you to some friends of mine there."

Lizzie could hardly refuse, after all Claudette was doing for her, but she had to find a reason not to partake of the alcohol, she had yet to tell her about the pregnancy.

For the first week, Lizzie wandered around the neighbourhood getting her bearings. At the end of the street was Quai de Valmy the road either side of the canal, little pedestrian bridges connecting one side to the other. Parking looked to still be a nightmare, but a tree lines path ran the whole length of the waterway as far as her eyes could see, with benches for people to rest or just gaze at the passing traffic on the water. Trendy bars, shops and galleries lined the avenue, people sheltering from the still hot weather under canopies in the shade, sipping their cool drinks.

She found a hospital, just in case it was needed on Rue Bichat, a small park Jardin Villemin in the same area. The post office was located on Rue du Faubourg SaintMartin with the Police de Paris on the opposite side of the road. She had thought about hiring a car, although Claudette had told her she was free to use one of hers; she was not confident enough driving in Paris traffic to do so and decided whilst she was still not showing, she would get herself a bike, the exercise would serve her well anyway. After the second week, Claudette found her in the main kitchen making an omelette.

"Would you like one, Claudette?"

"Not for me yet, it takes my stomach at least an hour to settle before food. So, when are you going to tell me what has been happening and why you are here? In truth, Lizzie, you have not come just to see an old friend."

"Pour us a coffee, it's on the table and I will fill in all the details."

They sat for nearly two hours whilst between bouts of tears and pauses of quiet thoughts, Lizzie told her about Billy, the disinheritance, the accident, the funeral and at last the pregnancy.

"*Mon Dieu!* You have been through the…, how do you say…, the washing machine and back."

"The wringer and back", Lizzie smiled, "I feel I need to make a new start and where better than Paris. Find myself and my independence, like when we were girls, recover from my sadness. Now with the baby, maybe have another family, my own family. I have Billy's family back in the UK and they are wonderful, but I think if I put myself in their hands, it will be the same as my parents, in a nice way, but I will still be relying on others to make choices for me, and I want to start making my own choices, good and bad."

"Well, the first thing we need to do is find you a decent gynaecologist, as you said, you are no spring kitchen and you will need professional care."

"No spring chicken", Lizzie pointed out.

"You know, I never did get that one, a spring kitchen. This always had me confused." They both laughed.

Claudette made an appointment with her gynaecologist, who turned out to be a lovely lady that spoke English. Lizzie bought herself a bike with a basket attached to the front and a satchel on the back. She would get some bits and bobs to eat and drink during the day and bike around. She had bought herself a decent camera as well and started taking photos of the local scenery. She was in contact with Dorrie, John and the rest of the Johnson family on a regular basis. She had found places she liked to shop at for groceries and had totally given up coffee and alcohol. She met many of Claudette's friends and often went out with them to different bars, museums, art shows, and visited their homes outside Paris in the countryside. Claudette's friends were a lot younger than either of them, the average being twenty-five; there were some older ones, but age with this lot just didn't matter, neither did appearance. There were nerds, Goff's, punks, hippies, models, professors, the sleek and the shiny and everyone got along the same. It was all so refreshing.

Lizzie phoned Penelope. "Hello, Penelope, how are you? And John and the boys? I'm just ringing to let you know, I'm going to be travelling for a while."

"Are you alright?"

"Yes, I'm fine. A friend was going on holiday, and asked me to join her, so I have."

"How long will you be away?"

"I'm not sure yet. I need time to think and recover. I'll let you know, when I decide. I'm just taking things as they come, at the moment."

"That's sensible." Penelope responded. "You take some time. Enjoy yourself a little."

"Has father sorted out the estate and who it will go to?"

"Yes, Daddy has made Steward heir, as Anthony is John's heir being the eldest."

"How is Mother?"

"Mummy doesn't seem to be her old self any more. I think Billy's death and you leaving, has hit her hard.

"Yes, it hit us all hard. Well, I have to go Penelope. I have a train to catch." This was a lie; Lizzie just didn't have anything else to speak about.

"Oh, Okay. You stay safe now."

"I will. I'll speak to you soon. Give my love to John and the boys."

Lizzie didn't tell her where she was, or that she was pregnant. After three months in Paris, Lizzie had two challenges in front of her, one was to decide whether she would let her mother know she was going to have a child, the other was to find a permanent home for herself. She was beginning to show, and as the months went on, she was beginning to feel more and more worn out by the constant comings and goings at Claudette's. She asked Claudette and her friends to keep an eye out for any bar gains that might arise. The consensus was that she wouldn't find anything in this area, and she explained that she would be quite happy to look in lesser trendy areas.

Whilst she could still ride her bike, she took to looking for À vendre, or for sale signs, but riding into lesser-known neighbourhoods were out. One place she really liked the feel of was the Haut Marais district an up-and-coming neighbourhood. It was one of the oldest parts of the city, with many 17thcentury stone mansions, one of which was the *Hôtel Salé* housing the *Musée Picasso*. It had a beautiful covered market which she later discovered was the oldest covered market in Paris, the *Marché des Enfants Rouges* (dating from 1615). It had a mass of cafés, bistro bars, art galleries like the Galerie Thaddaeus Ropac. She searched online and enquired through agents, asked her friends, but found nothing in her price range. She knew she would have to invest just about every pound of her inheritance in order to buy a property even in a lesser-known part of the city.

She eventually found a three-bedroom apartment above a shop on Rue de Menilmontant, both were for sale as a package. The place had been trashed, graffiti sprayed all over the outside walls and interior of the shop; it was an up-and-coming area and the right price. The owner had previously had two sales, fall through, so he was eager to sell. Lizzie was prepared to put some effort into the property and thought she could rent the shop out below for a small income. The building also had an underground car park for residents, all be it very narrow and difficult to park in. All her friends pulled together to get the place shipshape, painted and cleaned, donated bits and bobs, and someone even found a reliable tenant for the shop. A young couple wanting to start a store selling organic, ecological produce with no animal testing or force feeding in sight.

As she settled into her new routine and got to know the area, she found an abundance of charming corners such as the Parc de Belleville and its panoramic views, or the area around Place St Marthe, where the laid back ambience combined a cosmopolitan vibe full of people and families. There were also many art galleries cementing the emergence of a young original art scene. She found some delightful cuisine from Sicilian and Brazilian to Rwandan. Her Rwandan meal did cause a bout of heartburn that went on all night and a rather foul smell in the bathroom the next morning, not because the food wasn't good, but her body just wasn't used to such richness.

***

March passed and she knew she had to make the trip back to England, for Lee and Fetu's wedding, which was the 28th of April. She was going

to look like a beached whale, but one of Claudette's friends was a new de signer and had made her a lovely maternity dress for the occasion in oyster satin with a full-length jacket that matched. Tally and Stephen had been over to visit a few times, but their last visit was in January after the Christmas holidays and it was time to catch up again. They would Skype every week to make sure she and the baby were safe and then there was the most important life changing event, the birth of her son or daughter due on the 16th of May. She had been given the choice of knowing the sex, but decided she wanted it to be a surprise.

Her gynaecologist had been in touch with a colleague in London at Saint Mary's Hospital, in Paddington, where the birth would take place. She had asked Dorrie to be present at the birth and had an unusual request from Derrick to be present also.

"Jenny and I couldn't have children and Lee won't have another, so would you allow me the honour of being present to see the birth of Billy's child?"

She had been taken back a bit, but after thinking about it, and dismissing the horrible imagine of what this was going to look like, she told him he could. On condition the rest of the family, except Dorrie, wait outside, because she was afraid, they would all start making requests. She would be staying with Dorrie and John while in the UK, apart from some time she would be spending with Tally.

She booked her ticket on the Eurostar from Paris' Gare du Nord for the 20th of April; this would take her into St. Pancras, where someone from the family would collect her and take her home. The journey would take around two and a half hours.

Her apartment was ready for her return. She had decorated the lounge in off-white walls and wooden furnishings upholstered in warm earth colours: deep reds, greens, oranges and yellows. She had chosen some of her favourite intimate photos, close-ups of facial expressions, an old lady's blue-veined hands, two people sharing a secret kiss, and had them elegantly framed. Two large green ferns stood in terracotta pots that Claudette had given her from her courtyard. The nursery was a combination of yellows and purples. One solid yellow wall had a white stripe down the middle with three huge yellow-and-purple flowers that another friend had made for the baby. The grey kitchen had been installed and child protected as had any sharp corners, although, all the tables were oval, bar the writing desk where the computer sat. She was looking forward to returning.

***

Lee had chosen to have her wedding at St. Peter and St. Paul's church at the junction of High Street and New Road, not far from the house. It was a lovely little church and was the ancient Parish Church of Grays. The beautiful Grade II listed building had a lovely clock tower to the side of the main nave. Wooden beams adorned the arched ceiling and the carpeted passage leading to the sanctuary, alter and pulpit. Lee looked amazing in a thirties style silk cream gown with a Bateau neckline. Her hair was dressed with spring flowers that matched her bouquet. She looked so happy and so radiant. As Lee entered, she saw Fetu standing lean with a look of pride on his face in a single-breasted silver-grey suit, his yellow silk tie, tied with a café knot. Who had tied it for him? She had no clue. Lee on the arm of John knew there wasn't any two men prouder on Earth than John and Fetu. Thankfully, John had been aware enough to walk her down the aisle.

***

The wedding reception took place at the Royal Feathers that had closed to the public for the day. Charlie had brought in staff to cater for the one hundred guests. He had set up dining tables in the lounge bar for the overflow from the restaurant, and in the beer garden, a tent was erected for dancing to a live band. Lizzie lost count of how many people came up and rubbed her tummy saying,
"It's a boy."
"It's a girl."
At midnight Lizzie spoke with Derrick,
"I'm taking Dorrie and John home. We're all pretty tired."
"I'll walk you back."
"There's no need, you stay here and enjoy the party."
"There's no way I'm letting the three of you go home alone. The streets aren't what they used to be. A heavily pregnant woman and two pensioners walking alone, is asking for problems."
"It's ten minutes. We'll be fine."
"A lot can happen in ten minutes. I'll walk you home."
Derrick escorted them and then went back to the celebrations. Lizzie kissed her adopted parents' goodnight and made her way to Billy's old room. It still had his things there as though he would walk in at any moment, and in a strange way it comforted her. His enormous bed taking up a good portion of the room. His clothes had gone but there was still so much of him present.
There was only one place Fetu and Lee were going to go on their honeymoon. Lizzie had asked.
"So, where are you two going for your honeymoon?"
"Samoa of course. Fetu has a huge family there and as very few of them could make it to the weeding, we are going to celebrate the marriage with the rest of the family there." They popped around the house to say bye to Mum, Dad and Lizzie, having already said their other farewells at the party, when they left for their first night, as husband and wife.

"Make sure you're back in time for the new arrival. A fortnight away is cutting it fine."

"We'll be here, don't worry. We wouldn't miss this for the world." For the next couple of days, the only thing the family did was laze around, all of them, including Sofia, feeling totally exhausted after all the planning, arranging, dancing and dinking.

Six days after the wedding, on May 4th, Lizzie awoke at six am feeling unsettled. She crept down the stairs to make a pot of tea. She had got ten used to making a pot with tea leaves and was just lifting the boiled kettle when an excruciating pain shot through her back. She quickly put the hot water down and sat on one of the kitchen chairs. She breathed in through her nose and out through her mouth as she had been shown, mainly to calm herself; she wasn't due for another two weeks. After a few minutes, the pain subsided and she moved to put the hot water in the pot. Bringing the tea to the table, she collected some milk from the fridge and sat down again. During her first sip she felt another pain. She let it pass as before and then went and gently knocked on the backroom door which had now been changed into a bedroom for Dorrie and John as they could no longer manage the stairs.

"Dorrie", she tried to whisper quietly in order not to disturb John. "Dorrie, are you awake?"

Immediately there was a rustle and Dorrie opened the door ajar.

"I hope I haven't woken you", Lizzie said.

"You are all right, lass; we old folk don't sleep much. Doesn't look as though you are sleeping either, are you all right?"

"I'm getting pains, strong pains."

Dorrie went back into the room and put her dressing gown over her nightdress. She came out and quietly closed the door.

"Let's go to the kitchen", she said.

As they made their way, another pain struck, this time all around her abdomen, and Lizzie had to put one hand out to Dorrie's shoulder, the other against the wall to steady herself.

"It's not due yet, Dorrie; I think something is wrong."

"Don't you fret, girl. I'm surprised you've carried this long. You're a mature mum, so things can work a bit differently. I've been waiting for this for the past few weeks. I even thought, you would be having the child in France with you leaving so late to come home. Now don't panic. You've had a good thirty-six weeks and the babe will be fine. Now let's get you comfortable while I call the hospital and let them know what's going on."

***

This had all been rehearsed. Dorrie had all the contact details by the telephone ready. First, she had to phone the hospital. Being a paying client, Lizzie had arranged for an ambulance to collect her as neither John nor Dorrie drove any longer.

"Now when did the pains start, Lizzie?"

"I woke up at six and the first pain came about six forty-five, while I was making tea. The next one came about fifteen minutes later and then the last one, which again, was about fifteen minutes."

Dorrie asked her to describe the pains, which she did, then Dorrie left to relay the information to the hospital. She had all Lizzie's patient references on the same page as the phone numbers. Her next call was to the consultant, who sounded very chirpy for a man woken at seven am; he was probably used to it. Dorrie gave the doctor Lizzie's name and he knew straight away who she was.

"Ah, Mrs Johnson, I've been expecting your call. How is our girl doing?"

"She's a little bit worried, doctor, but I've tried to calm her a bit by telling her this is normal. It is normal, isn't it? My mother had eleven children right into her forties and the latter ones all seemed to come early."

"Your perfectly right, Mrs. Johnson, this is quite normal given Elizabeth's age. Have you phoned the hospital?"

"Yes, doctor, I did that first and they are sending an ambulance."

"Lovely, well it looks like you have everything under control. If you can help Ms Dowels-Hudson get ready. There will be no need for her to get dressed if she doesn't want to. She can come in her nightwear, but make sure she has a set of clothes, just in case it's a false alarm. Bring the baby bag with you as well and I will meet you at St. Mary's. Well done, Mrs. Johnson, keep up the good work."

Dorrie went back to the kitchen to make sure Lizzie was still OK and put the kettle back on. She sat down for a moment and held Lizzie's hand.

By her estimate another pain would come any minute now, and it did. Lizzie gripped the edge of the table and breathed until it passed. Dorrie threw away the contents of the teapot now stewed a dark brown and made a fresh pot.

"I'm just going to leave another moment, Lizzie. You are doing so well, good girl; just keep doing as you have been and everything will be fine. I'm going to call Brenda to come over and get John ready and then I'll call Derrick to let him know to make his way to Paddington."

Lizzie nodded her head. After the calls Dorrie asked if Lizzie wanted to go as she was or get dressed. Lizzie looked horrified at the thought of go ing in her pyjamas and said she would dress.

"Well you stay there and I'll fetch your clothes from your room."

She made her slow progress up the stairs holding onto that balustrade and placing first one foot on the step then the other until she eventually reached the top. Damn these knees. She gathered some clothes, underwear and shoes then went through the same process to descend. Given the amount of time she was upstairs, she knew Lizzie had another contraction while she was away. The front door rang; it was Brenda. Dorrie explained what was happening and asked her to get John up, wash and dress him. Brenda held Dorrie's hands.

"How exciting, not long now then", she said and disappeared into the back bedroom.

"Dorrie phoned her taxi driver, Richard, who knew he was on call for this occasion. He would come to the house and take John and Dorrie to St. Mary's.

***

As it turned out, Billy was wealthier than anyone knew, probably even himself, being as laid back about that sort of thing as he was. The four properties Billy bought for investment had in fact turned into eight when Billy, asked what he wanted to do with the profits accumulating from them, told his accountants to do what was best; they invested in four more.

The villa in Fuengirola he left to Derrick and Jenny. His tattoo sketches, he left to Sofia, valued at approximately one to two-hundred pounds each; there was over a thousand of them. He had left one hundred and fifty thousand pounds to Lee, to put a deposit on a house of her choice. To Fetu he had left a collection of wristwatches that nobody knew he had. There were seven watches in total, two Patek Phillipe, two Audemars PK Gubelin, one Blancpan, one Rolex and one Cartier, all made in the early sixties through to the mid-eighties; their value for insurance purposes was seventy thousand pounds. He left half the business to Noel, while the other half and all other interests, including the rental properties, were to be managed for Dorrie and John so that they wouldn't need for anything in their latter years.

To Lizzie he had left a house he had purchased as a surprised for their wedding, before the separation. It was in Kew, Richmond, facing the river in Cambridge Cottages. Hardly a cottage, the stone house boasted five double bedrooms, four bathrooms, three en-suite and one shared, two reception rooms, a dining room, a large American-styled kitchen, laundry, study. Attached to the back was an annex extension of three more rooms: one a sunroom and two studio-type rooms, which Elizabeth had thought he intended as a studio for him to draw his designs and the other for her as an office. The two were connected and could be opened into one large space by opening grand sliding doors. It had a huge, mature back garden, a rarity in this neighbourhood. When she had first seen it, in fact, the only time, she had seen what he had seen when visualising their life together and it had broken her heart.

"Rent it until I decide what to do with it." She had instructed a property agent.

With Dorrie and John having so much money they could never spend in this lifetime, they had contacted a private-car hire company and after having several drivers, taking them out on day trips, they met Richard. A lovely young man about forty, with a great sense of humour, who would always have Dorrie in fits of laughter, and John, on a good day, really enjoyed his company. If John were struggling, Richard would be patient and calm with him and make sure he was all right. Now, the hire company knew that Richard had become the Johnson's driver and always made sure he was available to take them where they wanted to go. Richard had been booked to take them to Paddington, for the birth of Lizzie's baby.

The ambulance arrived and so did Richard; the group made their way to Paddington. At the hospital, Dorrie realised she hadn't contacted Lee, so sent a WhatsApp message telling her to video call them at the hospital for news. Sofia was making her way to Paddington from Milton Keynes where she had been to see a rock concert in a bowl or something like that. Lizzie was taken to a private room and examined while Dorrie waited in the foyer for the others to arrive. When Derrick arrived, she asked him to keep an eye on Dad while she found out how things were going.

She asked the receptionist if she could speak with Dr. Benson. He made an appearance five minutes later. He shook her hand.

"Mrs. Johnson, I presume?"

"Yes doctor, how is she doing?"

"She's fine, she is about sixty percent dilated, so there is still some time to go yet. You are one of her attendees, I believe. And Mr. Johnson,

I assume the father, the other, is that correct?"

"Not quite, I'm afraid my son, the father, died last year in an accident. His brother, Derrick, that man over there, is the other."

"Oh, I am very sorry to hear that. How tragic for you all but what a blessing and miracle to be having his child born. It is very strange how these things happen; sometime us men of science are astounded."

"Someone leaves us and someone comes to us, that's Gods way", she told him.

"Yes, indeed. Would you like to go to her room and sit with her? I'm sure now that the examinations are over and she is hooked up to her monitor, she could do with the company. You can all go in if you like, then when she is ready, the non-attendees can leave."

She went to fetch the others and they followed to Lizzie's room. Lizzie seemed relieved and happy to see them all as they came through the door. She said she was parched and wanted something fruity, so Derrick went off to the vending machine. They sat around chatting, talking about the wedding and how it was a shame Lesley would miss the birth.

"We could film it", suggested Derrick to which Lizzie declined. "It's bad enough I have a strange man in here instead of Billy. There's no way your filming me like this and at my age." They all laughed.

"Well, hardly a stranger", sulked Derrick jokingly.

"No, not a stranger, but if I had a brother, I would not invite him in to film me either. But I'm glad you're here, Derrick, truly I am. This baby is as much all of yours as it is Billy's."

Lizzie's pains were coming more frequently, and the nurse had left some gas and air for her to help with the contractions. Derrick's mobile buzzed.

I'M IN RECEPTION. WHERE ARE YOU?

"It's Sofia, I'll go and fetch her", offered Derrick. He was glad to leave for a few minutes, seeing Lizzie in pain made him want to cry."

Sofia bounced in.

"Hi, everyone, well, how long until my cousin arrives? He's taking his time", she said.

"HE! It might be a girl."

"No", replied Sofia, "There are too many strong women in this family already; we need another male to boss around. Besides, I'm not sure I want competition on being the prettiest of the family."

The nurse entered. "Everyone out for a moment, please, I need to examine Elizabeth."

"Dorrie", said Lizzie, "would you phone Tally and let her know I'm here. She's in London so I'm sure she'll want to come after the birth."

"Of course, I will, pet."

The troupe made their way back to the waiting area. After phoning Tally, it took all of twenty minutes for her and Stephen to arrive, just in time for the nurse coming out to ask the attendees into the room.

"Let her know we are here, would you, please?" Talia asked Dorrie. "Of course, I will. She will be so pleased."

In the room, the midwife had prepared Lizzie to give birth.

"Talia and Stephen are outside", Dorrie told her.

"Goodness that was quick", replied Lizzie as another pain hit her. The nurse positioned the attendees at the head of the bed to help sooth Lizzie through the birth and encourage her to breathe correctly. Once the birth started, the nurses knew breathing would the last thing on Elizabeth's mind. Dr. Benson arrived and pulled up a chair between Lizzie's legs.

"Now, let's get the new member of your family into the world."

Forty minutes later Derrick went out to the waiting area grinning and blubbering at the same time.

"It's a boy."

"What does it weigh?" Asked Tally

"I have no idea, it's a boy."

They all hugged and congratulated.

"How's Lizzie?" Asked Stephen.

"She was crying when I left with the baby on her chest. The doc was doing some other things, you know, down there, so I came out here. She's great though. It all went smoothly, no complications. It's a boy."

"WE KNOW!" cried the others.

In the room the nursed asked Lizzie "Do you have a name for this lovely little fellow?"

"William Doran Dowels-Johnson" she Elizabeth.

"Why, what a splendid name" said the nurse.

"Can you do that?" Asked Dorrie

"I instructed my solicitors to change my surname to Dowels-Johnson by deed poll, six days ago. By the time the paperwork comes through, which should be any day now, and before Billy is christened, my name will be Elizabeth Magdalena Charlotte Dowels-Johnson. Quite a mouthful, isn't it?" she smiled. "But my surname will be Dowels-Johnson and so will Billy's. The solicitors are sending copies off to the appropriate authorities, DVLC, passport office etcetera, so yes, it's perfectly legal, don't worry."

"I didn't realise that. Are you sure you want to do that Lizzie?"

"Absolutely, this past year, with all that has happened, has been a new start for me. I have found out so many things about myself, how none of the old stuff is important. I want my son to have his father's name. Billy and I would probably be married by now if he hadn't died, and my name would be Johnson anyway. It's the right thing Dorrie and now Billy's linage will continue, as it should. William after his father, and Doran is the closest name I could find to yours Dorrie. The moment I read the meaning: fist, stranger, exile and saw it was Irish for Billy's birth Dad, it fitted perfectly.

"Fist for your strength, stranger for the way you welcome strangers into your heart and exile for me and William who were exiles but are no longer. I love you Dorrie."

"I love you too, my child. My Billy knew you were special before he had even spoken to you."

The christening took place in the same church of Lee and Fetu's wedding. Tally and Stephen were the only two there from Elizabeth's English friends. Claudette travelled over with her French companion, an art dealer, who was very suave and about thirty-five years old. He had business in London, so it was perfect timing, and Claudette, although very French herself, loved shopping in London where she could find far more adventurous outfits than Paris. Tally was named Williams godmother and Stephen his godfather.

Lizzie, decided to stay the first eight weeks of Williams birth at the Johnson household. Being a new mother, she needed all the help she could get in those first few weeks. Everyone mucked in and the bond with Billy's family grew strong, not just for Lizzie, but for Willian too. After two months it was time for Lizzie to return to Paris, and although sad about her departure, Claudette and Jean Luis had volunteered to come back to England and help her travel, which she couldn't refuse. Claudette insisted Lizzie would need the company and ease of transport in France. Lizzie made sure that the family knew any member could visit and were welcome at any time; she assured them she had plenty of room. She promised, as before, that she would be in constant contact with them and email them lots and lots of photos of William.

She still hadn't told her family the news.

Chapter Sixteen

Lizzie settled into her Parisian lifestyle and William, who everyone called *Billé*, became the darling of friends and neighbours alike and was spoiled far too often as far as Lizzie was concerned. Her French had always been quite good and was now near perfect. During Lizzie first months in Paris, riding around on her bike, taking photos, she developed an interest in photography. She decided to enrol in a photography course to learn about development, the technical aspects and presentation.

"*Je peux vous apprendre à produire de l'art, mais votre art viendra de l'intérieur, de votre âme.*" Their teacher told them. "I can teach you to produce art, but your art will come from within, from your soul." She loved it and had no end of volunteers to sit with Billy whilst she attended classes.

For the first months of his life Lizzie decided to buy a cargo bike to haul Billé and herself around Paris. She would place his car seat into the cargo bucket at the front of the bike and off they went. They became a common sight along the bike lanes, and she managed to meet some new friends with children William's age by doing so. She had bought herself a new camera and took photos of anything and everything that interested her.

When Billy was a year old, he got his first child seat; attached to the front of her old bike she had stored in the garage, and by the time he was five he was riding his own bike beside her.

She had received the call about John's passing when Billy was three.

"I'll be over tomorrow. I'll be bringing William with me. sorry, but it's such short notice to find anyone to look after him." The reality was, she thought Billy being there would lighten their sadness a little.

John was a good age when he passed and the family had been expecting it for quite some time. He was laid to rest alongside Billy's ashes in the family plot. Before John's death, Lizzie had managed to take Billy home on four occasions, when they would visit Billy's grave. William and Lizzie would tell Billy all about the things they were doing in Paris. Every week in between visits, William would talk with the family via Skype.

***

Her friends had started taking notice of her photographs and suggested she start selling them in Marais, Haute Marias, Le Nemours, the Metro and the Latin Quarter. She became a regular vender on the bridges of Paris and started to acquire a name for herself. Many of her friends and neighbours became her patrons, spreading the word.

Sofia would visit Paris regularly and was now planning to take a year off to travel after getting her degree. Derrick and Jenny had been over twice and whilst Derrick had enjoyed his stay, Lizzie got the impression it was just a little too cosmopolitan for him, however, Jenny loved it.

Some customers would request a theme and she and Billy would go on a hunt, producing several options, anything from a child standing in front of a wall with her dog to a human growing from a tree. Some of her most popular work was of people engrossed in their own world, full of emotion. Captured unaware, raw and sometimes vulnerable. She would take their photos and then ask their permission to use them. Some would say yes willingly, other refused point blank. The other popular photos were of tattooed naked bodies.

It was Jean Luis, still Claudette's companion after four years, quite a record, that asked her to send him a catalogue of her work.

"I have a friend in New York that is looking for new talent. I've spoken to him about your art, and he has asked if I could send him your catalogue."

"But I don't have a portfolio as such. I just have them scattered around in the studio mostly."

"Well I suggest you make one. You could get a few of us together one evening and we can go through your thumbnails and choose some to make one. I should think twenty, twenty-five would be plenty."

"Twenty-five good ones? That's a lot."

"I think you underestimate your work Lizzie. All those people buying your photos are not doing it out of the kindness of their hearts, but because they are amazing. The way you capture people's feelings, their spirits is incredible. They buy them because they love them and I think Fenton will love them too."

"I don't know what he can do for me over in New York. It's a long way from Paris."

"You'd be surprised. He has a few galleries and he's passionate about art. He's also a really nice guy and treats his artists well. If he commissions some of your photos for one of his gallery exhibitions, it could not only really elevate your name, but also your finances."

"OK, next Friday. Billy has a school play that afternoon. Some of our friends are coming to watch it, maybe we can go back to my apartment after and take a look."

"Great."

Jean Luis had watched Lizzie's photography go from average, when she started, to extraordinary now. Lizzie knew she had to take a leap of faith, and believe that this leap could secure her as a true artist and help her financially. William's play was a success, well for the parents anyway, and he was so proud he had remembered his lines. He had been an octopus in a musical of *A hole Under the Sea*, where a little mermaid became stuck in the hole and the sea creatures all had turns at rescuing her. The octopus with his eight arms was the one to succeed.

Lizzie cleared the main dining table and went to fetch the books of thumbnail negatives she had. Everyone took an eye glass or held them up to the light to look at the photos. They had narrowed it down to fifty by midnight. They went over the selected ones again and chose the twenty five for her portfolio, sometimes having to take a vote because opinions differed. Eventually everyone went home at two am. Lizzie promised Jean Luis she would name them and send them to him along with a catalogue number.

A month later Lizzie, Billy and Claudette were eating at Restaurant Philou, close to Claudette's house, when Jean Luis came over.

"Where have you two been? I've been calling you for an hour. Why aren't you answering your mobiles?"

"They're switched off while we eat. It's not good for Billé to see us talking while we eat."

"Well, I have news. Fenton Burrows wants to meet you.."

"Who me?" Asked Claudette.

"Not you, Lizzie. Fenton wants to meet Lizzie."

"Is he here?" Asked Lizzie, without much interest while wiping sauce from around Billy's mouth.

"Lizzie", exclaimed Jean Luis, please, this is important. Fenton Burrows likes your work and wants to meet you. Do you know what this means? He has seen your photos and he wants to know how many more you have. I have told him many, but he wants to meet you in person, probably to choose the ones he will exhibit for you. Your, first showing, in a famous gallery in New York."

Lizzie gave him her attention,

"That's great news, when is he arriving?"

"That is a slight hiccup, he wants you to go to New York."

Lizzie laughed.

"Me? Go to New York. I can't do that. What would I do with Billy and it's such a long way? I have things I have to do here."

"What exactly do you need to do here, that could possibly, be more important? Claudette and I can have Billy while you go. He is on summer holidays now; we can take him to the coast for a holiday. He would enjoy that. You have to go, Lizzie; I don't think you quite understand what this means. If not for yourself, do it for Billy and his future. This could mean a lot financially for him." He had her.

She agreed she would try.

"No, not try. I will be at your flat tomorrow, early. We will choose fifteen more of the original fifty, develop them to full size, tissue wrap them and buy you a nice expensive leather portfolio case for them. Claudette will take you shopping for some nice clothes. You will pack your bags and go."

"When do you think I will go?" she smiled at him. "He is sending a jet Saturday."

"He is sending what?"

"A jet. He is... what do you say? *Haute société.*"

"High society", replied Lizzie. *I hope bloody not.*

***

The flight lasted nine hours. Being a private jet meant she could walk around during the flight to stop her legs from cramping. The plane was straight out of Hollywood, white leather seats with a table in between, plush carpeting, a bar, soft up-lighting. She wasn't overly impressed; she had been here and done this all before and look what happened.

She had Googled Mr. Fenton Burrows. *Born 1969, the third generation of Irish immigrants from Pittsburgh. The family fortune began when Thomas Burrows formed a small loan bank in New York. His two sons took over the bank and multiplied the fortune. One son then invested in steel while the other in oil and the fortune grew and grew. Fenton himself invested in shipyards and building luxury yachts with a Dutch company. At the grand old age of forty, he left the business, selling most of his shares to his siblings, one brother and a sister. Since then he has worked in the art indus try, galleries, auction houses, fine art dealers.* She could just imagine him being a self-important jerk that felt he knew more about art than the masses. Photos of him showed him as tall, athletic, very handsome with mainly grey hair apart from dark flecks.

A white stretched limousine awaited them at the airport. *Gaudy. I'm not sure who he is trying to impress probably thinks he has some want-a-by-chic-ette arriving.* She smiled at the driver.

"The flight crew will take care of you bags, miss, and get them through customs. Mr. Burrows will meet us at your hotel." The Langham on Fifth Avenue was the venue. *This man is really pulling out all the stops.* She was handed a message from the receptionist that told her Mr. Burrows would meet her at eight pm for dinner. She looked at her watch, local time two pm. Time to relax, have a spot of lunch, probably in her room and unpack.

At six o'clock, she looked through what she would wear for this first meeting. Claudette, being Claudette, had taken her out for a few new dresses and outfits and chosen a few bright colours.

"You have to WOW him on sight. That way they become blubbering idiots and you can dictate what you want, darling, trust me."

Being a mother had suited Lizzie. She had reduced her weight and was now an elegant size UK 12. She wasn't sure what that was in American. She had joined a gym, tightened up her body after the birth of William, and with all the biking and rushing around looked easily three to four years younger than her forty-four years. After the trip over, she decided to show Mr. Burrows that she wasn't another wannabe, but a sophisticated, mature woman, who knew her own mind and self-worth. None of it was true, but she had put on a show of playacting since childhood; she was well versed in the art.

She chose a red satin dress that fitted closely, but not too closely to her upper body, with a scoop neck; the skirt of the dress flared from the waist down to just above her knees. She wore silk neutral tights that had just a slight shimmer and a pair of red slingback shoes with a slight heel. Around her neck she wore a single diamond chain, one of the jewels she in herited from her grandmother. She applied some subtle makeup by just lining her eyes with green pencil, a little swipe of blush and then a bright red left her room and made her way to the hotel bar for a cocktail.

***

Fenton Burrows arrived in blue chinos, blue jacket, white linen shirt and loafers with no socks. Expecting to see a typical Parisian woman similarly dressed in maybe cotton slacks, with an elegant blouse, high-heeled shoes and leather jacket. He had met Claudette on a few social occasions and well, wow, if they were friends, they may have the same fashion sense. He went to reception and asked to be connected with Ms Dowels-Johnson.

"She is waiting for you in the bar, Sir."

He scanned the tables looking for Lizzie, but didn't see her, so went back to the receptionist.

"Are you sure she's in the bar?"

"Yes, Sir, she's the striking woman in a red dress. I'm sure you can't miss her."

He went again and saw a woman at the bar with her back towards him; there were no others in a red dress.

"Hello, Ms Dowels-Johnso..." His voice trailed off, as she turned. He needed to pull himself together. "Err, Johnson, Ms Dowels-Johnson. Err, sorry, forgive me. I'm Fenton Burrows. I asked you here. I'm, err, really pleased you could come." *What the hell are you blubbering about?*

She stood, faced him and held out her hand.

"Yes, Mr. Burrows, it was very kind of you to have invite me. Such a fantastic city New York, so much life and lights. It's lovely to be here."

Is she taking the micky? Where on earth, did she get that voice? It sounded very English, educated English'.

"Do forgive me, Mr Burrows, would you like a drink?"

"I'd love one and please call me Fenton. Scotch on the rocks."

"Any particular brand Fenton?"

"You choose", he told her.

"Do you have any Macallan Sherry Oak 18?" She asked the bar tender.

Christ, where did this woman come from? I could be in trouble here.

"I'm afraid I didn't dress for dinner, Ms Dowels-Johnson. I assumed with you coming from the art culture of Paris, we would be casual. I'm sorry, I shouldn't have assumed anything."

"No, I suppose you shouldn't have and you can call me Elizabeth. It takes a little time for people to be able to call me Lizzie, and nobody calls me Ms. Dowels-Johnson. Such a mouthful, don't you agree?"

She was teasing him and they both knew it. When Fenton took her back to her hotel after dinner, he told her he would send a car for her the next morning to fetch her to his gallery in Chelsea. He wanted to discuss her photos.

"Should I bring any more?"

"You have more with you?"

"Yes, I've bought another fifteen."

"Then that would be great." He wanted to kiss her. *Where had that thought come from?*

"OK, see you tomorrow", she said wanting to kiss him, which surprised her as she had never even thought about anything like that since Billy.

***

The next day, Lizzie was dressed in cotton slacks, a blue and coral stripped silk blouse, high-heeled shoes and leather jacket. Fenton had told her at dinner what he was expecting, obviously she was making a joke of his comment. Not that the outfit was in any way funny, it was very Parisian chic. As she walked through the smoke-glazed windows of the gallery, he saw her immediately, in fact, he had been looking at the door distracted every few minutes waiting for her to arrive. His heart stopped in his chest. He didn't understand this and, to be honest, he didn't like it. All night at dinner he had a weird sensation of falling, a light headiness, and he was experiencing it again, here and now. He stood from the desk he had been looking at her photos on and came around to meet her.

"Did you sleep well, Elizabeth?"

"I did indeed", she had not, being anxious about this visit. She was out of her comfort zone and it reflected in her waking four times during the night. However, she was not going to let Mr. Burrows know that. "Who could not, sleep well at the Langham?"

Fenton always felt as if she were teasing him, *why was that?* After talking for an hour about her portfolio and how he felt she, given the right exposure, could become a very sought-after artist and could earn an amazing amount of money, she stopped him.

"Fenton, may I be honest with you?"

"Yes, of course."

"I would like to make money from my art. The opportunity to make this, these photos, my passion, my career is amazing. I have a young son whose father is no longer with us, thus his upbringing and the costs associated with that are mine. However, what I don't want is anyone, and I mean anyone, directing my career in a way I think to be unsuitable just for money. I'm not, and my art is not, a collectable trinket. Maybe if we collaborate and you get to know me better, you will understand why. We all need help along our paths, but I don't believe our paths should be driven by others' needs or desires at the detriment of ourselves. Can you understand that?"

All he could do was nod. No unknown would be so forthright, especially on only their second meeting.

"I would like to work with you and I am truly happy you like my work. I really am; you can't imagine how happy it makes me, so if you're up for it, so am I, under the provision I keep control of my career and work. If you agree we can look at the other photos and the ones you have and choose the ones you want. Oh, and by the way, do you really think I can make a decent living at this? As it would make my son Billy very happy; he wants a new bike."

"I think you will make money and I am perfectly happy to accept your conditions. Now let's have a look at those other photos."

After another hour Fenton said they should call it a day and get some lunch. At lunch Lizzie asked if he had decided which pictures he wanted.

"All of them, I want to give you a one-man exhibition."

"You must be joking? You can't take a chance on an unknown artist. What if nothing sells?"

"They will sell", he told her, "they will sell." He didn't tell her he would buy the whole bloody lot if they didn't sell, just to keep in contact with her.

"Can I take you to dinner tonight, Elizabeth? This time I promise to wear socks."

She laughed

"I would love that and now that we are in business together, you can call me Lizzie."

***

Claudette collected her from the airport two days later.

"How is Billy?" was the first thing she asked, even though she had spoken with him twice a day since she left.

"He's fine, just fine. He and Jean Luis have been having a ball. The two days at the beach saw Jean Luis get a bit of sunburn, but we kept Billy well creamed with factor thirty-five. Now tell me, how did it go? Is he going to take any of your pictures? Where's your portfolio, have you left it?"

"I've left it with Fenton, he wants to take them all and give me a show of my own."

Claudette jumped up and down, "Oh, the is wonderful news, fantastic. Jean Luis is going to be over the moon."

She was glad to be home and slotted easily back into her old routine. She had realised meeting Fenton and the feeling that she wanted to kiss him, that maybe time was moving on, and she may be ready for a new relationship. She hated the thought. She still loved Billy and always would, but she also missed being held in someone's arms, someone's kisses and touches. She knew Fenton had found her attractive, even desirable, which had boosted her self-esteem no end. She decided if the opportunity arose in the future and she was asked on a date, which had happened many times, but she had turned every one of them down, next time she would go.

Her happiness and peace were not to last long. It only took two days back in Paris when the phone rang. It was Derrick telling her something horrible had happened to Dorrie. She was in the hospital after having a heart attack. She left for England on the next train, leaving Billé once again in Claudette's care. Once she confirmed Dorrie was stable and would be allowed home after ten days, she went back to Paris for two weeks to pack up Billy and take him to see his grandmother. They all had a lovely summer holiday, and Dorrie was well on the mend. Derrick now retired and Jenny only working part-time, decided they were going to move back to the family home and take care of Dorrie. In the middle of August, Lizzie took Billy back to France, in time for the new school year.

September saw a message from Fenton.

Need you in NY for opening 16th, get here, the buzz is incredible.

The few selected previews have stirred a buzz I haven't seen in years. Everyone who's anyone is scrambling for an opennight ticket.

I think I may have priced these too low, need your approval to increase price.

You won't object once you see the guest list. Can't wait to see you. I'll send the jet on 14th. Bring that red dress.

Fenton x

Lizzie showed it to Claudette and Jean Luis.

"Will you come with me as my guests?"

"You couldn't keep us away even if we weren't invited. Who will you get for Billé?"

"I'm going to ask Sofia. She was saying last week she wants a break. Not sure what's going on, but I think she has just broken up with a boyfriend."

The three friends flew in together. This time Fenton himself met them at the airport and took them to the hotel, one in Chelsea near the gallery. He ran across the tarmac to the plane and hugged and kissed everyone, as excited as a puppy with a new toy.

"You, my dear, are the toast of New York and people haven't even met you yet. It's unprecedented for an unknown to have such an anticipated crowd waiting for her."

They all dined together. Fenton fitted in as though he had always been there and, of course, he had known the others for some years, but the company was all so relaxed and happy. Lizzie felt happier than she had in years. In fact, six years. Her light-headiness at all the praise and atmosphere allowed the wine to go straight to her head. Fenton called a cab to take them back to the hotel.

"Are you coming back for a nightcap", Lizzie asked him.

"Are you sure it's not too late after your flight?"

"No, don't be silly, do come and we'll have a drink at the bar."

After one drink, Claudette and Jean Luis left saying they were exhausted but gave Lizzie a wink as she touched Jean Luis' bum.

"Would you like another drink?" Fenton asked. Lizzie looked at him.

"Would you like to stay with me tonight?"

"I, I would love to, more than anything in the world" he stammered bewildered at the request.

They made their way to her room; she didn't touch his bum.

The next morning Lizzie awoke feeling a little disorientated, and it took a few seconds for her to realise where she was and who she was with. She looked at Fenton in her bed, lying on his stomach, out to the world. They had made love until four in the morning, exhausting each other until finally neither could stay awake another moment. She looked at her watch, eleven am. The others would be wondering where she was. Would she go down with Fenton? Would Fenton want to go down with her? Oh, my God, what have I done? *You've slept with the boss, you hussy*. She smiled to herself.

She went to the bathroom to shower; Fenton joined her five minutes later. He opened the shower screen, "How is the sexiest woman in the world today?"

"I've been called many things, but not that", she replied. "But she is feeling pretty damned wonderful and you?"

"Better than wonderful." He kissed her neck.

"Let me go, it's gone eleven, we need to get our arses downstairs and to the gallery to look at these prices you mentioned."

"Shit, is it really? You're right, we need to move, and what is a nice proper English lady doing using words like arse, very unbecoming", he joked.

"Sod off", she said.

They found Jean Luis and Claudette in the coffee bar, both were gobsmacked at the sight of Fenton walking in with Lizzie, but recovered well.

"Come on, you two, we're on our fourth cup and that's after the two at breakfast."

***

Lizzie saw the guest list, she recognised some of the names, so did Claudette.

"Have you seen the guest list?"

"Yes."

"Do you think any of them know it's you?"

"I don't think so, but who knows, anything is possible."

"Did you see Penny Barchett is on the list?"

"Yes. That could be a problem. I'm not bothered about her, but as soon as she is back in the UK, she will spread the word like wildfire, which means Mummy and Daddy will know where I am and have my new name to trace me."

"What are you going to do?"

"I don't know. I could tell Fenton I don't want to meet those specific people, I guess, or I don't know. It's not just Penny, Lord Anthony Blunt is coming and Stella will be there. We've both bought so many of her designs; she'll know us both straight away. Mind you, I'm sure we can get her on board to pretend she doesn't know us."

"Lizzie, you know the cat is going to come out of your handbag, don't you? At some point or other, if you become well known, the cat will appear."

"Cat out of the bag", corrected Lizzie, "and, yes, I do know."

Lizzie looked around her surroundings and had to admit her photos, now developed, framed, hung and highlighted by different up lights and downlights were stunning. Window shades had been placed at the windows to stop people from looking in, huge announcements in these same windows declaring the most inspiring show in years, by the new name on the block, and a gigantic black question mark. *That was it!* If her name hadn't been announced yet, and they were changing the price catalogue anyway, was there time to use a pseudonym? She went to find Fenton; there were some things she needed to tell him.

She found him with Jean Luis walking around the gallery. Asking to speak with him privately, he took her into his office, where he immediately took her in his arms and kissed her. *Well, at least last night wasn't a one night stand.* She sat him down and explained her family history, omitting the disinheritance; she didn't go into details about Billy, the way her family treated him or his accident, but did tell him in order to protect her son from their influences and why she had left England and made a new life in France. She pointed out several of the guests for the opening knew her personally and how she didn't want a traceable name to get back to her family.

"I know it's a lot to ask, but if you have any publicity with my name on it…? By the way, I think the question mark in the window is adorable.

Can we change it to a pseudonym? I can actually avoid meeting the people I don't want to talk to; Claudette has said she can intervene."

Fenton thought for a while as to what could be done. This was a lot to take in. He knew she was hiding something, or at least not really telling him all of her story, which most artists loved to do.

"The posters and publicity for the grand reveal aren't too much, as I was using your physical presence as your reveal and was going to say your name as you entered the gallery. There's the price list with your name on the front, which would be handed out to guests on request. I want to change the prices anyway so that's not a problem. There are two large posters for the window for after the opening and about ten smaller ones for my other galleries. Those are easily replaced. I'm sure given twenty-four hours; my printers can produce new ones. All the other stuff ready to explode on the world are digital, so I can get the staff to change that. So, I think we can do that. Let's think of a pseudonym. By the way, I knew you weren't just another struggling Parisian artist."

"Actually, that's exactly what I am, but I'll tell you about that another time. So, what shall I call myself?"

They called in Claudette and Jean Luis and outlined the solution.

"They are still going to recognise you", said Claudette

"I know, it's a possibility. They haven't seen me for years, so if I can get amongst the crowd quickly, maybe I'll be lucky. Maybe the ones that could possibly tell my family, won't see me. Worse scenario, at least not having my real name will delay the inevitable, and give me time to come up with a plan. If and when my family find out about William, they will have no hold on my son. I've heard about grandparents taking parents to court to gain access and even custody of their grandchildren, and knowing my father, if he were interested in doing so, even just to make a point, would do so. Just be sure, tomorrow, not to use my name with the people we know, just keep using the *nom de plume*."

They started writing down mixtures of her name.

Sofia Mary Jones

"Simon Boris Rabbit", laughed Jean Luis.

"Harry Barry Pigeon", laughed Claudette.

"Now let's not get silly", smiled Lizzie.

"Jenna Georgina Vadar", suggested Fenton, "sounds American and at the same time eastern European."

"No, none of these, work. I'm going to call myself Doran. It means fist, stranger, exile."

"But that is Billés' middle name."

"Yes, which makes it even more appropriate. The new works by Doran", she said aloud.

"I like it", agreed Fenton. "Now let's agree on prices."

"We are going shopping", declared Claudette. I want to buy something in deep subtle colours for tomorrow."

"You? Subtle colours?"

"Yes, I do not want to outshine the star with my brightness." They all laughed. All hands hit the deck after that. Fenton contacted the printers, telling his staff to listen to instructions given by Lizzie. The caterers were hired and as yet hadn't been given any names of the art ist so they were not a problem. After two hours he asked Lizzie if she were hungry to which she told him she was.

"I'll make us something at my place, it's not far."

He took her to his penthouse on 6th Avenue overlooking Bryant Park, fed her, showed her the view and took her to bed. Early evening, she phoned Claudette to ask if she would like to join them for dinner, but she declined saying they were going to the theatre, and they would meet for breakfast the next day.

"If you are up for breakfast", she said suggestively.

"I'll be there, I'm not sure what Fenton is doing."

"*Mon petit ami*. I am the expert on love, remember. We have a match made in the sky."

"Made in heaven", corrected Lizzie.

"Wherever it is made, it is good, *ma chérie,* no?"

"Yes, *ma chérie*, very good."

She found Fenton in his kitchen making coffee.

"Do you have a laptop so that I can Skype Billy? He will be going to bed now and I want to speak with him before he sleeps."

"Yes, of course, through that door, it's my office."

She went through and logged on. Sofia answered.

"Hi, sweety, how are things going? Is Billy still awake?"

She heard his shout in the background, "*maman, maman, je veux parler, Sofia, je veux parler avec maman*" Mummy, Mummy, I want to speak with Mummy.

"Speak in English Billy, you should know better than that. Sofia is English and you try to speak with people in their native language."

"*Mais je parle avec toi, maman*." But I'm talking to you Mummy.

"And I am English too, when you are speaking with Mummy on her own, we speak in English, in French company, French and so on and so forth. Now do as you are told. What have you been doing?"

"Sofia took me to Disney Park; we have only just come home. Marcus came with us; he is so funny. He put me on his shoulders to see the fireworks because there were so many people there and he held me tight on a big, fast train ride that went around corners so quickly I thought I would fall out and Sofia bought me some candy floss and..."

"Slow down, Billé, take a breath. Well, it sounds as though you are not missing Mummy at all."

"Ah, no, Mummy, I always miss you", he lowered his voice, "Sofia cannot make milkshakes as well as you."

Lizzie laughed, it was such a pleasure to hear his sweet voice and see his beautiful face.

"Who is that mummy?"

Fenton had come into the office to place a coffee on the desk. Lizzie looked up and smiled.

"This is my friend Mr. Burrows. The man I told you about who has put Mummy's photos in his gallery for people to buy."

"Hello, Mr. Burrows."

"Hello, Billy, and you can call me Fenton." He turned to leave, but Lizzie caught his hand.

"Stay, stay and chat a moment more. This rascal will go to bed in a few minutes; he has been telling me about his day."

The three spoke for another ten minutes until Billy made a huge yawn."

"Get yourself to bed now darling. I will speak with you in the morning, first thing, when you awake from your beautiful dreams, of your wonderful adventure today. Daddy's angel wings will protect you and keep you warm tonight."

"Daddy's angel wings will protect you and keep you warm tonight" he repeated the passage they told each other every night. "Will Fenton be here tomorrow Mummy? I would like to talk with him again."

"Maybe, sweetheart, now get yourself to bed."

Sofia came back on line with a sheepish look, as Fenton left the room. On the way out the door he looked back, and knew he had fallen in love.

"Marcus? *Ooh la la*, Sofia"

"It's not like that, we're just friends. He's nice and Billy adores being with him."

"Not only William, I suspect. You know he has been in love with you since you both first met, don't you? He is always asking when you will visit again. Anyway, I'll let you get Billy to bed and we'll speak tomorrow. Billy's angel wings will protect you and keep you warm tonight", she said. She disconnected and went to find Fenton. He was sat on his sofa looking out at the expanse of New York; the city lay below low-laying clouds, or what was more than likely smog. She went and snuggled beside him and placed his arm around her shoulder.

"Penny for your thoughts."

"You have a wonderful son there, so intelligent. How old is he?"

"Five, he is rather special, isn't he?"

"French and English at five and so polite. I guess he gets his etiquette from his mother. You are very lucky."

"Without sounding boastful, well actually, yes sounding boastful, he speaks French, English and Spanish as fluently as a five-year-old can, with splattering's of German, Greek and Italian. My friends in France are a diverse crowd and they took him as their own when I took him there, so he has grown up hearing and mimicking all the languages they speak. The manners? Well, you can't have enough good ones and he does have a few bad ones which he hasn't shown you yet."

"Yet? Does that mean there will be an opportunity for him to do so?"

"Well, I certainly hope so, and if you like, I can show you a few of my naughty manners now." She took his hand and pulled him back to bed. *Who needs food?*

Chapter Seventeen

"How should I look tonight?" Lizzie asked Claudette
"Radical, rebelle, mystérieux, fort." Radical, rebellious, mysterious, strong.

She asked the same question to Jean Luis

"Élégant, séduisant, sensible, seduction." Ellegant, secretive, sensitive, seductive.

And to Fenton

"Be yourself, but I do have rather a strong liking for a certain red dress and adornments you wore the first time I saw you. It was certainly Éle*gant, fort, rebelle, seduction, et surprenant*. Ellegant, strong, rebellious, seductive and surprising."

"You speak French?" Lizzie said.

"You know I do, especially if you Googled me."

"Yes, I do know, along with all those others, so unlike an American Billionaire."

"Are you teasing me? You do realize I'm the luckiest man alive to have found someone like you, Lizzie, right? Before meeting you, my absolute policy had always been to not get involved with the artists. Having a relationship with a person you're going to be working with can seriously dam age you, the artist. People start gossiping about the agent being between the artist's legs and not take her art seriously. I've majorly broken that rule. There are a lot of different scenarios that could turn disastrous if what we have doesn't work out, more so on you, and William. I can only hope we'll be together forever. There is something we need to talk about though."

A flashback hit her to when Billy had said the same and split up from her. She had lost so much precious time with him, only weeks, but with what happened, too many precious weeks. She sat and he expressed his concerns and laid out the things, especially in this business, what could hap pen, he didn't tell her his fears of losing her and Billy if they became a serious item, although he thought that horse had already bolted. She thought for what seemed a lifetime, not saying a word, then she said,

"I've been in love once before in my life. I'm forty-four years of age and never thought I would find that feeling again…"

He went to interrupt her.

"Let me finish. I don't know whether you have ever been so much in love that your whole life depended on it and you were willing… No more than willing, to give up everything you had and were, to keep that love. I have. However, I lost that love and it has been hard, so terribly hard to live with that loss. I expected you to be someone totally different to whom you are. Since I've met you, those feelings I had before, have returned and I never ever thought they would. I would never do anything to harm my child, but the other day when you came into your office when I was speaking with William, it was just natural for me to include you in that conversation. Why? Because I want to see where you and I go. I want this, everything you are offering, the show, the opportunity to spread my images, feelings, my thoughts, to the world; it's not something I want to jeopardise either. Having said that, neither of us know whether, this thing we have, will last or not, but it doesn't mean we give up on it because of outside influences. I learnt that the hard way."

She continued

"Someone once said to me, a very wise woman, in life, some people are destined to leave and others to enter. You have entered my life and after everything in my history, I want to keep you there. I believe there is a way for us to do that. Our relationship is new, so for the time being we keep it between the few that need or will know. If you believe, which you have expressed, I have a good chance here to make a name for myself, then let me do that. People don't need to know yet, let me establish myself as an artist, get my followers, establish my reputation, my reputation, **not yours** or your galleries, but mine and mine alone. We will act professionally in public and quietly together. My life is not an open book in Paris or England, so I don't have paparazzi stalking me like Princess Diana. I have a quiet life and I believe we can make this work. Once I have my name established, then, will be the time to tell the world." She took a deep breath, hoping she hadn't been too forceful, or too open. "What do you think?"

He was over to her holding her in his arms; he knew there was no more escaping.

Lizzie went back to her hotel alone to get ready. Claudette knocked on her door just before they were due to leave.

"*Mon chéri*, you look perfect, *magnifique*. How are you feeling, *ma douce* Rose?"

"Nervous, really, really nervous. What if they hate them, what if they think I'm a fraud, what if they are too expensive to buy? Did you see the prices he set? Who the hell is going to buy at those prices? But he's confident they are right. He said too cheap and nobody of self-importance will buy, not just that and I do understand this, fifteen thousand dollars to these people it's like buying at Penny-Mark. He has, with some, tripled the price for my first showing. I'm so worried."

"*Mon ami*, he is right. How do you think this man has made fortune after fortune? By being right, by knowing what he is doing, or at least speculating he knows what he is doing. His galleries sell some of the most expensive art in the world. His patrons are some of the richest people in the world. He is your... How do you say, manager? No, not manager, mentor, he is your mentor. He knows what is right for you."

"What if I trip coming down from the upper gallery?"

"You will not trip, my god woman, look at those heels they are barely noticeable. What are they? Five centimetres? Try standing in these at our ages." She showed her long thin heels.

"OK, OK, let's get this show on the road. Remember être discret, be discrete tonight.

Lizzie knew Claudette was an expert after so many *affaires secretes*. Lizzie was to enter one hour after the official opening. When she arrived, forty minutes early, she was taken to a back entrance that allowed her to access the upper gallery. She was led upstairs and handed a glass of champagne. She stood on the upper balcony trying to listen to the buzz below; people were chatting and laughing but she couldn't tune in or concentrate enough to hear full sentences. She heard a microphone tapped and a glass clinking.

"Ladies, gentlemen and honoured guests, may I have your attention please."

Within moments, the chattering had ceased as everyone gathered redirecting their attention to the speaker.

"This is all exciting stuff; do you not agree?"

Soft laughter began.

"Hopefully I have no need to introduce myself. You're in my gallery, so I'm hoping you all know where you are."

The laughter increased before dying down again.

"Earlier this year I was sent some photos from Jean Luis Bisset-Sanchéz. If you are ever looking for a talent scout, this is the man. He sent me some thumbnails he thought I might be interested in. As you know, I have a passion for discovering new artists. A few haven't reached their potential; thank goodness, it has only been a few, otherwise I might be poor." Laughter, everyone knew how rich he was.

Again, the laughter commenced as the majority of the crowd more than likely knew how rich Fenton was.

"However, the artist you have been admiring this passed hour, and having listened to what you have been saying about the art that has been shown, allows me to conceive, this will not be one of them."

The gathered crowd applauded before Fenton held up his hand for silence. "My first glimpse of these photos took my breath away; it was diffi cult for me to imagine someone could capture, so intensively, the soul and feeling of the subject. And just like my first reaction, we have, in this passed hour, had enormous interest expressed in the purchase of these photos."

Clapping and the sound of clinking glasses could be heard.

"I'm telling you all now, this artist will one day be one of the greats. This is their first showing, and you all know me, I don't do exclusive showings for an unknown. However, in this case, I was so knocked back, and I have noticed this evening, you all have had the same reaction. When I first saw their art, I knew I had to present HER to the world. Next year, if you want one of these photos, you will be paying at least double or triple, and I know you all like a bargain, so buy now."

Louder laughter began as some people began quickly chatting with their neighbours.

"Be one of the people able to say they were one of the first to patron HER. I would now like to present to you… Doran."

***

Everyone in the room below chinked their glasses and applauded. Lizzie appeared at the top of the steps from the upper gallery and made her way down. She didn't trip. Once amongst the crowd, Fenton came over to her and took her arm, introducing her to the assembled guests; all praising her work, he helped control every question. She was so relieved everything was going so well.

***

Stella was the first person she knew who approached her.

"Elizabeth, is that you?"

Lizzie took her aside and asked her not to reveal her real name.

"Don't worry, if anyone knows what it's like to be associated with a name, it's me. I have your back. This is amazing. I would never have thought, my local MP would have such insight into human emotions. I'm amazed and I'm buying. I want to be one of the 'I knew her when crowd'."

They kissed and Lizzie went onto the next guest. A representative of the Beckhams'; luckily, he had no idea she knew them. After chatting, another sale had been made. As she turned, she saw Penny and ducked out of sight. She found Claudette and got her to ambush Penny. Lizzie's first show sold out that day, with reserves on future works.

Fenton and Lizzie managed to keep their relationship quiet for three years, until one day in Paris. She, Billy and Fenton were sitting enjoying a meal at *Le Comptoir Génèral* when a family entered and a young boy turned to her.

"Aunt Lizzie, is that you?"

Lizzie looked to see Penelope, Anthony, Stewart, John and her mother. She stood,

"Anthony, my goodness. Look at you, you're a young man and you too Stewart, so tall the pair of you. Penelope, John, how are you? Mother how are you all? My, what a surprise."

They stood by the table, waiting, but Lizzie said no more.

"We're all fine", replied John. "We're here for the re-opening of the Louvre; thought the boys could do with a bit of cultural expansion. Nothing much is happening until the summer season starts and work is pretty quiet at the moment."

"That's lovely, oh, not work being quiet, I mean the Louvre, although work being quiet could be a good thing, I suppose." She was fumbling and you could sense it.

Fenton stood and held out his hand.

"Hello, I'm Fenton, Fenton Burrows." Everyone shook hands including the boys.

"And I'm William" Billy said "but everyone calls me Billé. Are you going to Disney? I can attest it's splendid if you are. I go there at least once a year."

Lizzy watched as her mother took just the slightest intake of breath and looked at the young boy speaking. She was probably wondering how old he was, whose he was? She knew they looked very similar in appearance, although Billy was slightly darker in skin tone. There was no denying he was Lizzie's, that was for sure.

"Are you here long? Where are you staying?" Lizzie asked

"We're guests of the Merrimons'. We will only be staying a week, it's just a quick visit."

Penelope didn't use the titles of Duke or Count in public. The very idea of a caste of lords offended France's cultural zeitgeist and after the revolution the French *la noblesse* had learned to be discreet.

"That's lovely, do give them my regards. Well, we won't keep you, I'm sure you have lots to do."

"We should do lunch, whilst we are here Elizabeth", her mother said, "are you here for long?"

Her mother was fishing and you could cut the atmosphere with a knife.

"For a while at least, and yes, that would be lovely. Do you have a number I could contact you on?"

"Here, take my number, Lizzie. You know your mother doesn't carry a phone with her", said John as he took out a small leather case and handed her a card.

"Thank you, John, I'll call you, we'll arrange something. Yes, I'll call you."

The meeting was over; Lizzie sat down and the family passed on to their table.

"Merde", said Lizzie.

"Mummy, you mustn't swear."

That night in Lizzie's apartment, Fenton asked her what had happened at lunch. Elizabeth had moved to Haut Marais, having sold her first apartment over the shop and bought one in a 17th century stone mansion. Fenton, as promised, had made her a wealthy artist instead of a staving one, now ranking just below greats such as Annie Leibovitz, Richard Prince and Cindy Sherman. It was time she knew. She had, during the first year of their relationship, been a little afraid telling him the whole story would scare him off, and things had been so busy that first year, travelling back and forth across the Atlantic and Europe to attend shows he had arranged for her. Then the second year she did less shows and more work on commission, and the subject just never seemed to come up, and again on the third year, she just made excuses.

They had up until now kept their relationship quiet, but had of late taken to being seen in public along with Billy. She knew the time had come. She knew it had come last year when articles about the mysterious Doran started circulating, but she had managed to stay out of public scrutiny. Now as Claudette had said would happen, the cat was out of her handbag.

She sat down and relayed her relationship with William's father, Billy, told him about how her parents had reacted and plotted against it, how she had found out later that her father had even instructed her ex campaign manager to enter her home and put dating sites and pornography on Billy's laptop for her to find. Unfortunately, Billy had died before they could run their exposé plans. She told him about race day, Stewart falling in, Billy jumping in to rescue him and losing his own life for it. She told him about her denouncing her inheritance and her finding out she was pregnant and then moving to France. She told him everything and he listened.

"And you've never told them about William?"

"No. I know, I know, I should have. I've kept in touch with Penelope, post cards, letters that I would get friends to post from different parts of Europe, not saying much, but letting her know I was fine and enjoying my new life. I would send her photos of me and friends on holiday as proof that everything was going well, but, no, I never told her about William, and I never gave her a return address."

"So, do you think it's time to tell them what has been happening over the last... What? How many years has it been? Eight, nine years?"

"Nine", she said pulling a face. "I saw it on Mummy's face, she knows. Did you hear her breathe in when Billy started talking and he told them his name? They all know William is my son. I could tell from the expressions on their faces. Well, not the boys; they were always kept out of the mess. They liked Billy; they didn't know the family didn't. But, yes, I guess I had better phone John and arrange a meeting, but if they think I'm going to start letting them have access to Billy, they can think again."

"But, by doing that, aren't you doing exactly what your father did to you?"

"What do you mean, I'm not doing anything to harm Billy, I'm protecting him."

"I know you think you are, but from where I sit, you're setting out his life for him and taking away his choices, just like your father did to you. You are trying to stop him having access to his own heritage, well one side of it anyway. I know he loves the Johnson family, especially Sofia, but you're not allowing him the chance to love the other side of his family, your side. It's kind of the same as your father but in reverse. His godparents are your side of the family. Can you imagine how thrilled

Tally and Stephen would be to be able to, at long last, be seen in England with him and show him some of their world? Well, that's just my opinion for what it's worth. Phone John, he seems like a decent chap, phone him and arrange a meeting."

"Why are you always so bloody right?"

Lizzie made the call to meet on semi-neutral ground, her gallery in Saint-Germain-des-Prés. She arranged for Sunday when the Galerie Du Doran would be closed for business. Fenton would be coming to take all three boys away while she talked with her mother, Penelope and John. She had been pacing for the past half hour waiting for their arrival, wondering how this was going to pan out, and what she was going to say. It had been so many years, but she didn't need to tell them everything, *I will just give them the gist and get it over and done with*. She heard the tap on the door and opened it to let them through. She had placed some refreshments on a coffee table in the middle of the two sofas and placed a couple of chairs around. She would sit in a chair to have a slightly higher elevation as she spoke. They sat, Penelope and the boys on one sofa, John on another and her mother in one of the chairs. Fenton came in from the storeroom at the back with Billy. Billy came over and stood behind his mother and draped his arms around his neck.

Lizzie took his hands, and brought him to her side.

"Billy, do you remember these people from the restaurant the other day? Well I'd like you to meet them all by name." She went through the names and he shook hands with them all. "You know how Aunties Jenny and Lee, Uncle Derrick and Fetu and your cousin Sofia come over and see you? Well, these are some more of your family. Penelope is your aunt, John your uncle and Stewart and Anthony your cousins. And this is your grandmother. Mummy hasn't seen them for a very long time, but now they are here and wanted to say hello to us, isn't that lovely?"

"My cousin Sofia is always here. She's in love with Marcus, and they are going to get married." He looked at Bethany, "My other grandmother, grandmother Dorrie died. We were all so sad, but Mummy said she went to look after Grandad and Daddy because they weren't picking up their clothes off the floor. Mummy makes me pick my clothes up. Do you have to pick your clothes up?"

"Yes, I do", said Bethany.

"We do too", put in Anthony.

"Now, Fenton is going to take you, Anthony and Stewart for some ice-cream. Would you like that boys while Mummy and grandma talk?"

They all agreed they would and started discussing the merits of different flavours.

"Is it all right if I come along?" Asked John. "I think it's a good idea for the ladies to talk and us men take a vote on the best ice-cream flavours, don't you."

"I think that's a good idea", replied Fenton. They left with the children.

"Why didn't you tell us?" Asked her mother, as soon as they were gone.

"To be honest Mother, I think at the beginning it was because I was angry. I felt the family had taken away or forced me to give up everything I loved at the time."

"You could have told me, in one of your letters" said Penelope.

"No, I couldn't. You would have told Mummy straight away. I was worried I guess that had any of you known you would have done something awful and taken him away from me."

"How could you think such a thing of your own family?" Asked Bethany.

"Oh, come on, Mother, after what happened with Billy? I thought Daddy might try it just out of spite, and I was still very vulnerable back then, I couldn't risk it. Then later, I stopped thinking about it really, my life started taking shape and grew to include the Johnson family and the many friends I made, and I just stopped thinking about it."

"When... Where was he born? America? Is that where you live? Are you married to Fenton?"

"He was born on the 4th of May at St. Marys hospital, in Paddington."

"You were in England for his birth?"

"Yes Mother, it had been planned that way. Billy's sister was getting married so I went for the wedding and stayed at the Johnsons home until he was born. He came two weeks early and I had him christened in Grays London, three weeks later. I named him..." Here goes. "William Dowels-Johnson."

"Dowels-Johnson?" queried Bethany, "but that's not even you name."

"Well actually, Mother it is and it was then. I changed my name by deed poll before the birth. He has Billy's surname."

"Oh, this gets worse and worse."

"Mother!" said Penelope infuriated. "Will you never learn?"

Her mother looked at her in surprise and somewhat indignantly.

"Thank you for that, Penelope. Anyway, to continue. No, I don't live in America; I live here in Paris and have since I left. No, I'm not married to Fenton, not yet anyway, but I do hope, maybe one day in the future, he will ask. Logistics are a bit of a problem because he does live in the States. Mummy, I want you to understand, I'm not the same woman that left. I've cut a new life for myself and for William here. I'm self-sufficient financially. I choose what I want to do, who I want to be with, where I want to go and everything else. I choose, nobody tells me any longer, what or who is good for me. I make the choices and sometimes they are good choices, other times bad ones, but I make them. It is the same for my son. I have brought him up to make choices about who he likes and merits his attention and who he doesn't like, and not on who they are in society or whether they have a name and money, but whether they are kind or funny or interesting. If I allow and, yes, choose for him to be part of your lives, I will not have anyone telling him who he should speak to, how he must behave, what he should look like. I advise him on those things and he makes his own choice. You may not want to have anything to do with him or me. We've all managed without each other up until now, and I'm sure we will manage again. But if you, and when you tell Daddy, want to know William, you can, as long as you do so with my rules."

Bethany felt she didn't know this woman in front of her, indeed she was not the same person that left nine years ago. She was the Bethany she had been for those few months in Paris with the man she loved, happy, determined, independent. But she had not been strong like her daughter and she had given in to what was expected of her. It had been the right choice for her and she realised now, it had never been the right choice for Lizzie. She and Omar had made a grave error in trying to mould Elizabeth into someone she was not, she knew that now. Now she needed to convince Omar of the same as she wanted to know this woman and her son. She wanted to know this daughter and her grandson. Bethany stood and went to her daughter, Lizzie stood and her mother gave her a heartfelt hug, something she hadn't done since Lizzie was twelve.

"Your rules Elizabeth, it will be with your rules. The right rules for this modern age of ours. I'd also like to get to know you again, this other you, who I think I am going to find is an extraordinary creature."

They hugged again. Lizzie put her arm out to her sister who was quietly crying and brought her into the circle.

"And you, Penelope, would you like to know us?"

"Of course, my darling, I've missed my elder sister so much; you can't imagine." They separated, "I'd also like to get to know Doran. This is her gallery, isn't it? Would you be able to introduce us?"

"I think I will be able to manage that. Let's go and find the boys. I know where they will be", Lizzie smiled.

Omar fought at first when he was given the news, so Bethany let him rant and rave for a couple of days. She knew he wanted to see Elizabeth, he hadn't really been the same since the death of Billy and Elizabeth leaving. She knew his rants where not really about forgiving Lizzie, but about forgiving himself, as she knew he felt ashamed of his actions. She brought him around by telling him she would leave him if he did not welcome them into their lives and although he knew she never would, it meant he could pretend he was being magnanimous for her. That was OK, they would all get what they wanted.

Chapter Eighteen

Tally couldn't believe she was bringing William over for a whole month and that they were going to be staying at Brookesley manor. Tally had offered her apartment for them to stay in during their visit, but Lizzie had declined stating she wanted to spend time with her family. Of course, Tally thought she was crazy and never believed Lizzie would even consider the notion. While she hadn't told Tally everything that was going on in her life, she knew her best friend would be eager and waiting to hear the details when Lizzie arrived.

Tally was going to be in London when she arrived, so they would spend a couple of days together before Tally had to go to Devon, and Lizzie would make her way to Norwich.

"Well at least I will have two days with my two favourite people before you go home. Don't tell Stephen I said that; he thinks he is my favourite person. Now are you sure you don't want me to collect you from the station? It's no bother, you know?"

"I know, Tally, but thanks, I've hired a car for the fortnight. I need to move around a bit, to see Derrick and Jenny, driving to Norfolk; if I get a chance, I want to see Sofia. I want to show Billy Grays and take him to see his dad, grandad and Dorrie, and I want to show him some of the country side of Norfolk and the coast, so thanks but I'm sorted."

"OK then, it sounds as if you have everything under control. Will Fenton be able to visit?"

"We're not sure yet, he's in Dubai. It depends on how the auction goes and how good the locals are at receiving and shipping the catalogue. I hope so, but we'll see."

"Right, well I'll see you tomorrow. I'm off to do some shopping to get Billy some of his favourite things."

"You spoil him too much."

"He's my godson, what else am I supposed to do?"

Lizzie, Billy and Tally hit the London sights the day after arrival, something Lizzie hadn't really had time to do on previous visits; those times had been more family holidays. The poor lad was exhausted by the time they finished and nearly fell asleep over his pizza. While Tally tucked him into bed, Lizzie opened a bottle of wine, as she and Tally needed to catch up. They each sat on a sofa in the lounge, their legs tucked up and cosy, ready to share.

"So, first of all, you have to tell how this all came about. How did you reunite with your mother in Paris?"

Lizzie told her the story.

"It's crazy, this world is getting smaller and smaller, I swear. You seem to be able to bump into someone anywhere nowadays. Oh, I can just imagine that first meeting. I wish I had been a fly on the wall", Tally laughed.

"It was rather strange, to say the least, but here we are, so it was obviously meant to be. Fenton helped me see it was time to let go of old wounds and mend bridges. I do hope he is right."

"He is, darling, he truly is. And what is happening on that front? You two have known each other for long enough now. Will we be hearing wedding bells soon?"

"Not for me to say. I've met his family on a few occasions and they are all very much like him, laid back billionaires. Maybe his sister has a little bit of grandeur, but she's bearable and quite a laugh when you can get a couple of drinks into her. Her kids are brats though; maybe it's just the rich American way, or all those nannies. Now you, what are you and Stephen up to?"

"Not a lot really, you know how it is, no children, lots of money, lots of travel and sailing. I envy you, Lizzie, I really do. What you have done with your life since shedding your shackles... it's nothing short of a miracle. You have so much purpose in your life. I just seem to look for one adventure after the other, but they are all the same thing in the end; it's getting quite boring."

"So, find a purpose, find something you're passionate about and make it a purpose of your life to do something or create something from that passion."

"But, I'm only passionate about Stephen and boats."

"So, take Stephen and sail the world, or design a boat, a new type of sail or engine. You know enough about them; you have money. If that's too much, paint them. I don't mean the boats themselves but pictures of them, like I have the photos. Teach kids to sail, underprivileged kids. I don't know, there's so much you could do if you let yourself do it."

"Now that you mention it, there is something I've been dabbling in, but I'm not ready to share yet. Soon though."

"Oh really? Well you must tell me first when the big reveal happens." Tally just smiled and nodded, before redirecting the conversation.

"How do you think you will feel seeing your father again?"

"To be honest, Tally, I have no idea, but I think it will be alright."

"And have you told Penelope who you are? Doran, I mean?"

"No, not yet, but I have brought her a couple of my photos, signed. I'll tell her when I give them to her."

***

Lizzie drove Billy to see Derrick and Jenny, then to the cemetery to see his grandparents and Dad. She showed him where he was christened and took him to meet some of the old neighbours, then they had lunch at the Feathers with Chris and Charlie. The drive to Brookesley Manor was surprisingly clear, and as she approached the gates, she wondered whether her entry code still worked, it did. When they pulled up outside the doors, the housekeeper Mrs. Douglas and her husband the butler Mr. Douglas came out to greet them.

"Oh, Miss Elizabeth it's so lovely to see you here again", said Mrs Douglas, "and this must be Master William. It's so nice to meet you, young man."

Billy held out his hand

"Oh, how sweet", and Mrs. Douglas shook it.

"Hello, Mrs. and Mr. Douglas, it's good to see you both and I must say you are both looking very well."

Mother came out the door, bent down and gave Billy a hug, she then proceeded to hug Lizzie. Mr. Douglas raised an eyebrow in his wife's direction. This was something they hadn't seen before, not at the front entrance anyway.

"Come on in you two, the family are out the back on the terrace." Lizzie held William's hand as they made their way through to the back terrace and garden. Nothing had changed from that awful day she had come with Billy, the last time she had been here. It was as if time had stopped, the tables and chairs, lemonade set on the table instead of tea.

The boys kicking a ball around, while Penelope sat in a chair, Omar in another. The boys stopped what they were doing, and although a lot older still came up and put their arms around Lizzie and gave her a hug. They shook hands with Billy and asked him if he liked football and if he wanted to play. Billy looked at his mother.

"Yes, go ahead, you can play." She looked in the direction of the chairs.

"Hello, Penelope, John, Father."

Omar started to stand from the chair and wobbled a little; John went to help him.

"It's OK, John, I can manage. He stood and looked at Elizabeth.

"Well, let me take a look at you. Your mother and sister tell me you have been on quite the adventure. The boy looks strong; that's good. We need all the strong blood we can get. And you, Elizabeth, you look extremely well and fit, although how on all that French food and pollution is beyond me. It's good to see you, Elizabeth, welcome home."

Lizzie went to him and placed her arms around him.

"Hello, Daddy, be good to my William won't you. I'm glad to see you, glad to be home."

He held her tight.

"I'm glad you're home too, Lizzie, I really am. I've missed you."

Around the dinner table that night the family talked about the people they knew and what had been happening in their social world.

"Have you heard Simon divorced Penny Barchett, not that I can blame him, she is such a terrible gossip and stir monger, she must be very difficult to live with?" Penelope asked.

"No, I didn't know. I saw her in New York a few years ago, not to speak to though. She was at the opening of a Doran show. Now that you come to mention it, I didn't see Simon there at the time."

"It happened, what is it Mummy, four years ago now? He left her for a woman they had met on holiday in the Greek islands. By all accounts they swapped contact details and he began a long-distance affair with her after he got home. Within six months he left. Well at least she has the children for company, although I believe they attend St. Andrews in Scotland during term time."

"That's a shame, they had been married a long time. It must be very difficult for her", suggested Lizzie.

"I shouldn't feel too sympathetic; I hear her solicitors wiped the floor with Simon."

"Your gossiping, Penelope", said Mother, "it's unbecoming."

"It's not gossip. It's telling Lizzie what has been happening." She sulked

They had avoided any conversation about Billy senior and Lizzie had skipped a lot of details of her life, preferring to give a broader picture. She told them about the first apartment she bought and that she had taken a photographer's course, that she used to sell her photos on the streets and bridges of Paris along with other artists. She told them about Williams school and some of the plays he had performed in and how his grades were fine and he was doing well. She told them about how her friends spoilt him and she sometimes had to admonish them for giving him too much.

"Is that how you met Doran?" Asked Penelope.

"Who is Doran?" Asked Omar, it sounds like a fish.

"She's this really famous photographer, Daddy. She took the art world by storm at the beginning of her career and became very sought after in a matter of months. When we bumped into Lizzie in Paris, it was at one of her galleries we went to talk. Lizzie was working there. Are you still working there? I assume you are; it was only a few months ago. What's she like? Nobody seems to know much about her private life."

"About that", said Lizzie "But before I tell you, I have brought some thing for you, Penelope; let me just go and get it. May I be excused for a moment, Daddy?"

"Go if you must, I suppose." Daddy had always been a stickler for not interrupting a meal, he seemed a little less stringent now.

Lizzie removed herself and went to the great hall. She had brought the two pictures down from her room and left them there as a surprise, telling Billy he should not talk about Mummy's work until she had given Aunty Penelope her present. He still wasn't really aware of what a Doran meant or how it affected his mother; he just knew mummy took photos and people bought them. Lizzie came back with the two obvious frames, covered in brown paper.

"Are those what I think they are?" Penelope asked in an excited voice.

"Yes, they are", she looked at Billy and put her finger to her lips to tell him not to speak. She knew he was dying to tell them that he had help choose which ones to bring. "They are signed and authenticated, but before I give you these, there is something I need to tell you. You asked me if I could introduce you to Doran when you were in Paris."

"Am I going to meet her?" Penelope asked hugging herself like a little child.

"You *have* met her, Penelope; you met her the day you were born, and Mummy took me to the nursery to see you."

"What? I don't understand, what are you talking about?"

"I am Doran, it's my *nom de plume*. I am the person you wanted to meet. We talked in *my* gallery."

"Mummy let me help choose them" piped in Billy no longer able to contain his words.

The room was silent for many seconds whilst everyone took in what Lizzie was saying. Bethany and Omar were slightly stupefied as they didn't really know how successful this Doran was, or that fine photographic art was as much in demand as a fine art oil painting, which is what they considered art.

"I, I don't know what to say Lizzie, are you serious? But of course, Fenton, Fenton Burrows was the dealer that discovered her, you. It's beginning to make sense now. That's why Fenton was with you, he's your agent."

"He's a bit more than my agent. He's my partner, boyfriend, co-habitant, whatever you want to call it. We have been together three years now. We have kept it quiet until such a time as I made a name for myself without being associated, personally or as a couple. Since that has now happened, we have started making public appearances, and going out with Billy so that people see us as an item. I do hope you're not disappointed you won't meet Doran, but you still have me."

"Mummy, please", said Billy exasperated, "can she open them now? Please, I want her to see them."

Lizzie went over to her sister, "I hope you like them."

Penelope couldn't believe her own sister was Doran.

"Crikey, wait until this gets out, it will set my social circle alight." She opened the first package, John rising to take a look with her, then the boys got out of their seat. Omar looked as though he had given up trying to control the table and stood also; Bethany followed him. The first photo was a dark monochrome, a broken, dead, half stump of a tree in the middle of a desert. Atop the tree was a naked woman crouched down into a foetal position, but looking as though she were just about to rise, her long hair flowing in what the picture told you was a gust of wind. The light in the back ground caught the faraway hillsides and the side of the woman's body which was tattooed over one shoulder and down her arm. It was signed at the bottom, *Elizabeth Dowels-Johnson 'Doran'*.

"My goodness, it's beautiful", said John "how do you get the lighting like that? Was it actually taken in the wildness?"

"Yes, it was, the model wasn't too happy after I got her to climb the stub for the enth time, and it took many hours of hanging around until I found the light I wanted. The rest was done in the processing studio and, hey, presto. Do you like it, Penelope?

"I love it, I don't know what to say, it's amazing.

The second was of a ballerina, the bodice of her tutu having fallen from her breast, her arms above her head placed on a descending ceiling, the walls of the room closing in. She was posed in a grande plie, bent down by the weight of the ceiling. Her side profile showed the pain she was suffering, her face contorted into a grimace, struggling to hold her stance when everything around her was closing in.

"They are both so beautiful, Lizzie. I just don't know what to say, I'm lost. I have no words, thank you, thank you so much."

"That one," said Billy pointing at the ballerina " is Chantel. She takes me to the park and Mummy goes to see her dance."

"My goodness you have changed so much", her mother said in awe. Penelope placed the frames against the wall and they sat around the table once more. After dinner they went to the drawing room.

"You know next week is the regatta, don't you, Elizabeth?" Asked Omar. "Will you be coming?"

Everybody was quiet except the boys who had wondered off to the far side of the room to look at comic books and could be heard talking about the impossible feats their heroes were performing.

"Yes, father, I will be going. Talia and Stephen have a new boat they have entered this year and I'm going to cheer them on. They went to Devon to arrange its transport to St. Olaves and have asked me to be there for its launch."

"Will you be OK?" enquired John.

"John, the time has come to put old ghosts to rest. So many things have happened since that day. I will never forget Billy. William knows his father died helping another child, but I've never told him who that child was; I don't believe he needs to know." She looked at her parents and sister, "If it had been any other child, I would not seek him out and tell William—that's the boy your dad saved. I think it's best left as he thinks now that his dad died a hero and that is all there is to it. If one day, when he is a man, he asks, I will tell him, but for now I'd ask you all to just accept it as a gift. I can't say it will be easy and I will skip Joe's Hole. But Talia and Stephen are here, and they are William's godparents and two of my dearest friends. They have asked me to be there knowing it would be difficult, so it must be important to them. I think maybe they are going to pull out all the stops to put a woman's name on the trophy, and I hope they manage it. I wanted to ask you, Mother, father, if you would look after William at the marina while I make the run. Will you do that for me?"

"Of course, we will", replied Bethany.

"It would be our pleasure", said Omar.

With that no more needed to be said. Lizzie stood.

"It's been a long day and I think it's time I put William to bed. I'll say goodnight and see you in the morning.

She called Billy to her and took him upstairs feeling happy Fenton had encouraged her to do this. Everything was now out in the open. Forgiveness in both directions had taken place, and now was the time to heal. When she had Billy in bed, she Skyped Fenton even though in Dubai, it was one in the morning.

"How is it going?" He asked.

"Better than I had thought. I feel calm as though I don't want to punish them anymore. That there is nothing to punish them for. Billy is getting along with everyone, especially, the boys. Will you be able to get here for next week's regatta? I miss you; I miss you so very much."

They spoke for an hour until Lizzie was too tired to stay awake longer. Fenton promised he would try to get to her.

The following Saturday, opening day of the regatta, she travelled with the rest of the family and accompanied them around the usual groups of people saying hello as was custom. After an hour of hearing Omar saying,

"You remember my daughters Elizabeth and Penelope, my son-in-law John, and my grandson's Anthony, Stewart, and I don't think you've met my grandson William, Elizabeth's boy," which promoted polite astonishment and as soon as they were out of ear shot, lots of wagging tongues, Lizzie was glad when her phone rang and it was Tally.

"Where are you?" Tally asked

"Walking around with the family. It has been fun watching the faces when father and Mother introduce me and Billy to the in crowd, but it's getting very repetitive and boring now, can you rescue me?"

"You bet your arse. We are in bay seventy-two and we will be unveiling the new boat in about thirty minutes. Stephen has just gone off to get the champagne from the clubhouse where they have been keeping it cool. There is already a crowd gathering to see her. I even saw someone trying to peak a look under the tarpaulin five minutes ago. Bring your family, I want them to see the boat as well."

"Do I have to?" Lizzie moaned.

"Yes, and I want Billy here too, so bring them all."

"This all sounds mysterious, what's going on?"

"It's a surprise, just get over here."

Lizzie relayed the request to the others and told Billy they were going to see Tally, Stephen and the new boat. He immediately lost interest in what he was doing, took her hand and asked the bay number. As they made their way, the crowd was gathering. The unveiling of a new boat, not seen before, was always a crowd pleaser and everyone was interested, especially the competition.

The family pushed their way through the crowd to Tally and Stephen. A long foldaway table had been set with white linen and at least one hundred plastic flutes. In the middle of the table was the champagne for the launch, the bottle before being used would have been scored with a cutter to weaken the glass. Although the boat was already in the water, it still needed blessing. Inviting a priest to bless the vessel died after the reformation, and now the honour fell to a 'noble or invited person known to the captain. Beside the table were six coolers containing the bottles of champagne.

There was a very small podium set up on the dock with a micro phone. This would be for the blessing and naming so that everyone could hear. The boat was covered in a tan tarpaulin with a rope leading from the main mast to the podium on the dock. At the appropriate moment, the owner, captain or invited guest would pull the rope to release the cover.

You could see the sails had not been erected yet; that would be too dangerous while moored, but once the naming had been done, the boat would ease out to open water and set her sails, always an incredible sight to see.

"WOW, you have really got all this sorted", said Lizzie. "You must have been here all night. Why didn't you ask me to come and help?"

"We managed and I thought it better you spend time at Brookesley than here."

"Who's speaking?"

"I thought I would ask your father", Tally said with a mischievous smile.

"You're not serious? Daddy takes these things very seriously indeed and would need at least a week to prepare."

"No, I'm pulling your chain. Stephen and I met this really nice guy some years back, and he and Stephen have become really good friends, so Stephen asked if he could do it."

"Have I met him?"

"I don't think so, darling, you've been away, remember? I do have a favour to ask of you though. Would you do me the honour of unveiling her? There's nothing to it, you don't have to speak or anything, just pull the rope. Will you do it, Lizzie? I can't think of anyone else I would rather have, and I know you hate being in the public eye, otherwise I would have asked you to do the blessing. Will you, please?"

"If all I have to do is pull a rope, of course I will"

Tally took her over to show her what to do. She spoke with her parents and asked them to keep an eye on Billy whilst she performed her duty, something her father was very happy and proud to see her do.

Stephen tapped the microphone.

"Ladies and gentlemen, thank you for being here today. Before we start, some people are going to come amongst you with glasses of champagne to toast our launching. If you are one of those strange people that do not partake, tough; you don't know what you are missing. There are soft drinks for the kids. If we run out before we get to you, sorry, you arrived too late."

A laughter from the crowd filled the air.

Champagne corks started popping and the caterers moved among the crowd.

"Most of you know me and my wife, Talia. Talia and I have known each other all our lives, but it took until later in life to fall in love. Since then, and when she agreed to become Mrs Stephen Byrne, she not only made me a rather rich man"—again laughter could be heard—

"She also made me a very happy man, a man that has found my other half. So, please give a round of applause for the owner and captain Talia."

This time along applause, whistles and hoots could be heard.

"Now I would like to introduce you to a dear friend of ours, some one that has proven himself a true and loyal friend and made another dear friend of ours a very happy woman. None of you bachelors out there were good enough for her, but she has now found someone who is. Mr. Fenton Burrows."

Lizzie's head shot around looking for him, so surprised he was even here, she wasn't sure what to do. He appeared from the crowd and took his place on the podium.

"Good afternoon", he looked at his wristwatch, "depending on your time zone, ladies, gentlemen and honoured guests.

"I was honoured to be asked here today to help launch this new vessel onto the open waters of the United Kingdom."

"As you can hear from my accent, I'm an American, and for those who do not know me, and I believe that is probably all of you, my name, as Stephen said, is Fenton Burrows. I'm one of those Americans, whilst proud of my country, who is always striving to do this sort of ceremony right and in a manner that you, Brits, have a natural knowledge to perform with ease. I have been terrified for weeks."

"I met Stephen and Talia just a few years ago, and in that time, I have come to know them well. They are passionate about life, giving love and, of course, sailing."

"The boat they launch today has been in the making for years, before they even met me. One of my industries is shipyards and building yachts. It was after we met, Talia came to me with some plans for a new design of sloop and I liked what I saw. She and Stephen, the great team they are, worked with my engineers to develop this vessel. This boat is a one-off and will never be built again because this boat is dedicated to a very special man that lost his life here whilst saving another life.

"I know there is a very special lady here today that lost more than anyone can imagine that day, however, before he died, Billy Johnson gave her a most precious gift, her son William. William is here with us today and will grow with pride in his father's name, a man that selflessly gave everything he had. William is there with his grandparents, Lord and Lady Dowels-Hudson. Please show him a round of applause."

Along with smiling faces and clapping, "hear-hears" sounded from many in attendance.

"So, without futher ado, please bow your heads in a blessing for this vessel and all who sail in her."

I launch my bark forth on unknown waters,
with thee O father as my harbour.
Watch over the travellers of this vessel
With guiding love.
Keep them safe from torments, squalls and all dangers.
Let them feel your spirit in the wind and the sea.
Free from harm in the sanctuary of thee.
O father be my harbour,
O son be my helm,
O spirit fill my sails,
Amen

"Raise your glasses please to…" he nodded and smiled at Lizzie as she pulled the rope and the tarpaulin descended. **"Billy's Ink."**

Talia smashed the magnum against the hull, and it splattered into a thousand pieces, white foam exploding after release from its confines. The tarpaulin fell to reveal a sleek, elongated vessel; on its hull scrolled Billy's Ink.

A group of boys and girls rushed to pull the tarpaulin free from the vessel. Stephen hopped aboard and started her engine. She caught the first time, and Talia released her ties, while Fenton jumped down from his podium, grabbed Lizzie's hand and pulled her aboard with him. Stephen jumped off and Talia moved away. Fenton took control of the boat and they eased out to wide water, as Lizzie stood dumbfounded on what was happening around her and had lost all sense of things. As they reached open space, Fenton called her to release the sails as he idled the engine, and came over to help her. An onboard motor hummed and the sails started hauling as they gathered volume. She saw it—the sails had Billy's Manawa and Korus lines embedded on the white sheets.

Fenton came over to her and wrapped his arms around her under Billy's ink.

About the author

Born in Kingston-Upon-Thames in 1958 aged 1 second. **Nina Grasia Rennd** passed the next few years, getting into all sorts of mischief until the age of sixteen when she left school. The workplace was to prove a disappointment, no adventure there, so Nina left England aged seventeen to be an au pair in Greece to find it.

She returned to the UK for a brief period while she gave birth to two children. She lived in Tenerife with her young family, for eighteen years.

Nina and her husband purchased their utopia in mainland Spain, unfortunately the house fell down after a year, literally. Her husband decided life was too difficult so moved to another country, she is now divorced.

She has, in her lifetime, travelled a decent portion of our world, met fascinating people, some good, some bad, and mixed with many different cultures.

Nina gets her inspiration to write from these people, about the fender benders, the blessings and in the belief that everything will still turn out right in the end. Nina never learns from her mistakes and still thinks this world and the people in it are amazing. She now lives in Seville, writing and maintaining a sense of humour.

Nina writes under the *nom de plumes* of Nina Grasia Rennd and A Griffin. https://www.facebook.com/NinaGrasiaRennd373810283273186

Look out for future books from

Nina Grasia Rennd and A Griffin
works in progress.

Just Breathe – The causes
Nina Grasia Rennd

Just Breathe – The affects – Maggie
Nina Grasia Rennd

Just Breathe – The affects – Sahara
Nina Grasia Rennd

Just Breathe – The affects – Laura
Nina Grasia Rennd

The Butcher of Kingston
A Griffin

The Not Business
A Griffin

Printed in Great Britain
by Amazon